Quick Change
Volume 2: Spire

C. T. O'LEARY

Cover design by: Jon Dunham

ISBN: 9798688897272

For my wonderfully supportive parents
Thanks for all of the sacrifices and encouragement

STORY SO FAR

Spoiler Alert for book one! If you're just previewing this on Amazon and haven't read book one, ABORT!

Seth Andersen is driving home from a bad day at work when he's transported to a new world, Morgenheim, where every resident lives with RPG-like elements: classes, statistics, and named attacks, all as part of their daily lives.

Seth chooses warrior as his class, then is given a free divine boon. He's allowed to choose from a very long list of some incredible powers, but accidentally chooses *Quick Change Artist,* not realizing that the selection is voice-activated.

He knows he's an *Adventurer,* though doesn't know exactly what that entails, so his first order of business is to seek out the "local adventurer" in the area he arrives in. He meets Aurora, but her adventurer title is misleading; she isn't from Earth like Seth. She seems powerful, so Seth tags along with her to get some answers to his questions, but ends up helping save her from an assassination attempt. It costs him his life, but his status as an adventurer allows him to revive less than a day later.

Seth travels with Aurora to the regional headquarters of her guild, in the closest major city, and accidentally bonds with a magical mount, Pahan, a wise, ancient, and somewhat prideful lion.

The trio arrive in Vardon to discover that there's been an attack on the Adventurers' Guild headquarters, and are captured by the group responsible, the Howlingshields, and taken to their leader, Ybarra. Ybarra is looking for one of the guild leaders, who he expected to be present during the attack, but wasn't. When Seth and Aurora don't have the information he wants, he tells his people to toss them off of the wall.

Seth, Aurora, Pahan, and Ivon, another Adventurers' Guild member, escape and make it safely down the wall, though Seth dies again in the ensuing fight. The four of them travel to a guild safe-house, and then follow a lead from there to Slyborn Stronghold, where the guild is trying to recover from the devastating attack on their Vardon headquarters.

Seth formally joins the guild, but the wild spirit that controls the mountain range pulls Pahan down to its dungeon core, trying to reclaim his essence. It turns out Ivon is feeding information to Ybarra and the Howlingshields. He knocks Seth out and escapes. The Howlingshield force is bearing down on the fortress as Seth, Aurora, and a healer named Dominick delve underground to save Pahan.

The group fights through dozens of zombies, including one large and furious one, and finally makes it to the core of the dungeon where the dominating spirit resides. It seems hopeless; the spirit is too strong, but then Seth gives his energy to Pahan, losing levels in the process. Thanks to the extra power, Pahan defeats the spirit, and usurps its place.

Seth, with his levels back and then some, Aurora, Dominick, and Pahan's first creation, his son Verun, head back to the surface to help fight the encroaching Howlingshields. Seth ends up in a duel with Ybarra after the man slays Ramses, the Adventurers' Guild commander, but it isn't going well. Aurora flies into battle on Pahan's back, and with their help and Ivon's, they take Ybarra down.

Guild members begin referring to Aurora as *The Liberator* due to her resemblance to a prophetic painting as she flew into battle, but she isn't receptive to the title, brushing it off. Weeks later, the group is back in Vardon, mothballing their old headquarters and planning to move their operation out to Slyborn more permanently. A giant peacock is seen descending from the sky, and the woman who steps off of it, Riley, speaks to Seth in English.

CHAPTER 1

Seth Andersen awoke to a miniature sun shining in his room. The light was so intense that it felt like it was shining straight through his closed eyelids. He let loose a befuddled grunt as he shaded his eyes, trying to figure out what the source of the light was.

Seth's eyes finally resolved a giant white lion, radiating light. Pahan, Seth's ex-mount and current dominating spirit of the Broken Bones mountain range, stood crammed into the corner of the small room. The top of his white furry mane squashed against the ceiling and his rear end butted against the room's only window.

Pahan's voice streamed directly into Seth's mind, <Seth, wake up. We have a problem.>

Seth grunted, sat up, then said, "What is it?" He started pulling on his chain and leather pants as Pahan spoke.

<I've still been unable to create a champion. I thought perhaps I could ask for assistance. As you're aware, that's something I'm not used to doing. I sent one of my dragon creations to fly to the border between my territory and the next territory over, to the south. You remember the one with the giant...what did you call them? Elephant men?>

Seth was getting a bad feeling in the pit of his stomach. He'd spent some time in the zone that Pahan was describing training with Verun in the past few weeks. The monsters were tough. "Yes. I remember the place. What happened?"

Pahan shifted from one paw to another, looking uncomfortable crammed into the tiny space. <Well, it seems the spirit may not be so amenable to talking with me. That was two days ago. It didn't send a response, but now a large group of the elephant men has crossed the border into my zone and is heading for Slyborn. I think they're after my dungeon core crystal, but the stronghold will be the first thing they hit. I'm creating more constructs as fast as I can, but I can't match their numbers without more time.>

Seth was pulling on his chest piece when Pahan finished, and said, "I'll go alert Aurora, when you say a large group, how many do you mean?" He was afraid of the answer.

<I've counted forty-three in my territory so far. I can't see very far past the border, so there may be more.>

If Seth had been drinking something, this is where it would've come fountaining out of his mouth. He yelled, "FORTY-THREE? What level are they!?"

Pahan closed his eyes and stopped moving altogether. Even given the news he'd just received, Seth couldn't help but marvel at the fact that Pahan could see anywhere in the mountain cluster in real time. It had led to some uncomfortable thoughts more than once as Seth used the restroom.

Pahan's eyes snapped open, and he said, <They are all around level forty-five, just like the ones you've fought there before.>

Seth cursed. While he and Verun, his current familiar and Pahan's offspring, could handle one elephant man, or even two, at a time, they were some of the most powerful fighters in the stronghold at the moment. Other guildmates would have a harder time.

Pahan said, <I must go, this avatar is taking too much of my energy, I will continue to make constructs to fight the invaders.> With that, Pahan vanished in a flash of white-gold light. Seth rubbed his eyes, trying to see in the now pitch-black room as he unceremoniously shoved his feet into his boots. He walked to the window that Pahan had been blocking and looked out. It was still dark, but he could see some light beginning to crest the horizon, so the sun would rise soon. He found the doorknob and left his room, heading toward Aurora's room at the other end of the long hall.

Seth's room was on the second floor of the main barracks building in Slyborn Stronghold, which joined to the main bulk of the fortress by a stone bridge. He'd moved in when the guild had moved their regional headquarters to the stronghold, a little over two months previous. Many of the guild members felt that the government of Vardon had betrayed their trust when some city guards had taken bribes to stay away during Ybarra's massacre. Slyborn had seemed an easy to select, nearby alternative. No one was sure if the arrangement was permanent, and Aurora had mentioned that there had been pressure from the guild's ruling council to make amends with Vardon and return to their location there.

Seth reached Aurora's door and banged several times. Quicker than he expected, he heard heavy footsteps approach, the click of a lock, and the door opened. Aurora was in her full plate armor and had dark rings around her eyes. Seth saved his questions about why she was awake and battle-ready before sunrise, and said, "We have a problem. A large group of monsters is approaching from the south. They aren't Pahan's, he's making some constructs to fight them, but he needs help. They're heading for the stronghold."

Aurora, to her credit, stayed remarkably calm at the news. She said, "South...Giant elephant men?" She'd actually said something that translated more literally to giant men with trunks and tusks, but Seth's ever-impressive in-head translator subbed in the word elephant for him.

Seth nodded, and Aurora said, "How long until they're here?"

Seth felt embarrassed. "I don't know, I didn't think to ask that." Why couldn't he ever think ahead? Aurora would've thought to ask Pahan that before he vanished.

She didn't chastise him, though, just grunted in acknowledgement and walked toward a metal lever on the wall in her room and yanked it down. Seth heard a deep thud through the wall, and then the whine of a pulley as rope spun it, the counterweight plummeting down a chute tailored for the purpose.

In seconds, a loud BONG noise rang out throughout the building. The contraption in Aurora's room could only ring the bell in the tower atop the barracks building once without being manually reset, but someone would be up there on guard duty like always, and if they hadn't been awake before, a bell tolling three feet away from them would have fixed that in a blink.

Sure enough, only around ten seconds later, the bell started ringing every few seconds, summoning all hands to the main courtyard. Aurora looked at Seth and said, "Let's go."

***

Seth and Aurora reached the main courtyard before many others, as most people had been sleeping. Verun had been asleep atop one of the walls, and swooped down to settle next to Seth, already filled in on what had been going on through his link to Pahan. Whoever was in the barracks tower was still ringing the bell, and another guild member on guard duty had rung one in the main part of the fortress, too.

Drowsy guild members started filing out and filling the courtyard, all wearing various amounts of battle armor and carrying weapons. They knew the alert wasn't a drill. There were more people at the headquarters than Seth had realized, before seeing them all together. When he'd first arrived at Slyborn, the guild was still reeling from Ybarra's surprise attack, but there had been some backfill since then. Members deployed to various posts or in another region had returned to the headquarters. Other regions had sent trainees to help fill the ranks. To Seth, it looked like there were over a hundred Adventurers' Guild members. He looked around, craning to see over the crowd, but didn't see Riley or her mount, Zuh. That wasn't uncommon, as she hadn't joined the guild. She was the only other person from Earth that Seth had met in Morgenheim, and she tended to go wherever she felt like, sometimes disappearing for days at a time.

Before Seth could ask if anyone had seen Riley, Aurora started speaking, describing the situation in short, concise sentences, wasting no words. Everyone in the guild already had pre-assigned "battle teams" that they were to form into in an attack, and they trained together twice a month. Seth invited the five other members of his to a party, and they all accepted within moments.

Seth looked over his own, and his party members' summaries, refreshing his memory of everyone's statistics.

```
Seth
Main Class: Level 48 Warrior
(659,430/949,224)
Second Class: None
1,728/1,728 Health Points
0/100 Fury Points
Factions: Adventurers' Guild
Stamina: 96
Dexterity: 100 (96 + 4)
Strength: 171 (144 + 27)
Intelligence: 48
Wisdom: 48
```

Dominick
Main Class: Level 29 Priest (1,235/29,712)
Second Class: Level 21 Knight
1,755 / 1,755 Health Points
2,466 / 2,466 Mana Points
Factions: Adventurers' Guild

Isaac
Main Class: Level 25 Scout (11,236/14,328)
Second Class: Level 14 Rogue
788 / 788 Health Points
100 / 100 Concentration Points
Factions: Adventurers' Guild

Baltern
Main Class: Level 48 Knight (143,246/949,224)
Second Class: Level 21 Rogue
3,852 / 3,852 Health Points
1,728 / 1,728 Mana Points
100 / 100 Concentration Points
Factions: Adventurers' Guild

Farolt
Main Class: Level 21 Mage (5,934/6,910)
567 / 567 Health Points
756 / 756 Mana Points
Factions: Adventurers' Guild

Tela
Main Class: Level 19 Rogue (4,432/4,798)
599 / 599 Health Points
100 / 100 Concentration Points
Factions: Adventurers' Guild

Baltern was technically the member of the party who'd been in the guild the longest, but even though he and Seth tied for the highest level in the group, Aurora had made Seth the squad leader since she'd worked with him. Baltern hadn't come right out and said it, but Seth thought the man was a little bitter about that.

Isaac, Ivon's son, and Dominick had both been members of the guild for longer than Seth, too, but his huge level advantage over them seemed to make it easier for them to accept his position.

Farolt and Tela were both newer recruits to the guild who'd relocated from other territories to help fill the depleted ranks of the Vardon region's branch.

The other five members of the party filtered through the crowd to stand near Seth, and Aurora spoke again, "We'll spread our battle teams out in a line and head south. If your team spots any of the elephant-men, someone in your team should shoot a fire spell or flaming arrow skyward. Two consecutive flares should be sent skyward if you need immediate assistance. If you see one flare, be ready to move in that direction, if you see two, you'll head to your comrade's aid if at all possible. Understood?"

There was a collective agreement from the gathered battle groups, and the mass of people started filing out of the stronghold and across the stone bridge onto the mountainside. The sun was peeking between two of the Broken Bones, slowly eliminating the chilly fog that clung to the behemoth mountains.

Seth's battle group was to be on the far right of the formation. There wasn't much room to spread out on the mountain immediately near the stronghold, but as the mass of Adventurers' Guild members moved away from the stronghold and started heading down the south face of the mountain, the groups could get farther and farther apart. Eventually, Seth could barely see the next group to his left, headed by Molly, one of the higher-level mages in the headquarters.

As they walked, Seth said, "Ok, who has the best eyesight? I think I have the highest dexterity stat here." Seth had learned that the immediately obvious benefits of the stats weren't the only effects. Dexterity, for instance, made one faster and more nimble, but also subtly increased the intensity of most of the five senses. Warriors, like Seth, gained two dexterity points per level. Mages gained one and a half point of dexterity per level, and knights and priests only gained one. Scouts and rogues were the dexterity kings, gaining three points per level, but Isaac and Tela were both so far below Seth in level that it meant he still had more.

Baltern, who was walking at the front of the group with his back to the rest of them, snorted, shaking his head from side to side but not turning around or speaking up.

Isaac said, "I just got access to *Eagle Eye* when I reached level twenty, so I think I can see the best." After a moment, Isaac shared a log with Seth, which appeared in the bottom of his vision.

Eagle Eye - Passive - Cost: none - Cooldown: none
Your eyesight is now greatly enhanced. You can see farther, and with more detail. You can pick out camouflaged targets more easily and track fast-moving targets.

Seth grimaced, that must have been why Baltern was laughing at him. The scout level-twenty class skill gave them incredible eyesight, and Seth's question had exposed his lack of knowledge. He said, "Alright, Isaac, keep an eye out and tell us if you see anything."

The group kept walking. Verun walked in the back of the group next to Seth, and Seth considered hopping on his back and taking to the skies. Surely he could see more from up there, but then he'd leave his group unattended, and he wasn't ready to do that. Seth was the strongest damager in the group, and they'd need his help to take down the elephant men. He'd have to trust Aurora's plan of walking in formation.

Fifteen minutes later, Seth saw a *Firebolt* spell streak into the sky to his left. It was hard to tell how far it was, but he didn't think it was Molly's group to his immediate left. He watched tensely, but no second signal appeared. He hoped his guild members were safe.

Seth was rocked out of his reverie when Isaac broke the silence. "Movement ahead." Each member of the group snapped their heads upwards in unison, following Isaac's gaze to the southwest. The trees had grown thicker as the group lost elevation, and Seth could see the tops of several of them were moving. The movement was getting closer.

Moments later, five of the monsters broke through the trees. They saw the guild party and altered course, heading straight for them and picking up speed.

They were huge, Seth estimated around fifty feet tall, but scale was hard at such a distance. They had heavyset humanoid bodies, but it was obvious that massive muscles resided under the wrinkly gray skin. Their faces looked almost exactly like elephants that Seth was familiar with, except for the tangled gray beards of varying length below all of their chins.

All five of the giant men were bare-chested and wore light-blue cloth wrapped around their midsections. Three of them wielded tree trunks like staves, and the other two held shorter wooden clubs with white ivory tusks sticking out at sharp angles, matching the menacing white tusks jutting from their faces.

The situation worried Seth. He didn't know if his group could take on five of the monsters. He stepped forward, putting himself between the enemy and the rest of his group. He jumped a little when a *Firebolt* spell went whizzing into the sky. Farolt had shot it to signal to the other groups that they'd come into contact with the enemy.

The elephant men looked, from a distance, to take slow, ponderous steps, but each step covered so much ground that they were advancing quickly. His group's lives were in Seth's hands. It was different when it was just him and Verun. Maybe he could take most of them out himself. He took off at a trot down the mountainside, Verun loping behind him.

Seth finally reached *Charge* range and activated the skill. He heard Farolt yell something behind him, but he didn't catch the words due to the wind whipping his ears as he practically flew toward his target. Seth and Verun struck the elephant man on the far left at near the same instant, Seth sliding *Fearless* into the meat of the thing's improbably thick calf, and Verun raking his claws along the monster's exposed chest.

You hit level 46 Forest Tusker with *Charge* for 843 damage.

Your familiar Verun hits level 46 Forest Tusker for 547 damage.

The beast locked up, all of its muscles tensing at once from the stun effect on Seth's *Charge* skill. Verun, through some feline magic, was clinging to the giant's chest, wicked claws attached to gray flesh and bits of loincloth as his white wings flapped in jerky motions behind him, keeping him balanced.

The other four enemies passed him, and he heard Baltern's voice carrying as he yelled orders, "Kid, shoot another flare, we'll need help. I'll try to keep their attention. Dominick, keep me healed as much as you can. Seth apparently has the left one. Focus fire starting to the right, but disengage if you pull its attention away from me! Go!"

The other four enemies reached Baltern, led by one of the two with giant spiked clubs. Faster than seemed proper for such a large frame, the monster had the club raised and descending rapidly toward Baltern, who was dwarfed in the shadow of the monstrous humanoids.

Baltern raised his shield skyward just before impact, and a massive *whoomp* slammed into Seth's eardrums as the shield held, but the knight below it was shoved six inches into the rocky dirt below his feet.

Seth's target swiped a massive tree trunk at him, chunks of dry dirt still clutched by the roots. Seth leapt out of the way, avoiding both the tree and the small crater it made on impact. He rushed inwards, wrapping the thing's uninjured leg in a bear hug as it struggled to dislodge its tree from the rocky ground. He heaved with all his massive strength. Seth's one hundred seventy-one strength showed. Not only did the elephant man go tumbling down the slope, it lifted around a dozen feet into the air before gravity took control again. He heard the air whoosh out of its lungs as it landed squarely on its back and started rolling. He looked back at the rest of the group.

A large ball of fire, around the size of a basketball, arched over Baltern's head and hit the central elephant man directly between the eyes, before exploding in a mass of expanding liquid fire. Farolt's hand was smoking where he'd thrown the powerful spell, and Seth could see in his party menu that the young mage's mana bar was almost a third depleted from the single cast.

It may have been worth the cost, however, because the elephant man let loose a pained grunt from its tusked mouth and staggered backwards down the mountainside, gray feet struggling for purchase as it tried to put out the inferno on its face.

Less fortunate, however, was the fact that the three others switched their gazes from Baltern, still struggling to get his plate-clad feet dislodged from the ground, to the source of the powerful spell: Farolt.

All three took a single step each, almost perfectly synchronized, toward the mage before Baltern let his *Taunt* skill loose. *Taunt* was a skill that knights used frequently, as it forced most enemies in the area to focus on them. It was voice activated; something had to be screamed in conjunction with the activation of the skill to have effect. Most knights tended to just yell "Hey" or some insult at whoever they fought, but Baltern yelled, "I *said* the right, you imbecile!" The *Taunt* skill gave his voice a strange echoing quality, and he'd yelled much louder than should be humanly possible.

Many things happened at once. Farolt scrambled backwards and squeaked, "Sorry!" The central monster finally put out the flames on its face, except for a few small patches in its now-singed beard, and started trudging back up the mountainside. Verun took to the sky, dodging the tree-weapon of the giant he'd been fighting. The three others stopped and looked at Baltern, who'd finally freed himself from the hole he'd been hammered into like a human nail.

Dominick shot a sphere of golden light at the knight, whose health had only dropped by around five percent from the hit, his shield soaking most of the damage. Tela appeared behind the elephant man at the far right, twisting her dagger into its Achilles tendon and activating her *Backstab* skill, eliciting a rumbling groan of pain. Seth hadn't even seen her vanish into *Stealth*. Isaac loosed an arrow at the far-right enemy, but it whistled harmlessly over the behemoth's head as it took a knee, forced to collapse from the triple damage Tela's surprise attack granted.

Seth started for the closest enemy. There were only three still standing. Several more heavy blows thundered onto Baltern's upturned shield, which was showing more and more cracks, but he was still on his feet, and his health bar was at roughly eighty percent. The giants had hammered him into the ground again, only his hips and above were visible, and he'd plastered a furious snarl on his red face as he screamed his defiance at the giant men raining blows on his upturned shield.

Isaac was firing arrow after arrow at one titan, but his quiver looked to be running low. Farolt was clumsily uncorking a bottle filled with blue liquid, having already burned through his entire mana supply using powerful spells, and Seth couldn't spot Tela at all. Dominick's mana bar had dipped below the fifty percent mark. The party couldn't keep this up. They needed to end the fight.

Just as Seth was wracking his brain, trying to figure out the best move, a *Fire Bomb,* looking identical to the one Farolt had started with, sailed over Seth's head and struck the central remaining giant in the chest.

Despite the spell looking the same as the one cast by Farolt, the effect was profoundly different. Whereas Farolt's *Fire Bomb* had knocked the giant it hit backwards down the mountainside, this one detonated like a grenade, the shock wave of the explosion tossing all three of the giants backwards in different directions. A roaring fireball, centered on where the spell had struck the middle giant's chest, mushroomed into the sky, making the rest of the world seem temporarily darker. As the smoke cleared, Seth could see Baltern's shield was still pointed skyward. He dropped it, the translucent shield disintegrating into shimmering dust, and began struggling out of the hole he'd been hammered into.

Everyone's eyes turned toward the source of the powerful spell, and Seth was unsurprised to see Molly, the red-haired fire mage stalking towards him. She said, "Everyone alive?" She didn't wait for an answer, just continued, "Follow me, we need to head towards the main group." With that, she turned and headed in the other direction.

Seth followed, then stumbled as Baltern shouldered past him. The man looked back and hissed, "Someone more experienced won't always be around to save your hide. You need to learn when to man up and take charge, not run like a headless chicken into battle. You left your team helpless." He didn't give Seth a chance to answer, immediately stalking away after Molly.

Dominick patted Seth on the back as Isaac and Farolt passed him. Tela materialized near Molly, dropping her stealth ability. Seth was staring at the back of Baltern's head, fuming. Rage was building in the pit of his stomach and rising. It'd been happening more and more lately, his temper besting him, but he was powerless to stop it. Baltern was a bully. He was unhappy he hadn't been put in charge of the battle squad, but that didn't give him license to disrespect Seth in front of the entire team. He shrugged off Dominick and took off after Baltern, who was still just walking away, not looking back.

"Hey!" Seth yelled. Baltern stopped and turned around, a cocky smile on his face. He knew he'd crossed a line, and he was happy Seth had taken the bait. It was too late, though. Within seconds Seth was in his face. No more words came to Seth's mind, but the rage was there, so he wound back and punched the knight in the face, not pulling his punch in the slightest.

Seth's strength score was formidable. He'd lifted boulders, punched through trees, and more amazing feats over the previous few months. However, through whatever twisted physics governed Morgenheim, punching Baltern—who likely had more stamina than Seth had strength, and had astronomical physical defense—was like punching a solid steel beam.

Baltern turned his head to the side at the last second, and Seth's fist connected with his cheek instead of his nose. A bang like a gunshot went off, but the big man barely reacted to Seth's punch, not even taking a single step backwards from the blow.

> You hit level 48 Knight (Baltern) for 112 damage. Level 48 Knight (Baltern) resists the knockback effect of your strike with passive skill *Immovable*.

Seth's rage immediately diminished, half from realizing he'd just slugged a team member, and half from sheer surprise at how little effect it had had on the man. Baltern spit some blood on the ground and then grinned at Seth, red smeared over his teeth on the left side of his mouth, and said, "Is that all?"

Seth almost took the bait again. His vision was hazy and his heart was hammering, adrenaline roaring through his system as his caveman brain screamed at him to draw his sword and run the pompous man through. With immense physical effort Seth reined in his rage and said, through gritted teeth, "We'll settle this when the guild is safe."

Baltern just turned and kept walking, calling over his shoulder, "I'm sure we will." Molly had stopped to watch the altercation, and she caught Seth's eye, a dissatisfied look on her pale face.

Verun's voice broke into Seth's mind, <I want to eat that man's stupid head.>

Seth mentally shot back, *Me too, buddy...Well, not literally.* Joking with Verun helped his rage subside more, but it didn't disappear. It turned ice cold and settled deep in Seth's belly.

***

By the time Seth's team made it back to Molly's team, which she'd left at their double flare, the fighting had all concluded. Seth saw four dead elephant men at different levels of wholeness scattered down the mountainside. Molly's and Seth's squads linked up and kept heading inward in case any of the other teams needed help, but thankfully they had all succeeded too. There weren't any casualties, though there were injuries. The various priests could heal most, but not all.

A knight named Silvia had lost an arm when one of the giant elephant men had decided to stop hitting her shield and simply pick her up and yank on her limbs. Her squad had killed it before it killed her, but the priest in her party had only been able to close up the stump of her arm as he wasn't high enough level to use the *Restore Limb* spell yet. A higher-level priest would heal it when they returned to the stronghold.

Before long the entire force had reunited, and they all reported their kill counts to Aurora. The battle squads had killed a total of forty giants, meaning that at least three were still on the loose in the area. At least, that was the thought, until one of Pahan's lung dragons screeched overhead and dropped something.

People backed up as the lumpy shape plummeted to the ground, landing with a wet *thwack*. It was one of the elephant men's heads, eyes glassy, tusks gleaming white. Pahan appeared in the flesh soon after, confirming that his constructs had taken out seven of the giants and he could sense no more in his territory. He seemed tired, and vanished less than ten seconds after he'd appeared, needing to rest after stressing his magic so much in such a short amount of time.

The Adventurers' Guild hiked back to Slyborn feeling victorious, but Seth only felt hollow and confused.

CHAPTER 2

One week after the incident with the neighboring wild spirit, Seth shoved the heavy iron door open as he exited the cave system that wound through the Broken Bones mountain range below Slyborn. He'd been down there for hours, in the very deepest part of the cave that held Pahan's dungeon core crystal.

He had been looking at his quest log screen while he made the long trek back up through the cave, and had noticed that the *Impress me* quest from Djinia said one out of one hundred, as opposed to zero out of one hundred like it'd said since he'd entered Morgenheim. He wondered who had completed it, and what they'd done to impress the goddess of expensive suits.

Pahan was still struggling to master his powers as an etherean, which is what Seth had learned the wild spirits called themselves. He'd asked Seth to come down and try fighting the champions he was trying to construct several times in the previous week. Something was missing, Pahan just couldn't seem to get it right, and instead of creating tough champions to guard his dungeon, he just ended up making larger versions of the same few constructs he'd made that weren't any stronger; in fact, they tended to buckle under their own bulk.

The big lion was growing frustrated, and his displeasure could be felt throughout the entire mountain range. When Pahan was angry, his constructs were more likely to attack humans, as if he lost his grip on them slightly.

Pahan was desperate to create a champion, like a big boss to guard his dungeon crystal, but there was more to it. He'd explained to Seth that he could level the Broken Bones up, which was just a rank one domain, but he had to have at least one champion to qualify. The etherean system seemed alien to Seth, having both an individual level, and a domain rank independent of one another.

Having a friend who was a wild spirit had answered a lot of questions for Seth, but Pahan could only stand to take a corporeal form for a couple of hours per day before running out of magic, so Seth didn't get as much face time as he would have liked. Pahan had also started to regain all of his memories of his time with different *partners* over the centuries. They'd all been of the ancient adventurer race, and he described that ancient world as markedly different from the one they lived in now, though his memories were still fuzzy. The other ethereans were angry and aggressive, as evidenced by Pahan's attempt to try talking to one of his neighbors. He said that was new, too.

Seth walked out of the room that held the six empty jail cells, up the spiral staircase, and across the stone bridge that connected the two sides of Slyborn. He'd wanted to head for his room and take a nap, but had a few errands to run first.

He'd been conflicted over the confrontation with Baltern for days. Every time he thought about it he got angry, but he remembered how he'd failed the team under his command. He'd intended to try to take out all the enemies himself, but it hadn't gone nearly so well; he'd only ended up killing one. He couldn't blame Baltern for being annoyed, but he could blame the man for how he'd responded. It was the disrespect that had gotten under Seth's skin.

He'd debated, first with himself, then with Aurora, over whether he should challenge Baltern to a duel. He wasn't sure what it would accomplish, but he was sure swinging his sword, *Fearless*, at the man's face would make him feel better. If he could beat him, at least.

Knights were almost exclusively defensive in nature; they could take a beating but weren't great at dealing damage. Baltern's secondary class was rogue, though, meaning he did have a higher physical attack score than an average knight, and could likely put out a decent amount of damage. Seth was a physical attacker, and a knight's plate armor gave them a hugely inflated physical defense score, meaning that Seth might struggle to get through. He could use his *Quick Change Pierce* skill to get through Baltern's armor, but he had to be careful he didn't kill the man in a duel. Jerk or not, the man was a guildmate, and they were on the same team.

Seth had eventually told Aurora he wouldn't try to duel Baltern, but in his head, the jury was still out. It had helped that he'd hardly seen the man in days, as Seth mostly spent his days down in the dungeon with Pahan, or in a neighboring territory fighting constructs to try to increase his level. If he'd been stronger, he could have simply killed all five of the enemies and protected his groups.

He desperately missed *Djinia's Blessing,* the spell granted to him when he'd first entered Morgenheim that let him gain ten times the normal experience rate. He'd leveled at an astounding rate, passing Aurora, a career fighter, in only a few weeks.

That wasn't only due to the blessing, though, and Seth still had his other edge: he wasn't *nearly* as afraid of dying as normal humans in Morgenheim. He could afford to be reckless, and all he would lose if he died was some time and some experience points.

When members of the guild wanted to grind their levels, they had to jump through hoops. First, they had to identify a zone where monsters were around their level, preferably a few above to increase the amount of experience they'd gain per kill, but not too strong. This often meant travelling long distances.

Second, guild members wishing to level up had to form a team, as fighting monsters in the wilderness by oneself was much too reckless. What if two monsters showed up? Typically, six-person teams would go on week-long levelling expeditions. The experience from every kill would be divided six ways, and the group always had to be ready to run if they encountered a group of monsters or a wandering champion.

Another strategy Seth knew some guild members employed was that of quantity over quality. Members could venture into a low-level zone on their own, equipped with dozens of health potions, and slay literally hundreds of low-level monsters. This was better in some ways, as there was a low chance of dying to monsters vastly under-levelled to yourself, but worse in others. Most monsters took days or weeks to respawn, meaning it was technically possible to "over-hunt" an area. The amount of experience someone would receive for defeating an enemy much lower in level would be low in the scope of how much they needed to advance again.

These facts worked out to Seth having a much easier time levelling. He and Verun could fly, getting to great hunting grounds faster. Verun could help him fight, but didn't take any of the experience away (except for the ten percent diverted to their bond level), and they didn't have to worry about dying for good.

Seth snapped out of his reverie on levelling as he walked across the fort's main courtyard and into the crafters' building. It was a three-story behemoth filled with the tools of all the major levelable crafting skills. Seth had learned about all of them as they'd integrated him into the guild. While he'd been almost completely focused on increasing his combat level for his first several weeks in Morgenheim, there were actually other levelable skills. One could level their combat, like he had, and level their armor crafting ability in one of three areas, smithing for metal, leatherworking for leather, and tailoring for cloth. People could also level carpentry to improve at building structures. The guild had transported a master carpenter who specialized in stone construction to help rebuild the partially collapsed tower at Slyborn.

There were still more levelable skills. Farming, mining, and herbalism skills affected how much output someone would get when harvesting things from the planet. The cooking skill could rank up, and high-level cooks were quite sought after. Slyborn's head cook's cooking skill was level twenty-three, and her food was delicious every time.

There was also enchanting and alchemy, which Seth was very curious about. Enchanting was almost exclusively the realm of mages, but that wasn't a hard restriction. One could work together rare and expensive materials with armor, weapons, or even structures along with magical power to create an immense number of effects. Seth had asked Aurora if it was within their budget to hire an enchanter to enchant the walls of Slyborn with defensive magic. She'd barked a single laugh at him and left the room. Apparently it wasn't in the budget. Seth did find out that Barnett, the rituals master, had dabbled in enchanting, but his specialty was in enchanting armor, and he was only level fifteen.

Alchemy could be used to create potions, and there were several guild members moderately skilled in it. Herbalists would spend the day foraging plants from the Broken Bones, and the alchemists could use them to crank out a variety of potions. Staples like health and mana potions were always in high demand, but more niche potions, and even poisons were possible with the right plant ingredients. Ivon's son, Isaac, had actually made Seth a potion that instantly gave him thirty fury points upon ingesting it. Seth had begged for more, but the young man had said he only found one plant. He described it to Seth in case he ever spotted more of them out in the world. It was apparently a brown mushroom that looked, in Isaac's exact words, "Startlingly like a mound of feces." That bit of information mollified Seth.

The crafting building was packed with tools and equipment for many of those different disciplines, but Seth was there to speak with someone specific. He walked into the building and headed down a flight of stairs. He could feel the heat coming off of the forge from across the room, and saw Landers, the newly arrived guild smith, pounding away with a hammer on a red-hot piece of metal. He waited until the man drenched the metal in water, steam pouring out, and then approached.

Landers didn't even turn around, just said over his shoulder, "It ain't ready yet, boy. Come back next week."

Seth sighed, and said, "Is there a reason you aren't working on my project right now? I thought the commander sent down a note saying it should be top of your priority list." He fought the rage trying to bubble through his consciousness.

Landers finally looked at him. The man was in his upper forties, with thinning brown hair and a burly brown beard threaded with the occasional gray hair. His bright-blue eyes seemed somehow incongruous in his face, especially with that angry expression. He glared at Seth for a moment and said, "Yes, there is a reason I'm not working on it right now."

Seth waited, but Landers just turned around and started heating another lump of metal. Seth, flustered, said, "And that reason is?"

Landers ignored him for a few beats but then said, "None of your business, boy. You aren't my commander." Seth wanted to yell, but the man was right, he didn't have to listen to Seth any more than any other guild member. He spun and left, fuming.

Seth had gotten approval from Aurora to commission a new set of defensive armor for himself to wear on his second outfit slot. It'd been over a month now, and from what he could see by talking to Landers, the man hadn't even begun work on it. He wasn't sure why the man disliked him, but he obviously did.

He shoved the door open, probably harder than strictly necessary, and exited the crafting building, entering the main courtyard again. There were two guild members manning the walls at all times. He walked over to the front gate and called up to one, "Hey, have you seen Riley?"

The woman looked down at Seth, suddenly nervous, and said, "We did. She was trying to...fly again earlier. By jumping off of the wall. I'm afraid she's...Just for the time being..." She drifted off, unwilling to say it.

"She's dead?" Seth said. The woman flinched and then nodded. He sighed, audibly, and said, "How long ago?"

The woman seemed to relax, now that she didn't have to describe Riley's death. She said, "About three hours ago."

Seth thanked her and started walking to his room. He thought Riley was at around level thirty-eight last time he'd joined a party with her, so it'd be another thirty-five hours before she was back, as time in the void after a death directly related to level. Seth and Riley had revealed their adventurer heritage to the entirety of the fortress within the first two weeks of returning to Slyborn. Seth wasn't sure he'd wanted to, but Riley had forced his hand when she'd gotten herself killed with some kind of experiment with a huge metal lightning rod during a storm and then walked back into the fort less than two days later. There had been a big commotion, but most of the guild members were emotionally past it a couple of months later, at least if they didn't have to see the deaths.

Riley was one of the more reckless people Seth had ever met. She was also the only other person from Earth he'd met in Morgenheim at that point. She'd flown into the old Adventurers' Guild headquarters in the middle of Vardon, one of the most populous cities in the region, like it was a walk in the park. Seth, Aurora, and others had been there cleaning out the place and packing everything they needed to take to Slyborn. She'd heard rumors of Seth flying on Verun over the city and assumed it must have been another adventurer. It hadn't even occurred to her that they may kill her, take her prisoner, or any other negative consequences; she'd wanted to see if he was from Earth, so she'd just gone.

Aurora had offered to allow Riley to go through the trials and join the guild too, but she'd refused, saying something about having bosses not being "her vibe." Aurora let her hang around Slyborn only because Seth assured her that she really was from Earth like him, and because the girl seemed to mean no harm. She'd occasionally party up with them and help them out. For all the unfocused air she had about her, she was quite a powerful mage, rivaled only in the fortress by Molly. While Molly focused on fire magic, Riley focused on wind magic, which included electricity-based spells. Seth still shivered at the thought of Freya roasting him with lightning outside of Vardon every time he saw Riley use the *Redirect Lightning* spell.

Seth had learned more about how mages worked in Morgenheim from working with the two intimidating women. All mages had access to both fire spells and wind spells at certain levels, starting with *Spark* and *Jolt* at levels one and two, respectively. At level five, though, all mages had to choose between taking *Fire Mastery* or *Wind Mastery*, which would triple the damage associated with that school of magic. So while Molly could technically cast *Redirect Lightning*, and Riley could technically cast *Fire Bomb*, they'd be much weaker than casting spells in the school of magic that they'd chosen at level five. That was not too far from changing for both women, though, as mages gained access to whichever mastery they didn't choose once they hit level forty. Molly was at level thirty-nine, and Riley at level thirty-eight. Seth mentally corrected himself; Riley would be back down to level thirty-seven once she respawned.

He'd gotten used to not seeing her for days at a time due to the deaths. Lately she'd obsessed over trying to learn to fly by blasting one of her wind spells, *Windstorm,* downwards and leaping from the wall. It hadn't been working, though she seemed convinced that she was travelling further and further every time. Thankfully, she didn't die every time she leapt from the walls, and a priest was usually around to heal her broken bones.

Seth had been the first one to point out to her that she didn't need to learn to fly, since she had Zuh, her familiar, to fly her anywhere she wanted. She'd retorted with some nonsensical answer about a hypothetical scenario where Zuh was busy and she needed to get somewhere super fast. Seth had given up trying to make her see reason.

Zuh was the giant peacock bird that Riley had ridden into Vardon on the day they'd first met. Seth had spoken to him many times since then, his mental voice very distinct from either Verun or Pahan's. Seth couldn't help but think of Zuh as an old man. He wasn't terribly emotionally intelligent, and mostly just wanted to be lazy and comfortable, not gallivanting all over the country on adventures like Riley wanted. Even so, the two of them got along great, and Seth could tell they really cared about each other.

Verun and Zuh got along too, even if Verun had been mildly intimidated by the bird at first. Seth often saw the two familiars flying around the fort together. Seth had only seen Zuh and Pahan interact once, and Pahan had fallen into his normal routine of acting like everyone was younger and less experienced than him. The two had talked about it, and it had come out that Zuh was at least one hundred years older than Pahan. The bird didn't let him live it down, so Pahan mostly avoided him.

Seth got back to his room, stripped off his chain armor, and lay down in bed. He hadn't slept well the night before. He was almost asleep when three quick knocks sounded on his door. He gasped and sat straight up in bed, heart thudding from the noise. He groaned, "What is it?" loud enough for whoever it was to hear.

He heard a slightly muffled voice say, "Commander wants to see you." and then footsteps receding. Of course she did. Seth rose, dressed slowly, and headed down the hall to the stairs that would take him to Aurora's office.

CHAPTER 3

Seth was in a glum mood as he walked down the hallway toward the staircase. His room was on the first floor, and Aurora's office was on the second. He took a look at his statistics window as he walked; it'd become a habit when he was levelling so fast. It was much less rewarding when he took weeks to gain levels.

Seth
Main Class: Level 48 Warrior (782,125/949,224)
Second Class: None
1,728/1,728 Health Points
0/100 Fury Points
Factions: Adventurers' Guild
Stamina: 96

Dexterity: 100 (96 + 4)
Strength: 171 (144 + 27)
Intelligence: 48
Wisdom: 48

Seth sighed audibly at the second class line of his statistics page. He'd been agonizing over what second class he should pick for weeks. The guild had master-level people in every class if he was willing to travel to them, which was made considerably easier by the existence of Verun, who could travel much farther in a given day than a horse. There was already a scout above level forty in Slyborn, a woman named Kifri, who'd been one of Ramses' escorts at the battle with Ybarra. Liora, Aurora's mother was also above level forty, so Seth could get a secondary class of scout or mage within the next two weeks. Baltern was above level forty, too, but Seth wasn't sure if he'd ever stoop to asking the man for any kind of help. He just wasn't sure what to do.

He'd talked with a variety of members about it, over his time in Slyborn, but had gained no clarity on the matter. Randolph, the warrior primary, rogue secondary that Seth had fought during his trials, had raved about having a rogue secondary. It allowed the use of two weapons very effectively, granted use of a rogue attack called *Bleeding Slash* that did damage to opponents over time, and increased dexterity, which had the effect of raising physical attack power and making the person overall more agile and quick.

Just as convincing as Randolph had been, though, Seth could find someone who'd rave just as strongly about adopting a different secondary class. Adopting a knight secondary gave one a huge health point boost and made them overall harder to hurt. Taking on a mage secondary granted several magical ranged attacks, scout secondaries could use bows exceptionally well from day one, and priest secondaries could heal their own damage, making them much more self-sufficient without having to rely on limited health potions.

Seth still didn't know what to pick, and he was getting the feeling that agonizing over it wasn't getting him any progress. He'd debated just picking scout and having Kifri grant it to him just so he could stop worrying. Then he'd worried about that all night and decided against it. He could safely ignore the problem once more, though, when he reached the door to Aurora's office.

People had expected Aurora to take over Ramses' old office, but she hadn't. That room had been converted into a meeting room, and Aurora had taken the one next door. Seth stood outside that door now, wishing he'd still been sleeping.

He knocked on the door, and she yelled for him to enter. He did. "Hey Aurora, someone said you wanted to talk." He glanced around the room, noticing the two whisper sigils framed on one wall. The little stones allowed communication over any range, and were worth a fortune. Ivon had used one to communicate the location of the Adventurers' Guild hideout to Ybarra. When they'd finally defeated the man, they'd kept them. No one had any clue where he'd gotten something so rare.

Aurora smiled at him, but it was tense and didn't reach her eyes. "I did, thanks for coming."

Seth let the silence hang for a moment before saying, "...And what did you want to talk about?"

She sighed, exasperated, and said, "This...is difficult for me to do, but I need someone to talk to. I'm feeling very stressed out, I received word today that my mother will be here within a week."

Seth tried to hide his cringe. Aurora had been stressing about this for the past two months. It was only a two weeks' travel time from Agril, where the guild's head office was, to Slyborn. Liora, Aurora's mother, had delayed the trip several times because of guild business, and so the threat of her arrival was ever present, but constantly pushed off. It seemed like she'd actually embarked on the journey though, so likely wouldn't be turning back. Seth said, "Have you talked to Isaac about it?"

Aurora blushed and looked away. The two of them had only met after the battle with Ybarra and the Howlingshields, which, looking back, Seth thought sounded like an excellent band name. Isaac and Aurora had had an instant romantic connection, but had kept their relationship a secret. Seth was one of the few who knew, and only then because Riley had spotted it and said something about it in front of him. For all her apparent silliness, the woman could be quite insightful, perhaps due to her high intelligence stat. Seth wasn't sure if Ivon knew or not. Aurora cleared her throat and said, in a low tone, "Well, I have talked to Isaac about it, but he doesn't seem to understand the gravity of the situation. It's *my mother* we're talking about. This is a nightmare. I get my first command post and she comes to look over my shoulder just two months in."

Seth could sympathize. He imagined how Geoff Treso, his boss on Earth, would have reacted if Seth's mother had showed up to his presentation to the board. Thinking of Earth made him a little sad, as it did most times, and thinking of his mother did too.

Aurora read it in his eyes, and said, "I'm sorry. I'm being selfish. You don't even know where your parents are."

Seth said, "No, no, I'm okay. Tell me, aside from just looking over your shoulder while you run the place, is there some other reason you don't want your mother here? I mean, it seems like you'd have spent tons of time with her growing up, right? Didn't she like...birth you?" Seth wanted the topic back on Aurora, and off of his family.

Aurora grimaced. "My mother is...hard to be around at times. Have you ever met someone who always seems to know the right answer, and everything just goes well for them?" Seth didn't say that it reminded him of Aurora herself. She continued after his nod, "Well, that's my mother. She's on the leading council of the Adventurers' Guild, one of the most powerful organizations in the entire country. People will literally do whatever she wants, almost always. It wouldn't be so bad if she didn't expect me to be just like her. She's a living myth, and it's difficult to live up to her reputation."

Seth said, "I hear you, but I'm sure it will work out. You've been running this place like a total champ. How could she not be impressed?" Aurora tried to look angry, but then a smile crept across her features.

She said, "Alright, I have to admit things are going well around here. Thanks, Seth."

He stood up and said, "Well, if that's all you needed, I really could use a nap." He started to walk out, desperately hoping.

She dashed his hopes. "Oh, that isn't all I needed to talk to you about, Seth." Ugh. Aurora had a bad habit of always having one more thing to ask of him. She said, "The letter that let me know Mother will arrive soon also said that she was bringing a scholar with her. His name is Siestal Pacora. He's the guild's foremost scholar on the wild spirits. He wants to talk to Pahan. Do you think you could make that happen?" "I've already asked Pahan everything they sent in the letters. We gave them everything he knew," Seth said.

She said, "I know we did, but the man seems to think he might glean some piece of information you weren't able to. Please?"

Seth thought it was strange that she'd say please. Couldn't she just order him to do it? But it wasn't quite that simple when he thought about it. Aurora may have been Seth's boss as far as the Adventurers' Guild went, but he was the one who'd bonded with Pahan. The lion was independent and didn't strictly have to keep his monsters from attacking the guild.

Seth was suspicious of this scholar that was coming. What were his motives? What if he tried to experiment on Pahan? He'd have to let Pahan make his own decision on the matter. He said, "I'll talk to him about it and let you know what he says. I was planning on heading back down there tomorrow morning. Does that work? That is, unless he happens to be listening right now?" Seth looked around the room, hoping Pahan might flash into existence and stop him from being message-boy. After a few moments of silence, Seth shrugged.

She nodded, a slight smile on her lips. Seth said, "One more thing before I go. I went by the crafting building today and talked with that Landers fellow again. He still doesn't seem to have started on the project for me and was super rude. Can you do something about that?"

She sighed and was silent for a few moments, thinking, before saying, "I've had multiple orders sent down for him to prioritize that. Have you tried to find out why he dislikes you so much?"

Seth looked at the floor. "Well, no, not really. I got so mad that I thought I'd better just leave. That's been happening a lot lately." He didn't have to say he was thinking about Baltern.

Some concern showed through Aurora's mask, and she said, "What is your strength stat up to?"

Seth was caught off guard by the dramatic switch in topic, but mentally opened his stat window and answered, "It's at one hundred seventy-one with bonuses from my armor. Why?"

She nodded thoughtfully, then said, "I should preface this by saying that I've not actually experienced anything myself, but there are rumors among the guild that people very high in a single stat may experience negative consequences. I've heard strength and aggression linked numerous times, but as far as I know it's just hearsay. You could try not wearing the armor with strength stat bonuses if you think it's affecting you day-to-day."

Seth hadn't thought about it, but the anger had seemed to increase as his level increased. He started to ask, "Well, what do the other sta-" but was cut off when Aurora held up a plate-gloved hand.

She said, "Like I said, none of my stats are high enough to feel anything, and I don't like to spread rumors. Talk to Barnett if you are curious, he might find you a book or two that mention the phenomenon."

Seth, feeling mildly chastened, just nodded and made his way out of Aurora's office. He was sorely tempted to go find Barnett and ask more about the statistics immediately, but his bed was calling him. He had exhausted himself fighting Pahan's creations that morning. Barnett could wait until after an afternoon nap.

Seth ended up sleeping through the entire night, missing dinner. The sleep was mostly restful, but there were more strange dreams mixed in. One of a little boy negotiating with a businesswoman in some high-rise office, and another of two brothers, fighting with swords and throwing knives over their father's inheritance.

CHAPTER 4

Seth had spoken to Barnett, the guild branch's rituals master, the next morning, and the pudgy little man had complained, mumbling something about "unsubstantiated drivel" as he'd fetched a book for Seth before shooing him out of the stronghold's library, saying he didn't care if Seth brought it back or not.

Apparently Barnett wasn't a fan of the small, purple book. Seth looked at the unfamiliar golden runes on the cover, which shimmered as they usually did when he tried to read anything in Morgenheim, before being replaced by perfectly legible English. He was grateful the translation magic also worked on the written word, as he doubted Barnett would've wanted to read the book to him aloud.

The book was titled *A Thesis Examining the Adverse Effects of the Five Great Statistics on the Human Psyche.* The stuffy language turned Seth off, but he wanted to know more about what his strength score might be doing to him. He found Verun curled up atop a length of the wall surrounding Slyborn, and sat down in the early morning sun, back against the adolescent lion, to do some reading.

The book led with massive, overly wordy explanations about the experiments that the authors had engineered to try to prove their thesis. It came down to having people fill out written tests about their mental state, waiting several weeks, and then giving them *heavily* enchanted items to wear, radically boosting one stat, and giving them the survey again. Why couldn't they just have written that instead of two dozen pages on the topic?

Finally, Seth found where the results of the different stats were described. Again, there was an enormous amount of flowery-worded explanations for each of the five statistics. He skimmed over them, trying to get the gist.

The authors found some changes when they boosted all the statistics, though some were more nebulous and hard to pin down. First, radically increased strength scores tended to make subjects more aggressive and quicker to anger, according to the books.

Second, a very high stamina score positively correlated with a decreased concern for one's own safety. High-stamina individuals were more reckless and prone to high-risk behavior.

Dexterity was a strange one. The authors couldn't find any mental changes in high-dexterity individuals except for an increase in irritability, but it had a very specific cause. For people with very high dexterity, everyone else seemed to move and speak slower than normal. They had to struggle to slow their own words down when they talked to someone with average dexterity, else people may struggle to understand their words. Conversely, from the frame of reference of the dexterous person, most others seemed to speak painfully slowly, like an audiobook on three-fourths speed.

Intelligence produced perhaps the most dramatic mental changes in an individual. People who had their intelligence boosted dramatically with enchanted items solved puzzles much quicker than before, but they eventually discovered a negative effect. With an increase in intelligence, came a commensurate decrease in empathy. People turned cold.

The book listed a negative effect of high wisdom, too. Where an increase in wisdom typically carried an increase in empathy and emotional intelligence, it was a double-edged sword. High-wisdom people could become over-emotional, prone to wide mood swings and the tendency to "go with their gut" even when direct proof to the contrary of whatever feeling they had was plain to see.

The last section of the book described more experiments that the authors wanted to conduct, such as hugely increasing both wisdom and intelligence on the same individual, but they needed more funding if they were to have such highly effective gear enchanted. The last page implored the reader to send donations to an address in a city called Cragos. Seth briefly wondered if he should try to donate, as he had gained some valuable insight from the book, but then he saw the letter asking for donations was dated almost seventy years in the past. The authors likely weren't alive any longer, or if they were, they probably weren't keen on continuing their experiments.

Seth closed the book, still trying to digest the information he'd received, and toed the great lion he'd been leaning against. Verun let loose a massive sigh, but didn't show any signs of unfurling from his sleeping position. Seth toed him again, a little harder, and said, "It's time to head down to see your dad."

Verun immediately rose, grunting and stretching, and Seth smirked. The lion loved going to see Pahan. Seth let Verun get the stretching out of his system, watching the lion's wicked white claws scissor out of his huge, fluffy paws and impale themselves in the stone making up the outer wall. Verun didn't even seem to notice he'd done it. He waited while Seth climbed onto his back and then leapt from the wall, white and red wings popping out and catching the air.

Seth had gotten more comfortable flying, but the initial gut-drop still scared the monkey within him. Verun beat his massive wings and the two of them soared up the mountain a way, heading for a cave entrance that hadn't been there a month before.

At first, for Verun to get down into the cave system where Pahan's dungeon core resided, Seth had to banish him to the void and then re-summon him when he was in the cave, as the door leading from Slyborn's small jail room into the cave system was much too small for the massive lion to fit through.

Verun still refused to admit it, but it was obvious to Seth that he was afraid of the void. He preferred to always be in the real world, even if he was far from Seth. Verun had apparently talked to his father about this, because there was a slight rumble on the mountainside one night, and the guild had discovered the cave opening the next morning, a fresh tunnel burrowing a few hundred yards through solid stone and dirt to connect to the pre-existing cave system. Pahan's new power was frightening.

They reached the cave entrance, Verun tucking his wings back as the mountain swallowed them. Fifteen minutes later they arrived at the end of the dungeon. It was amazing how quickly Verun could traverse the cave system when he knew exactly where to go, and when no monsters blocked their paths.

The cavern was just as Seth remembered it from his first visit, months ago, where he and his friends almost met their end. His would've been temporary, but his friends' wouldn't have.

The cavern was massive, stretching up into darkness. The highest point wasn't even visible. The only light came from the massive, levitating white crystal floating above a small fountain that was as close to an actual body as Pahan had in his new form.

So deep underground, the air had a faint chill to it, and the whole cavern had a subtly earthy smell that filled the nostrils. Pahan appeared and something in his tone, if a mental voice can even have a tone, worried Seth. The spirit was too chipper as he greeted Seth and Verun.

Seth tried not to look at the half-formed monster limbs that littered one side of the chamber, mostly obscured in darkness. He knew from experience that if he looked too close, he could see them twitching or pulsing. Pahan was enthusiastic about getting the most out of his new status as a full etherean, and that meant creating monsters to protect his territory.

First, Seth broke the news that some fancy scholar was en route to Slyborn and wanted to meet with Pahan, wondering if it may ruin the lion's mood. Pahan made some crack about doing his best "not to eat the repugnant worm." Seth took that as acceptance, but assumed he'd still have to escort the man down and watch him at first to make sure he didn't have any alternate motives.

Then Pahan told him why he was so excited. Instead of trying to form a champion for Seth to fight today, he had something else. A magical item. Seth found the little metal contraption sitting on the fountain that Pahan's crystal floated above. It was around the size of his hand, vaguely egg-shaped, and hollow. There was an opening at one end of the thing. Seth said, "What is it?"

Pahan's voice said in his mind, <Since I've had such trouble conjuring up a champion, I figured it may behoove me to talk to my equals. As you know, that didn't work out with my neighbors, but what if I didn't ask? Constructs, when killed, will disintegrate within hours. This item will contain a piece of a champion's body and prevent it from decaying. My hope is that, if you can kill a champion from another etherean and sustain some of its flesh in that container, I can use it to figure out how the etherean made such a strong construct.>

Seth thought about it, then said, "Wait, you want me to do it?"

<Well, who else?>

"I don't know. What champion? And what do I get out of it?"

Pahan's eyes lit up, and his voice sounded giddy in Seth's mind, a stark contrast to the booming mental voice he projected, <That's the genius of my plan. You do get something out of it, so you'll do it for me.>

Seth said, "Well, yeah, that's how normal compromises work, Pahan."

Pahan just rumbled deep in his chest, his version of laughter, and said, <You'll travel to the Mistwood, near Bosqovar, and get me a piece of the Wandering Arborist. In return for finding and defeating him, you'll get one of his Mistwood Monolith seeds, which I know you've been coveting since I told you about it. It's good for both of us.>

Seth was surprised. He *did* want one of the seedlings to the massive mist-generating trees. He'd been dreaming about building a treehouse high in the branches of one since he'd first seen them, and if he could plant it wherever he wanted, it was all the more alluring. He thought about it for a minute, and then said, "But I could have done that whenever I wanted. You're not really giving me anything except a good reason to go to the Mistwood."

Pahan said, <That may have been good enough, but there's another thing. If you plant the seed in my territory, I may be able to help it grow faster. Those behemoths likely take centuries to reach full height, you'll be long dead before you have the

chance to see the tree in its full glory unless I help you. Do this for me, and I'll help it grow.>

Seth considered it a bit more, then agreed. It really was a great deal. He said, "Riley's due to respawn this evening. I'll see if she and Zuh want to come with us."

Verun rumbled a contented sound and said, <I want to show Zuh how good I've gotten at fighting!>

Riley and Zuh's bond wasn't high enough to get a second bond token yet, so Zuh only had the ability to fly, not to fight for her. It sounded to Seth that Verun might want to rub it in the cocky old bird's face.

Seth, Pahan, and Verun talked for a few more minutes before Seth and Verun headed back up to Slyborn to pack for their trip.

***

Riley and Zuh returned to Slyborn that evening, when the sun was still a couple of hours from setting. They landed in the center of the courtyard, but the guards didn't pay them much mind, they were used to it. Seth and Verun were there to meet them.

Riley said, "Howdy!" as she hopped off of Zuh's back and strolled towards Seth. She'd said it in English, as attempting to say "Howdy" in the language of Efril, the country they were in, translated to something like "How do you do?"

Riley was grinning, no doubt waiting for Seth to scold her about dying again. She seemed to think it was hysterical when Seth chastised her, which just made him more annoyed.

Riley was twenty-four, a few years younger than Seth, and stood slightly below average height. She had bright-blonde hair that she almost always kept in a bun on top of her head, held in place by one of Zuh's feathers. She wore thick-rimmed black glasses on her face. Seth also hadn't been able to figure out where she'd gotten those, but the guild members were absolutely fascinated. *Who cares if the woman comes back to life after she dies, right? I want to know about those glasses!* There were even several people at Slyborn whose vision was improved when they tried them on, and Riley swore she'd try to get more pairs for them.

Seth said, "How was the void?" He thought he was being clever, but she just grinned even bigger. Instead of responding, she just walked up to him and embraced him. Seth held his arms out to the side, feeling slightly awkward but not opposed to the contact. When she stopped and stepped back, Seth said, "What was that for?"

Riley said, "You looked like you could use a hug. Why are you waiting out here for me, dude?"

"I needed to talk to you about something and knew about when you'd be back. I wanted to catch you before you jumped off of another ledge." Riley was wearing her green robe. Seth still hadn't found out where she'd gotten it, but it was masterful. It was woven in such a way that, from a distance, it didn't look like cloth at all, but like knotted vines wrapping around her body. It had a formidable enchantment on it that raised both her intelligence stat, and her wisdom stat, meaning it made each of her attacks stronger, and allowed her to cast more of them before running out of mana.

Seth realized that it had been silent while he admired her outfit. Riley was just staring at him expectantly, eyebrows slightly raised, though not looking angry.

Seth cleared his throat and said, "Pahan's asked me to go kill a champion and collect a piece of its body for him, I was going to see if you and Zuh wanted to come along and back us up, since you two are the only ones who can keep up with us. We're planning on heading out first thing in the morning."

Riley pondered it for a moment and then looked at Zuh. They must have been speaking privately, because Seth didn't hear a thing, then the woman turned around and said, "I'd wanted to keep working on my flight spell, but I can hold off until we get back. You're going to be *so* jealous when I'm zipping around the skies."

Seth didn't mention that Verun and Zuh would fly them around wherever and whenever; he'd said it since she started obsessing over the flying thing, and she didn't seem to care. He said, "I'm sure I will be. Meet at sunrise?" Riley nodded and walked off, heading for the bridge that led to the other half of Slyborn where her rooms were. Verun and Zuh both took to the sky, and Seth caught something about the two of them racing to the top of the mountain Slyborn sat on through his bond with Verun.

Suddenly, Seth was alone again, with the rest of the night to burn before he went to sleep and headed out on his errand the next morning. It was too close to dusk to make it out of the mountain range and fight some monsters for experience points like he might have done another time, and he didn't want to bother Verun to fly him somewhere anyway, since the juvenile lion seemed to be having fun with Zuh.

Seth headed back to the crafting building. Inside, he climbed all the way to the top of the building to the enchanting room. It was abandoned, as it usually was, since few people took up enchanting. While intensely powerful if used right, the skill was one of the slowest to level, and one of the most expensive, as most enchantments required rare or expensive materials to create.

Seth, however, had a shortcut to learning to enchant and leveling up the skill. It was possible to take an already-enchanted item and destroy it with enchanting tools to glean some information about how the enchantment might be recreated. This was typically *ludicrously* expensive since enchanted items were so difficult to come by, but Pahan becoming a full etherean had changed things. He could make enchanted items at the cost of some essence. This was how champions usually dropped reward items to lure humans into the dungeon areas surrounding an etherean's dungeon heart. While Pahan hadn't yet found out how to create a radically stronger construct to be his champion, he could already create enchanted items, and he'd given Seth a few after he experimented with them. Enchanting, levels, and magic in general were vastly different for ethereans, and Pahan didn't actually need the rare items to make enchantments, he just sort of *willed* them into existence and lost some of his essence. Seth hadn't been able to get details on the entire process out of the lion yet, but he was understanding the dynamic between ethereans and humans.

The two races were like magical predator and prey, where the goal wasn't to get meat, but essence. Humans killed constructs and took the essence, converting it to experience and levelling up. Conversely, dungeons actively attempted to lure humans in with promises of magical items and treasure hoping some of those humans would die in the process, and the etherean could get a massive amount of essence from the perished human. Ethereans naturally, over long periods of time, drew in essence from the world around them, but getting it from a human, especially a high-level one, could advance them exponentially more quickly.

Pahan's dungeon had killed no one since he'd taken over, but he had tried to pressure Seth into literally dying for the cause a few times. So far, Seth had talked his way out of that.

Focusing back to the task at hand, Seth swapped to his second outfit, grunting as he struggled against the heavy plate armor that he kept there for defense, and pulled a pack off of his waist, setting it on the enchanting table in front of himself.

He swapped back to his primary outfit and started rooting through the pack, pulling out dozens of little sparkling gold rings. He called the pack his *Fortified Fanny Pack*, and he kept his most valuable belongings inside. Because of how his divine boon, *Quick Change Artist,* gave him access to two outfits, when he was wearing the primary outfit, everything that was part of the secondary outfit just kind of...ceased to exist. He'd discovered that if he *wore* a pack around his waist and swapped outfits, it disappeared too, contents included. Why this didn't also work for his large backpack, he couldn't explain. The rules of his boon seemed so arbitrary at times. The bonus, though, was that when things were stored in the *Fortified Fanny Pack,* they literally *couldn't* be lost or stolen, as they didn't even exist in the world.

The enchanting table in front of him was made of fancy dark wood, almost black with fine grain patterns visible throughout, stone and gem inlays spread around the perimeter, and brassy metal caps on all four corners. There were several metal bowls sunken into the table in various places on its surface. Arcane runes and lines reminding Seth of blueprints were burned into the wood of the table, connecting the little metal bowls. A huge crystal the size of Seth's fist was stuck out of the very center of the table, and it glowed with a dull blue light.

During normal enchanting, the item one wished to enchant was placed in the largest bowl, on the right of the table, and the resources required were set in the various bowls on the left. The enchanter then placed their hands on the large crystal, pumped mana into it, and attempted to create the enchantment, destroying the valuable resources in the process. The higher the enchanter's level, the higher chance that it would succeed, and the more potent the given effect would be. He hadn't seen one, but apparently structural enchanting required some sort of portable apparatus.

Since Seth had no mana points as a warrior class, he had to ask mages or priests to come up to the room occasionally and precharge the crystal so he could use it. That was another reason for him to consider taking mage or priest as his secondary class. It would give him access to mana points and make enchanting much less annoying.

Seth wasn't here tonight to do normal enchanting, however; he was there to disenchant. Disenchanting involved something akin to the opposite process. He picked up one ring Pahan had made for him. It was a thin gold band. Seth inspected it.

> Weakly Enchanted Gold Ring
> Jewelry
> - 3 Stamina

He hated to destroy the ring, but it was necessary if he was ever to learn how to enchant items for himself. It was either destroy free rings from Pahan, or become filthy rich and buy unicorn horns and phoenix feathers to create his own enchantments. That was an exaggeration, but the items that made enchantments, especially rare and powerful ones like the one on the cloak Ramses had given him that diverted arrows, were insanely rare. So far he'd resisted the urge to disenchant the valuable cape.

Seth set the ring in the large bowl on the right side of the table and then set his hands on the glowing crystal. It was warm to the touch. He willed it, and a menu appeared to him.

> Do you wish to Disenchant the item *Weakly Enchanted Gold Ring*?
>
> Table mana storage: 9,984/10,000
>
> Cost: 210
>
> Yes   No

Seth mentally selected yes, and the ring fizzled and glowed white hot for an instant before quickly cooling back down. It looked unharmed, though a little more dull than it had before. Seth now knew that the subtle glow on items usually hinted that it was enchanted. He observed the notifications that had appeared in his log.

Successfully disenchanted *Weakly Enchanted Gold Ring*!

You've discovered that stamina enchantments can be performed with steel, iron, and other hard metals. Rarer or harder metals will offer higher levels of enchantment, along with higher enchanter skill!

+210 enchanting experience, 255 experience until level 7.

Disenchanting gave a high amount of experience to the enchanting skill, but destroyed the enchantment on the item in the process, cost mana, and didn't return whatever material had been used in creating the original enchantment. For most people, that made it too expensive to use often unless they were determined to find out what material was used to create some specific enchantment that they had on an item. It worked out for Seth, however, since Pahan had made these rings for free, and was actively working to increase his own enchanting skill level.

Seth repeated the process with all the rings, forty-two in total, and increased his enchanting level up to ten, just barely below eleven. He'd used almost all of the mana stored in the enchanting table, so he'd have to ask Molly or someone else with mana to drop by and recharge it.

He returned all the gold rings to his fanny pack and then re-equipped it on his secondary outfit, stowing it out of reach of any thieves. He planned to try to sell them to jewelers next time he was in a city.

He headed back to his room and took off his armor, fitting it on the armor stand in the corner. He shot a message to Verun, who was sitting out on top of one of Slyborn's watchtowers, and fell asleep, dreaming of tree houses in giant trees.

CHAPTER 5

Seth woke up before dawn. It had been like that lately, since he settled into a routine while living at Slyborn. Nothing woke him up, but he tended to wake up right around dawn. His inner teen hated it. He put his armor back on and packed his larger backpack with some extra clothes, a fire starter, and a thin bedroll in case they had to spend the night out.

He dropped by Aurora's office on the way to meet Riley, but she wasn't there. He considered knocking on her bedroom door, a few doors down from the office, but didn't want to wake her if she was sleeping in. He settled for scrawling a quick note letting her know that he was heading on an errand for Pahan, and that the lion had agreed to meet with the scholar, if reluctantly.

He found Verun asleep in a corner of the main courtyard of Slyborn. The lion had taken to doing that, even though Seth knew that constructs didn't actually need to sleep, they still seemed to like it.

He nudged the adolescent lion with his foot, but Verun didn't respond. It took several more nudges before he finally opened his eyes, huffing loudly and kicking up dust in front of his nostrils. <It isn't time to wake up already, is it?> The thought came from Seth's link to Verun.

Seth said, "Unfortunately it is, my friend. I hope you're ready to stretch your wings. We have a long way to fly today." That seemed to enliven the lion, and he stood, stretching and grunting dramatically. Seth ducked as a huge red-tipped wing whooshed past as Verun spun in a circle.

Seth's jaw almost hit the floor when Riley walked out into the courtyard and Zuh landed on the wall, wind whooshing as he beat his wings to slow his descent. He'd expected them to arrive late. He said, "Nice of you to show up on time today!"

Riley just glared at him, but Zuh said, <I woke her up on time, I'm quite excited to get out of the mountains for a while.>

Seth smiled at the wise old bird. He gazed at the huge peacock feathers on Zuh's tail and wondered if they could create any enchantments. He'd have to ask for a few when they returned.

Seth marked the location they were heading on Riley's map, and the two adventurers climbed on their mounts' backs and took to the sky. At first, Seth had been afraid of flying, but that had receded with weeks of practice, and now he felt comfortable enough to hold on with only one hand as they soared over the mountainous landscape.

Seth looked behind and spotted Riley doing some yoga stretch on Zuh's back, both of her hands reaching for the sky. Her legs weren't even around his neck, but just planted on his back. Maybe he wasn't as comfortable flying as he thought he was, or maybe Riley was just insane.

They flew for two hours before Verun and Zuh wanted a break. The two familiars alighted in a rolling, hilly plain on the edge of a small forest of trees. Seth and Riley took turns heading into the forest to relieve themselves, and the two of them stretched and talked as they snacked on the sandwiches Seth had brought.

Riley said, "So what exactly is this champion we're going to fight?"

Seth said, "It's called the Wandering Arborist. I saw it once-"

Riley interrupted him by busting out laughing. "What kind of name is that? *Wandering Arborist!* Next thing I know you'll be asking me to help you fight the Chubby Mathematician!" She feigned fear and made the sign of the cross at some imaginary monster.

Seth said, "I didn't name the thing..." He tried not to laugh at the image of a massive chalk-wielding monster trying to explain Euclid numbers to his victims. He waited for Riley's laughter to die down and said, "I don't really know anything about how it fights, but it wanders the Mistwood and doesn't like people messing with the giant trees. Supposedly it will drop a seed to one tree if you defeat it. I'd hoped to plant one near Slyborn if we get it." He thought about telling her about his sky-high treehouse dream, but didn't want to be laughed at, so kept it to himself.

They chatted for a few more minutes, and then took to the skies again, heading for the Mistwood.

***

Five hours and two more rest stops later, Seth, Riley, Verun, and Zuh reached the edge of the Mistwood. They were somewhere west of Vardon, Seth could tell from his map, and he felt a little daunted realizing that he was looking for a single monster in a massive forest filled with giant wolves.

He cleared his throat and said, "I have to admit, I don't really know how we're going to find the champion... When we last saw him, Pahan could see him from the farthest away. Verun or Zuh, think you can do something like that?"

Zuh said, <I can sense champions from farther away than you can, yes, but that doesn't mean I

can lead you to the part of the forest where it currently is.>

Riley said, "We could just fly around until we find him, how long could that take?"

Seth said, "We can try to canvas the forest while Zuh and Verun look for him. I wonder if we should split up to cover more ground."

Riley said, "Wait, didn't you say that the champion protected the trees. What if I just lit one on fire?" A fireball appeared in her hand and she looked around for a suitable target.

Seth said, "No! I don't want to destroy the trees, but maybe that can be our last resort. Let's just search for a while. We can stay within sight range of each other. If you see him, just circle around the area and we'll head your way, and you do the same for us."

Zuh and Riley agreed, and the group started flying above the towering Mistwood Monoliths, the massive tops of the trees spearing a thick fog blanket around their bases.

***

It took only three hours of flying to spot the Wandering Arborist, or rather, to detect it. Zuh was the one who finally found the champion, and he and Riley flew in big lazy circles until Seth and Verun noticed and followed them.

The two flying mounts started their descent into the thick fog. It was cold on Seth's face as they entered the heart of it, and left a funny smell in his nose, earthy, like after a heavy rainstorm. He could barely even make out Riley and Zuh flying to their right as they descended, and he kept imagining the ground materializing out of the mist while they were still descending too fast, but to the mounts' credit, they landed lightly on the forest floor.

Verun and Zuh were both looking the same way as they touched down, so Seth looked that way too as he strained to see through the thick mist. He and Riley dismounted, both readying their weapons. Seth felt tense. Riley's voice almost made him jump as she whispered, "It's so spooky! This reminds me of a horror movie." She was smiling, as if excited at the prospect of being eaten in the mist. Seth rolled his eyes silently, not trusting his voice not to shake with all the nervous energy.

The four of them headed in the direction Verun and Zuh indicated, still not able to see anything through the impenetrable white-gray wall. Seth went first, and he tried not to be intimidated when the silhouette of the massive monster presented itself through the mist. It towered over him. The thing was laughably tall with proportions that were all wrong. It was pulling at some vines that had climbed one monolith. Seth heard them snap and fall to the ground, one vine even landing around fifteen feet in front of Seth. The Arborist had pulled it down as if it were just a cobweb, but the woody vine was as thick as Seth's bicep.

The champion was humanoid, but clearly not human. Its head was smaller than it should have been on such a large body, probably no larger than Seth's, but its glossy black eyes took up two-thirds of its face, so large they wrapped around the sides of its head. Conversely, the monster's arms hung much lower than a human's, its too-large hands almost dragging the ground as it stood at its full height. The thing had an emaciated look about it, skeletal structure clearly visible through its strange, barky brown skin.

The monster moved in slow, ponderous motions. When they drew even closer, it froze and turned toward them. No one moved for several seconds, the champion seemingly frozen in time, perfectly motionless.

Seth took a deep breath, hoping he wasn't about to bite the dust and spend the next two full days in the void, bored out of his mind. He started taking steps forward, approaching the towering figure, sword out in front of himself. It still stood, motionless. Finally, Seth took another step and was in *Charge* range. He grit his teeth together and activated the skill, feeling the muscle memory take over.

Seth's body coiled like a spring, crouching low in an instant, and then he shot forward like a bullet, gleaming sword point leading - and missed. For as slow as the Wandering Arborist had been moving before, it was far from slow. He'd barely even seen it move out of his path.

Seth gasped and spun. The giant, at least three times his height, stood behind him, looking down curiously, head cocked slightly to the side, like he was some interesting new discovery. Seth let out a small peep of fright. He thought Pahan had said the champion was only leveled somewhere in its twenties. Was it about to kill him that quickly, despite such a level deficit?

Then, a red and white streak, Verun, barreled into the monster, knocking it away. It took a few staggering steps backward and swiped one of its overly long arms at Verun, but the lion nimbly darted out of the way and swept in again, trying to sink his teeth in.

A blinding flash illuminated the area for just an instant, lightning lancing down out of the misty sky to strike Riley's robed form, leaving a huge tubular hole in the mist extending all the way to the blue sky. Electricity arced through her body and out the tip of her finger. However fast the champion was, it was slower than lightning.

The bolt slammed into its back, and it fell forward into a crouch. Seth started trotting over to the giant to try to rejoin the fight, but it stood up before he could make it there. There were chunks of dirt in each of its hands.

The Wandering Arborist used those overly long arms and whipped a chunk of dirt the size of a boulder at Seth like a fastball, its body working like a massive trebuchet, then neatly swiveled in place and chucked another one at Riley.

Seth dodged out of the way, only tripping from the dirt-clod shaking the ground beneath his feet on impact, but Riley wasn't fast enough. It struck her and she went flying backwards before barrel rolling on the ground to a stop. Zuh stood in front of her as she tried to get back to her feet, defiant, but the champion just ignored him, sensing he couldn't actually fight.

Seth saw Riley pull a red bottle out of her pack, fingers shaking, as he tried once more to engage the champion. Verun was up in the monster's face, looking much more like a winged kitten than the massive lion he was compared to the tall champion. Seth selected his *Quick Change Position* skill, which let him switch places with a living being, and took aim at the Wandering Arborist, lining up his hand in front of himself like sights on a gun. He fired the spell, and it landed. The towering figure didn't seem to notice. Seth then sprinted up to Verun, hopped on the lion's back, and said, "Hightower surprise!"

Verun was familiar with this ploy, as they liked to use this tactic on tough monsters in the wilderness, and shot into the sky almost immediately, his wingbeat sending the mist billowing in mesmerizing patterns. Verun said, <Good idea!>

They ascended dizzyingly fast for around eight seconds, pushing the ten-second effectiveness of his spell to the absolute limit. Seth leapt from Verun's back, using his legs to propel himself around a dozen feet away from the flying lion who immediately flapped and headed away.

Seth looked down as he fell through the mist, a mistake as far as his stomach was concerned, and saw the champion advancing toward Riley, who still sat on the forest floor. He'd only fallen for a fraction of a second, but when he activated the position-swapping spell the momentum carried over. He and the champion instantly switched places, and Seth crashed into the ground, which was now only a few feet below him, shaken up but not hurt.

He looked skyward and saw the silhouette of the champion falling through the mist. They'd flown straight up, instead of at an angle, as they typically did. Seth was standing dead center in the impact zone.

He scrambled to his feet, desperate to get out of the way, but it ended up being needless, as the falling figure lashed out with one of its lanky arms and snagged a vine growing between two of the giant trees. The vine directed the monster's momentum off to the side, having snapped from its connection to one of the two trees. It bled some of the champion's downward momentum off before breaking entirely, but it had done its job, as it had changed the fall's course to pass right by one of the massive Monoliths.

The champion's hands latched onto the bark of the tree as it fell, still trying to slow its descent, and it would have worked, if the monster hadn't let go as soon as a piece of bark broke off, more willing to be hurt itself than injure the tree.

The Wandering Arborist crashed into the ground several dozen yards from Seth. He felt the impact in his boots. It was motionless for a long moment, but Seth saw that it still had some health points left, less than a quarter. Its sickly-thin extremities worked to right itself.

Before the champion could gain its feet, another bolt of angry lightning lanced down through the fog into Riley, who was back on her feet next to an empty potion bottle discarded on the ground. The bolt ripped out of her outstretched arm, blasting the creature back several feet. Its health bar dropped to zero, and the fight was over.

Verun alighted on the ground next to Seth, abuzz with excited energy. If nothing else, the lion loved a good fight. Seth walked over to Riley and Zuh, breathing heavily, and said, "Nice job finishing it off. I'm surprised that it was so difficult. I fought a champion higher level than that in the caves below Slyborn."

Verun, who hadn't been *born* yet at that point but had heard the details, said, <You had Aurora and Dominick with you then, didn't you? Everyone here today is a damager, so we have no one to take the damage or heal it, right?> The lion was still young, but already becoming pretty insightful.

Riley said, "Verun, when will you ever impart some of your wisdom to Seth, so he stops making these silly comments?"

Seth just sighed and shook his head at the two of them, noticing how Verun practically glowed at the mage's praise, and walked over to the giant's body, glancing at his combat log.

You've slain Wandering Arborist (Level 26 Roaming Champion), +28,423 experience, 138,676 experience until level 49.

He almost felt bad for the creature; they'd hunted it down, and it had just been doing its job to keep up the forest. But it had something he wanted, something Pahan needed, and it would respawn in a few weeks anyway, if he could remember the information from Pahan's scan last time he'd encountered it.

Seth searched through the remnants of the large basket strapped to the giant corpse's back. It was full of basketball-sized seeds, but all of them turned to dust when Seth grabbed them, except for the last one. The seed looked perfectly unharmed. It was heavy, hard as steel, and Seth could almost swear there was a thin mist coalescing around it. He inspected it.

Mistwood Monolith Seed
This is the seed of a Mistwood Monolith. Plant it and watch the massive tree spring forth! All it requires is water, sunlight, and several centuries.

He walked over and deposited it into one of the bags hanging from Verun's sides, then returned to the corpse with the metal contraption Pahan had given him. He gritted his teeth as he cut off part of the giant's index finger with his sword and shoved it down into the little metal container. A piece of metal *snicked* into place, sealing the extremity inside, and a notification appeared.

Successfully preserved flesh of the Wandering Arborist! You may inspect this sample in an *_untranslateable_entity_name_* to begin learning how to create champions of your own! Error: Insufficient class to create additional constructs. Error: Creating additional constructs has been locked for this race. Sending error to Ausnahme, god of errors...

Error propagation halted by goddess Djinia, error has not been assigned.

Error deleted by goddess Djinia.

Quest complete: *Impress me* - 2/100

Seth only had a brief instant to say, "Wait, what?" before he vanished. Verun was banished back to the void, and Riley and Zuh stood alone in the Mistwood next to a dead giant.

She said, "That isn't normal, is it?"
Her familiar responded, <No, I don't think so.>

CHAPTER 6

Seth found himself in an expensively decorated room. The furnishings looked very Earth-like, which threw him for a loop for several seconds, having spent so much time living in a medieval-level society for the previous three months. He grabbed his head and squeezed his eyes shut, trying to fight off the nauseous disorientation from being teleported.

A ghost sat on a chair behind the receptionist desk that was placed imposingly to the left of the only door from the room. The transparent man kept shuffling papers on his desk, not even acknowledging Seth's sudden appearance.

Seth let the nausea from being teleported settle for a brief pause, and then approached the desk, clearing his throat louder than necessary. The ghostly man still didn't look up. Seth grimaced and said, "Hey dude. Can you hear me?"

The man finally made eye contact for a brief moment, irritation flashing over his translucent features. He replied in a slightly echoing voice, "Yes, *dude,* though I wish I couldn't. There's an idea, I'll deafen myself so you meat puppets stop pestering me." He looked back down and continued shuffling papers.

Seth said, "You don't have to be a jerk. I didn't exactly bring myself to this office did I?"

The receptionist said, "Well, neither did I, kid, yet for some reason she makes me deal with you."

Seth said, "She? Djinia?"

The man sarcastically said, "Who else would I be talking about?"

Seth practically screamed, "Literally anyone else! Any other *she* in the entire universe! I don't even know where I am!" He reached for his sword on his belt, but realized he wasn't wearing it or his armor, just the maroon clothing he usually wore underneath. The ghost receptionist had worked him into a frenzy though. He activated *Quick Change* and found that his heavy armor was still there on his second outfit. He struggled against the armor, trying to reach the huge longsword strapped to his back, but before he could do anything, all of that armor, and that sword disappeared too. Seth looked at the receptionist to see fear in his eyes.

A woman's voice thundered through the room, seeming to come from everywhere at once, "Esmund! Do you think I can't replace you? Send the man in!"

Esmund, the ghostly man, hunched his shoulders and simply pointed toward the big door and mumbled something indecipherable. Seth headed for the door.

Seth was a little disoriented as he walked into the room and let the heavy door close behind himself. All four walls of the room were large, floor-to-ceiling windows showing flowy, uninterrupted cloudscape outside, including the wall that should have shown the waiting room he'd just left. It was as if they floated in a box high in the atmosphere, completely unsupported. Dramatic oranges and reds were thrown across the clouds, as if during a sunset, but Seth couldn't identify which direction the sun was even coming from, and the colors were equally vibrant in all directions.

Djinia, the patron goddess of adventurers, sat behind an impressively constructed wooden desk inside the room. She was looking at him, anger tainting her features. Her hair was exactly the same as the last time he'd seen her, or the hologram of her at least. She had dark hair, with a shorter in the back, longer in the front, *I'd like to speak with your manager* cut. Where her expensive-looking business suit had been all black the last time he'd seen her, it was a dark navy now, otherwise, she looked exactly as he remembered.

Seth thought he glimpsed a flash of concern briefly on her face, and she reached up and grabbed a lock of her hair absently as she said, "Welcome to my office, and congratulations on being the second to impress me and complete the quest." She lifted up a manila file folder and pulled up a few pieces of paper, saying, "Let me just take a look at your file here..."

Seth stayed quiet as she skimmed the paper. She looked up after just a few seconds, eyes wide in shock, and said, "You already figured it out? I didn't expect anyone to solve that particular mystery for at least a few generations. How'd you develop the device to preserve the champion's body?"

She looked back down at the paper and Seth answered, "Oh, well I actually-"

Djinia interrupted him, "Oh, you didn't make the device yourself, you were given it by an etherean. Even stranger. Why would an etherean want to give you something like that? I see that it was one of the few who still haven't caught Ectocypher."

Seth said, "Ecto-?"

The goddess spoke over him again, "Wait, this etherean is a construct who you supplanted in place of an infected one. Curious."

Seth didn't even try to speak this time, but thought to himself, *Is this lady ever going to let me talk?*

Djinia's eyes snapped up to his as if she could read his thoughts. His hypothesis was confirmed immediately when she said, "You know, kings would give up their kingdoms for just a few minutes of my time. But really, if you think your time here would be better spent by blabbing your gums, please be my guest." She crossed her arms across her chest, adopted a stubborn expression, and kicked her red-bottom high heels up onto her desk. Her eyebrows rose up her forehead when he didn't immediately answer, expectant.

Seth slowly said, "My apologies. I didn't realize..."

She looked hard at him for a moment and then said, "That wasn't fair. I'm sure I'd offend all of my counterparts if they could read my thoughts too." Seth was intimidated, she actually came right out and admitted it. He waited in silence, doing his best not to think of anything insulting.

She said, "Alright, so here's the deal I gave the first guy who completed this quest. He turned out to be a little prodigy. In exchange for rising above all the noise of the thousands of reports I get through here, I'll answer one question for you. It could be about something in Morgenheim, about someone on Earth, or advice on what you should do in a certain situation. I can't see the future, but I can certainly weigh the odds better than you can." She tapped the side of her head as if to accentuate how amazing her brain was.

Seth said, "Wow, that's very generous of you. Um..." He trailed off, mind whirring. He wished he had more time to prepare an answer. Two things immediately jumped to mind, both things that had been weighing on him. He'd been wondering if either of his parents were in Morgenheim too, and he'd been agonizing over what to select as his secondary class. One was an obvious, emotional question, but what if the answer was no, and then he had wasted it? Or what if one or both of his parents had come to Morgenheim but died at level one?

Asking about what class to pick was a forward-thinking question. It would help him with the rest of his life, and take all doubt away about what the objective best choice was. He'd be able to take on the secondary class that she said, and it would help him continue to raise his station in his new life.

Seth felt trapped between old and new. Look forward, or look backwards? Earth and Morgenheim collided in his mind, and he could feel himself starting to breathe heavier. Was he going to have a panic attack? Here? In front of this goddess?

Seth started looking around for a chair to sit in, but there were none aside from the one Djinia occupied. He was about to sit his rump down onto the floor, courtesy or not, when Djinia spoke up, "Ok, I can't take it anymore. I'll answer both questions. It looked like you were about to give yourself a stroke!" She stood from her chair and put her hands spread out on her desk, palms down, leaning forward. She said, "It's actually convenient that the answers to your two questions are related. Yes, your mother came to Morgenheim with us. She's alive and well, for now." She squinted her eyes as if looking at something. "Your father and step-mother are still doing fine in Florida. Earth as a whole went into a bit of panic when thousands of people simply disappeared across the globe, but things have returned to some semblance of normalcy."

Her eyes refocused on Seth and she said, "Now, about your second class. There is one I think suits your class, fighting style, familiar, and Quick Change Artist boon. Interesting choice by the way. Did you know you're the only person on the planet with that one? I don't want to tell you which one it is, that'd be much too easy, but the class I think is best for you is specific to the region most recently known as Askua, not far from where you've been living. That also happens to be where your mother was deposited during the transition. A war is brewing there, though, so I'd get there as soon as possible."

Seth thought he remembered seeing Askua on the map Ramses had shown him. It was in the gray zone, completely unreachable without passing through extremely high-level zones. He said, "How will I get past the high-level monsters in those areas? I could fly, but Verun can't make it the entire way. We'll have to stop and rest. We'll have to set up camp."

She looked at him with one eyebrow quirked, as if scolding him for daring to ask a second question when she'd answered two for free. Seth started to apologize, but she held up a hand. "I guess that is a fair question. I need to see what you know." She walked forward and before Seth could react, pressed the tip of her index finger to the center of his forehead. There was a brief flash of pain, like a split-second migraine, and then Seth had the feeling that something *much* larger than him had brushed his psyche, like a whale cruising past a fish in the depths of a pitch-black sea.

It was over quickly, and she stepped back, her expression thoughtful. She said, "You smelled cinnamon once, when you were in the dungeons below that fortress of yours. Do you remember?" Seth nodded, and she asked, "What did you make of that?"

Seth pondered for a moment, a little thrown by the unexpected line of questioning, then said, "It seemed like the crystal was infected, if I had to describe it. Pahan said that there was something wrong with the wild spirit that had been resident there, that it was unnatural or something."

The goddess stared at him in silence for several awkward seconds, absent-mindedly drumming her fingers on the dark wood desk, then said, "I think that's close enough to classify, plus it's already mortal knowledge, anyway. Don't go telling any of the other deities that I shared it with you, just to be safe."

Seth *almost* thought about how he wasn't exactly in contact with any other deities, but tried to stamp down on the thought before the goddess could read it from his head. Djinia had turned away from him, now back on her side of the desk, and was looking out the windows at the ponderously slow-moving cloudscape. She held up her right hand, palm up, somewhat absently, as if she were holding something. A hologram-esque projection appeared above her open palm. Seth was no expert, but it looked like a 3D-render of some viruses he'd seen on television back on Earth, a slowly rotating reddish-brown globe with wicked spikes protruding in every direction. An ominous light flickered inside of it, half heartbeat, half candlelight.

Djinia spoke, "The Ectocypher contagion appeared sometime within the last two thousand years, after I left Morgenheim. It doesn't affect humans, it can't even penetrate their cell walls, but it is extremely contagious among the etherean population. It's infected almost the entire etherean population, except for some who reside in human-dominated areas, as the primary route to infection is by constructs from an infected etherean coming into direct contact with the core of an uninfected target. Humans have kept some of them safe by accident, just defending their homes from encroaching constructs.

"Infected ethereans aren't killed from the infection, their behavior is just modified. They become intensely aggressive toward uninfected of their own race, and all other sentients; humans and, recently, adventurers. Before you ask, no one knows where it came from. There are obvious signs of intelligent creation in its makeup, but we've not been able to trace it.

"Ygzotl, my counterpart over the ethereans, thinks Easium, over humans, created it, and they've been at each other's throats over it for centuries. I'm not convinced, though, as the extreme aggression of the infected has pushed the humans into ever-smaller pockets of civilization, which I'm sure you've noticed. The country you're in now is completely surrounded by overly aggressive ethereans who've grown in power unchecked for decades. Easium doesn't have a motive, it's negatively affected him more than it has Ygzotl."

She turned around and looked at Seth, eyebrows raised as if expecting a response. He said, "So those areas are impassable?"

Djinia smirked. "That's where the first person who impressed me comes in. He found that the high-level priest spell called *Purify*, when cast on an infected dungeon core, actually cures the infection. We've known this almost since the beginning, but it was classified as divine knowledge, so we couldn't let mortals know." She started speaking in a lower-pitched, melodramatic voice, imitating Seth, *"But great and powerful goddess, why don't you just cure them all?"* She returned to her normal voice, grabbing her snappy suit jacket by the lapels and straightening it. "We could, but it'd be breaking the rules. The three of us, the gods of sentient races, settled on a pact when we all ascended to godhood, and that pact strongly discourages us from meddling in mortal affairs. It's a slippery slope."

Seth started to speak up, but she cut him off again. He expended an extraordinary force of will to *not* think about how annoying it was. Djinia said, "Let's see," She paused and her vision unfocused for a moment before continuing, "There are a grand total of three priests in Efril with a high enough level to cast that spell. You'll need one of them, and probably quite a few other people, to help you get there and to fight to the center of all of those dungeons. Cured ethereans will still be a threat, but they won't actively try to exterminate you unless you draw very near to their dungeons."

Seth, speaking quickly, said, "How am I supposed to convince all of those people to come with me?"

Djinia looked irritated again, and said, *"Wow, wonderful goddess, thank you for all of this incredibly valuable information.* As far as convincing people, I can't help you much there. I can give you a quest, though, and allow you to share it with others. At least people will believe that it's really a quest from me that way. Hopefully my name still carries weight down there." She pointed down towards the plain gray carpet.

Djinia, patron goddess of adventurers, has offered you a quest!
Title: Unite them
Shareable Quest - may be shared with up to 60 others by the original quest owner
The goddess Djinia has requested that you create a safe travel route between the countries of Askua and Efril.

Reward: 200 gold and 2,000,000 experience for all who've accepted quest upon completion

Accept?   Decline?

Seth coughed violently when he saw the experience and gold rewards. They were massive! He didn't think he'd have trouble finding people to help him with that kind of money and experience on the line. He hurriedly accepted the quest, trying not to let his mind linger on how large the rewards were.

Djinia said, "I'll give you one more, too. I'm going to give this to everyone who completes *Impress me.*"

Djinia, patron goddess of adventurers, has offered you a quest!

Title: Wrapped in an enigma

The goddess Djinia has offered a hefty reward for information leading to the discovery of who created the Ectocypher virus.

Reward: Djinia will grant you a wish*

*Djinia reserves the right to deny any request deemed unreasonable.

Accept?   Decline?

Seth accepted that one, too, and said, "That-that's very generous of you. Thank you."

She said, "I know it is. Now, get back to work. We may talk again in the future." She raised her hand and snapped a finger, and Seth was back in the Mistwood.

A second teleportation was too much for Seth, and he emptied his lunch on the forest floor, stomach acid stinging his esophagus. He gathered himself and looked around. Riley and Zuh were gone, probably heading back to Slyborn to tell the guild about Seth's disappearance. He could sense her direction, so they were still in a party. That meant she'd likely know by now that he was back in the world. The sun was significantly lower in the sky than it had been when they'd killed the champion. How long had he been gone?

Seth looked at his beast bond menu for Verun and saw that Verun was in the void. "Crap," he said as he hurriedly summoned the lion. Verun appeared seconds later, an unhappy expression on his feline face. Had Seth really gained the ability to read feline expressions?

Seth said, "I'm sorry! I completed Djinia's quest, and she teleported me to her without any warning. I guess it must have banished you automatically! How long were you there?"

Verun said, <It felt like hours... Did you just get back?> Seth nodded and Verun said, <Thanks for bringing me back right away, then. Not that I'm scared of the void or anything...We should set up camp, then you can tell me about your visit.>

Seth looked at the sun getting low in the sky. Verun was right, they wouldn't make it back before the sun set. He hopped on Verun's back and started looking for a place to sleep for the night.

CHAPTER 7

Seth and Verun woke at dawn. They'd camped just outside the edge of Mistwood, not far from Vardon. Seth had considered trying to get a room for the night in the city, but didn't want to leave Verun alone outside the city, or try to convince the staff to let the giant lion stay too.

So instead, he'd slept on the ground in a thin bedroll next to Verun. Despite being somewhat exposed and in the open, sleeping next to a giant friendly lion had a way of making Seth feel secure.

At first, Seth had just assumed he'd tell the guild about the quest and try to convince them to accompany him, but he had doubts. He didn't want to drag people into danger, and the red zones that divided Efril and Askua were some of the most dangerous places he knew of.

His mother and a statistically superior secondary class for him both waited in the isolated country, so he certainly wanted to go there, but maybe he could try to make it alone. He and Verun could just do their best to fly straight there, landing only when they needed to and avoiding monsters at all costs.

He also sensed some ulterior motive from Djinia. She'd offered an insanely high quest reward; was that because the quest was incredibly dangerous, or because she *really* wanted him to go? What else would await him there? He didn't want to be a pawn.

Perhaps he shouldn't try to go at all. He'd gotten comfortable in Slyborn, surrounded by people he could trust to watch his back, only a short hike away from Pahan, one of his best friends in the world of Morgenheim. If he tried to travel to Askua, he would have to leave the lion spirit behind. He wasn't sure what he was going to do. He decided to make a trip into Vardon before returning to Slyborn, to give his brain time to crunch on the problem.

He'd been seen several times before the guild had relocated, flying over the city, so he and Verun just flew straight into the old Adventurers' Guild headquarters. There still a skeleton crew there, to make sure looters didn't pilfer anything and squatters didn't move in. There was one guard on duty, and he waved a hand at Seth as the two of them descended out of the sky, recognizing both man and lion.

The man who'd been waving was named Reinhold. Seth had only interacted with him briefly before the guild moved their headquarters to Slyborn. Seth hopped off of Verun's back and walked toward the man, who was trying not to look nervous at being so near to the multi-ton flying lion. Seth said, "Hey, Reinhold. How have things been here?"

The stout man grimaced slightly before plastering on the universe's fakest smile and saying, maybe too quickly, "Everything's going great!" Seth just narrowed his eyes and said nothing. Reinhold's eyes shifted for several seconds, not wanting to meet Seth's, before the nervous man finally sighed and said, "Well, things are fine, I should say..." He finally made eye contact with Seth and continued, "Relations with the city administration have been difficult. Even though the crooked guards who allowed the-" his eyes flitted to the central courtyard where bodies had been piled after Ybarra's attack, "-*incident* have been jailed, it's difficult to trust them."

Reinhold started pacing as he vented, "On top of that, the citizens seem to think we betrayed them by moving our headquarters. Vardon has more than enough guards on hand to fight the occasional monsters that crop up around the outskirts of their land, so I'm not even sure why they think they need us here. Personally, I think the blue capes are behind it with some kind of slander campaign, but I've no proof."

Seth kept silent, not ready to interrupt the frustrated man. Reinhold looked at him after the somewhat awkward silence and said, "Sorry to unload on you like that. There are just so few of us here, and my wife has heard it so many times she's forbade me to speak of guild business at all!"

Seth finally answered, "It's no problem, I'm sure it's no fun being stuck at the old headquarters. I wish I could offer some help, but I'm really not sure what I can do about any of that. You know, warrior class." Seth tapped the side of his head as Reinhold chuckled.

At first, Seth hadn't taken kindly to the insinuations from every side that he was dumb. It'd make him angry every time someone hinted at that, joking or not, but he'd realized it was just ingrained in the culture. The population generalized all warriors as dumb, even though knights technically tied them for lowest intelligence per level. The intelligence stat was more like IQ back on Earth; someone high in the intelligence stat would be quicker at solving problems and puzzles, and may have a better memory, but they didn't inherently know more information or always know the right thing to do at a given time.

Knights were always assumed to be goody-two-shoes, even though Seth had personally met at least one knight with terribly questionable morals. Rogues were always looked at with suspicion, like they may try to steal your belongings at any moment. Everyone seemed to think that all scouts were loners, and didn't want to be part of anything, so scouts were often simply not invited to events. Priests tended to be viewed as holier-than-thou, and full of themselves, and mages were the closest nerd analog that Seth had identified in Morgenheim. Society knew that mages were necessary, and they were typically pretty highly paid and sought after, but, paradoxically, they were ridiculed quite often. Seth broke out of his thoughts and said to Reinhold, "You're due to be rotated out in a few weeks though, right?"

The bearded man smiled. "Yeah, I am, and that day can't come quickly enough. Anyway, what brings you back here?"

Seth almost launched into a story about the fight with the Wandering Arborist, his abrupt transportation into Djinia's office, and the insane quest she'd given him, but he stopped himself. Aurora had told him several times he shared information too freely, and while he didn't want to become one of those cloak-and-dagger types, he was trying to heed her advice. He said, "Oh, I was just in the area and thought I'd stop by and do some trading. I'm not sure when I'll be near another city. That's the downside of the new headquarters, you know. It's still possible for the guild to conduct trade at a distance through messengers and caravans, but it's difficult for individuals to do shopping of their own."

Reinhold said, "Oh, I hadn't really thought of that. I should stock up before I rotate out there. I'll let you be on your way then, if you need anything from us just flag one of us down."

Seth said, "Great, thanks. I hope you don't mind if Verun hangs out here while I'm in the city. I don't want to startle the citizens, he's so terrifying and all."

Verun flexed his claws and stood up a little taller, before yawning, slowly walking to an unoccupied corner of the wall surrounding the compound, and began slowly spinning, trying to find the perfect position to sleep in. Reinhold just smiled a nervous smile in Verun's direction and nodded his head a few times before turning and walking the other way.

Seth walked toward the exit, then stopped and paused, removing his red cape and folding it into his bag. If the city's residents were harboring negative feelings towards the guild, perhaps he could benefit from some anonymity.

Feeling vaguely naked without red cloth that almost always adorned his shoulders, Seth slipped out through one entrance to the guild's defunct headquarters, headed for a market area he'd passed through on his first ever visit to the city.

It wasn't far to Utgar Way, one of the main promenades that ran along the cardinal directions through Vardon. He walked through a residential area, mostly three or four-story mini-mansions, the wealthy affording to live along such a prominent street, but before long he entered the merchant area.

Dozens of tents, wooden stands, and stone merchant booths lined both sides of the road in an overwhelming cacophony of color and flash, all vying for the attention of the citizens that perused the area. Merchants hollered at Seth, and other customers jostled him as he walked, their necks turned to the side looking at the merchandise and not focused on where they were going. Seth had a flashback to when he'd first walked this street with Aurora, and he remembered how everyone had seemed to part for her as she walked. Perhaps he should've left his red cape on, but it wasn't so bad. His stamina level was high enough that, to him, it didn't really feel like much when someone walked right into him. From some shocked looks he caught, it must've felt like walking into a tree trunk to the people who collided with him. Most of them weren't even angry or apologetic, just surprised. Seth chuckled and kept wading through the crowd, dodging aggressive salespeople and doing his best not to gawk at some of the curiosities for sale, intent on his mission.

He walked past the man who he'd bought his longsword from. The man was engaged in some heated haggling with an older woman who was trying to buy a dagger, so Seth kept going. His first priority was to find someone to buy all of his disenchanted golden rings. That'd hopefully give him a good amount of spending money.

After several minutes of peeking at different booths while trying not to engage the merchants, he saw one displaying an array of shiny gold and silver rings, earrings, and necklaces. The woman behind the low table looked to be somewhere in her forties. She was slender and deeply tanned, with dark features and an abundance of jewelry. A delicate golden chain ran across one side of her face, connecting an earring to a nose ring. There was at least one ring on each of her ten fingers, though many fingers sported upwards of three distinct rings.

Seth approached, and the woman spoke before he could. "Greetings, may I interest you in some fine jewelry? I have both enchanted and unenchanted, whichever you require."

She threw Seth off with her strange, breathy way of speaking, but he pulled himself together and said, "I was actually hoping to sell, I have some unenchanted gold rings that I no longer need. Would you be interested?"

The woman put a bejeweled hand to her chin and considered for a moment, looking over Seth's shoulder into the distance and muttering under her breath. Finally, she said, "I may be open to purchasing them, but I'll have to examine them first, and I'll need to make sure I can still turn a profit on them." The woman's abrupt switch into business mode surprised Seth. The whole mystic aura had been dropped like a stone.

Seth realized that he'd have to switch to his second outfit in the middle of the street to fetch the rings from his *Fortified Fanny Pack*. He needed to start thinking ahead. He looked around awkwardly but no one was paying him much mind, everyone focused on their negotiating, or staring at wares they couldn't afford. He shrugged and quickly swapped to his second outfit, straining against the heavy plate to grab his fanny pack and remove it from his waist, then switching back to his normal armor, smiling apologetically at the merchant woman. She actually didn't seem that surprised at what he'd done, but maybe that just came with the territory of selling in a big city.

He unbuttoned the pouch and fished four of the rings out, not wanting to reveal just how many he had quite yet. He handed them to the woman, who brought one of them within inches of her eyes, intense focus painted on her features. After repeating the process with the rest of the rings Seth had handed over, she said, "Just these? I could do one gold for the lot." She was trying to act nonchalant, but he could see she was closely watching his eyes, measuring his reaction.

The way the woman so casually said it bothered Seth. He knew that one gold piece was worth quite a lot; he earned one gold and six silver per month, totaling around twenty gold a year, for the work he did for the Adventurers' Guild, but even that was above average for the guild, and guild members were considered somewhat upper class by the general population. Then it struck Seth. Had she been trying to take advantage of him because he was a warrior? Did she think he would be too dumb to see it?

Seth let a little anger slip into his voice, and said, maybe slightly louder than necessary, "Surely you could do more than that. I could melt those four rings down into enough gold for two gold pieces, and that doesn't even take the craftsmanship into account!"

The vendor let some displeasure show in her features, and ducked her head as several other patrons and shop owners in the area turned their heads at Seth's words, making all of her fine jewelry clink together. Seth smiled at her, knowing full well what he'd done. She said, "My mistake, it appears I miscalculated. I could do three gold for the lot, but I really can't go higher, else I won't be able to make any profit at all on these." Seth's mind flashed back to some pawn shop show that he'd watched back on Earth, and he considered trying to get even more out of the woman, but he was already tired of the haggling game.

He said, "It's a deal if you're willing to extend that same rate to the rest of them, assuming they're of the same quality." He patted his fanny pack, which was potentially the lamest, most sacrilegious thing he'd ever done. If there was a god of coolness in Morgenheim, Seth was positive the deity had just felt a chill run up their divine spine.

The woman stared at his fanny pack for several seconds. Was that disgust in her eyes? Finally, she said, "You have yourself a deal. How many more do you have? I keep little currency at my booth, but can write you a certified withdrawal note for the central bank."

Seth started fishing out rings by the fistful, setting them in a little pile on the counter, and the woman's eyes bulged. It took several scoops before he had all the rings out, seventy-three in total. Seth thought he may want to enchant some of them himself at some point, so snatched three of them back and returned them to his fanny pack.

The woman finally got over her shock and started sorting through the rings, examining each with as much fervor as she had the first few. The merchant said, "Did you craft these yourself?"

Seth wasn't sure how to explain how he'd obtained all the rings, so just said, "Uh...no. A...friend did?" It was technically the truth. The woman gave him a supremely skeptical look and returned to examining the rings.

She must not have found any issues with them, for after several minutes they'd all been stowed away in a box she kept behind the counter. Seth saw a soft glow emanate from it as she clicked it shut and wondered what kind of enchantment was on it.

Seth was still struggling with the math when the woman finished and pulled out a small square of paper, starting to write the bank note. Maybe he really needed to find some way to increase his intelligence stat. She handed it to Seth when she finished, and then counted out ten gold pieces in addition. Seth saw that the note had an account number, signature, and the amount of forty-two gold and five silver. He thought the math was right and hoped that the withdrawal slip was legitimate. Her stand looked quite permanent, so he hoped there wasn't a chance she'd disappear if it was a fake. He shoved the gold and slip into his *Fortified Fanny Pack*, swapped to his second set of armor, grunted a bit while he put the fanny pack back around his waist, and then swapped back to his primary armor. As he walked away, thanking the woman, she said, "If you ever...come across...more of those rings, feel free to bring them here again." There was a greed in her eyes, and...was she insinuating that he stole them? Seth just smiled and nodded, before heading toward the center of the city to collect his bounty.

CHAPTER 8

Seth had never been into the Vardon bank, but he'd seen it several times, from both street level and the air. It was impossible to miss, as it had to be the single most defensible building in the entire vast city. It sat almost exactly in the center of the city, geographically, and was completely encircled by three rings of walls, almost as tall as the walls that encircled the city itself. As Seth passed through the huge open gates in the walls, he noticed that there were walkways on the outside, instead of on the inside like he would have expected. On the insides of the walls, there were wooden walkways that looked to have been added more recently. Had the original builders made the walls...backwards? To Seth, it almost looked like the builders meant the walls to keep something *in* rather than *out*.

He'd been told that the central bank was one of the oldest structures in the city, and if its geographical location didn't give that fact away, then Seth thought its architecture did. The building seemed to *grow* out of the yellowish stone that made up most of the structures in the city. It was huge and ornate, with massive pillars supporting a domed roof. A single sharp spire stretched skyward at the peak of the dome, made of the same sandy-yellow rock, but with swirly silver inlays spiraling around it.

None of the guards posted at the gates bothered him, though several of their gazes lingered on his sword pommel. The shining silver pommel was attractive, but it certainly wasn't subtle. When Seth finally entered the huge building, there didn't seem to be many other customers there. The room he entered was a long, somewhat slim hall. Desks lined either side, though around half of them were unoccupied. What really caught Seth's attention, though, was a massive stone arch that dominated the center of the long room.

It resembled cooled lava rock or obsidian. It had a somewhat organic shape and almost seemed to suck in the room's light around itself. As Seth drew nearer, he thought the arch was about large enough for three people to walk through abreast, and Verun could walk through if he tucked his wings in.

Seth wasn't aware of having crossed the distance to the arch until his finger touched the surface. It was cold, colder than the surrounding room. A prompt appeared in his vision.

You feel a connection to this place.

The unbelievably vague prompt frustrated Seth, but he didn't have much time to think about it, because someone shouted at him just then. "Sir! Please do not touch the priceless artwork!" Seth yanked his finger back as if it'd been burned and looked for the sound of the angry voice.

A portly man in fancy clothes was standing behind one desk, glaring at him. Seth muttered a couple of apologies and then headed for the man. The banker said, "That's alright, you're certainly not the first person to be drawn in by the piece's beauty. It's part of the building, we aren't even sure who the artist was. Now, what brings you here?"

Seth, after some awkward armor switching and fanny pack detaching and reattaching, handed the man his IOU from the merchant, praying that the man wouldn't say it was some kind of fake. After studying the note for a moment, the banker glanced at Seth and said, "Right, I'll be back momentarily with your payment," and scuttled through a squat door on the side of the room.

Several minutes later, Seth was hurrying back toward the merchant district. He'd been in Vardon longer than he wanted to, and wanted to make it back to Slyborn before nightfall. He'd just gotten significantly richer thanks to Pahan's rings, though, and wanted to do some shopping, as he had no idea when he'd be in a major city again.

Seth was cutting through an alley between two yellow-stone buildings, trying to make his way back to the same market area he'd been in before, when a man stepped out at the end of the alley, blocking his exit.

The man was tall and broad-shouldered, wearing patchy chain-mail armor. A cocky smile was plastered on his face. He crossed his arms over his chest, and he looked as if he were trying to appear nonchalant, but Seth could see a tension in his pose. He was ready to fight.

Seth, anger rising quickly, spoke first, "What do you want?" The man just smiled bigger in response, and Seth felt a sting in the back of his thigh. He read the notification as he whirled.

Level 16 rogue hits you for 15 damage.

A skinny young woman with lank, black hair backpedaled away from Seth, a thin spike of steel, like the end of a rapier held in her grip. Her eyes grew wide when Seth turned, and she shouted, "Forty-eight!" The woman leapt backwards, increasing the distance between herself and Seth in an instant, and Seth felt his attention returning to the warrior in front of him.

He turned again and saw the man turning to flee, any trace of a smile gone from his face. He considered letting the man go. Then the anger decided for him. Warriors weren't the most dexterous classes, but they did gain two points per level. That fact, plus a small dexterity bonus from Seth's armor, gave him an even one hundred dexterity, which was quite formidable. Most moderately high-level rogues and scouts could move more quickly than him, as they gained three points of dexterity per level, but not other classes, unless they were higher level.

Seth lunged forward, reaching the man before he had even taken five steps away, and slugged him in the back of the head. The man collapsed instantaneously, arms going stiff at his sides, and slammed onto the cobblestone street. Seth turned and heard what sounded like multiple people fleeing over the tops of one building next to the alley. The rogue was nowhere to be seen.

He turned around and looked at the unconscious man on the ground, anger leaving him as rapidly as it'd appeared. He hadn't noticed it before, but he was just a kid, maybe late teens, and while his shoulders were broad, he wasn't filled out, just skinny. He could see the health bar above the kid, sitting around fifty percent full. Had a single punch really done so much damage? One look at his combat log answered his question. The warrior was only level eighteen. Seth was lucky he hadn't killed him.

Seth looked around, but there was literally no one in sight. He didn't feel right leaving the kid there. On the other hand, they'd obviously intended to rob him until the rogue had pricked him to get his level. He was confident it wouldn't have happened if he'd been wearing his red cape.

Seth waffled around for a few seconds, torn between leaving the kid there and carrying him somewhere. His dilemma resolved itself, however, when the prone man stirred and then pushed himself up, rubbing the back of his head, facing away from Seth.

He slowly swiveled in a circle, a confused look on his face, until Seth came into view. The young man's face rapidly morphed from confusion to terror as he realized what had happened, and that the cause of his throbbing headache was still standing there.

Before Seth could say anything, the man ran away, and Seth didn't pursue him. He wondered how the interaction would've played out if he was only level ten or fifteen. Would they have taken his money and let him leave, or beat him to a pulp? He briefly debated putting his red cape back on again, if only to dissuade anyone else from trying to take advantage of him, but decided he didn't want to deal with the angry population that Reinhold had been talking about.

Seth gathered himself and continued on his way, making it the rest of the way to the market district undisturbed.

***

He spent around an hour perusing the shops and made several purchases. Seth knew that he'd probably paid more than he could have if he was better at haggling, but he'd talked them down at least slightly. He reviewed them as he stowed them in his backpack and Verun's saddlebags.

Wind Breaker Potion x 5
A strong wind buffets you from behind, increasing your running speed by 75% for 30 seconds. No speed-increasing potions may be used for 10 minutes after a successful use of this potion.

Mystery Potion x 3
The use of this potion is unknown. Talk to a master alchemist for more information, or drink it if you're feeling lucky.

Essence-Enriched Quartzite Nugget x 7
This quartzite nugget has been steeped in essence by existing near a dungeon core for

---

> centuries, it is incredibly hard, but almost impossible to meld into any useful shape without simply breaking it.

He'd bought the speed potions and mystery potions from the same potion seller, the man had practically given the mystery potions away after admitting that he wasn't high enough level to see their effects, and wasn't willing to sample them to puzzle it out.

The crystal nuggets were also picked up at a good price, as they'd been harvested around fifty years too late to be useful for most applications, since they couldn't be shaped with such high hardness. Seth, however, thought he could use them to put stamina enchantments on his new defensive armor, assuming Landers ever completed it.

He'd made it back to the former guild headquarters and was now about to head back to Slyborn. He waved goodbye to the member on watch, a female scout if he had to guess by her clothing, and he and Verun took to the skies, still wondering whether he should even tell Aurora about the quest from Djinia, or if he should just try to make the journey alone.

CHAPTER 9

The return flight to Slyborn was uneventful, with a few rest stops along the way for Verun to get his strength back. Seth and his familiar discussed what he should do about the Askua quest on the journey, and Verun showed some real wisdom, telling Seth that "The lion goes where his heart tells him."

Seth agreed that his heart was telling him he should go find his mother, but that didn't help him decide if he should try to make the journey alone, which was probably almost impossible, or risk the health of his friends and guild trying to get there.

The two of them landed in the stronghold's central courtyard, dust whooshing up in great whirls as Verun beat his massive wings to slow their descent. Seth patted Verun on the shoulder as he dismounted, grabbed his camping gear and the seed from Verun's sides, and headed for his room. Verun climbed up onto the stone wall surrounding the fort and started turning in circles. He'd be snoring in minutes, Seth knew from experience.

Riley was still in a party with Seth, and he could feel she was out of the fort, somewhere off to the east. He figured she was probably training or something and assumed she might return when she realized he was back. Seth headed for his bedroom. He stashed the huge seed and his gear in a trunk at the end of his bed, locked it up, and bee-lined for Aurora's office. He wanted to talk to her about his encounter with Djinia, though he still hadn't decided if he'd mention the shareable quest or not. He'd cross that bridge when he came to it.

He knocked on her door and tried the handle without waiting for her to answer, too excited to talk to her. It was one thing to walk into a woman's room without waiting, but Seth didn't know that the same privacy policy extended to an office.

The door was open, so Seth slid it open slowly, yelling, "Can I come in?" as he did. There was no response, so he pushed the door all the way open and looked in. A woman he'd never seen before sat behind Aurora's desk, papers scattered everywhere along the top.

The woman was probably somewhere in her fifties or sixties, and her hair was pure white and contained in a low ponytail disappearing behind the nape of her neck. Her skin was still relatively unwrinkled, except for some around the corners of her eyes. Her armor was a strange mix of cloth and plate that Seth hadn't seen before. It was primarily white robes with golden accents, but metal pauldrons and bracers were worn overtop. She was staring daggers at Seth, her mouth a hard line.

Seth said, "Um... I'm sorry. I thought this was Aurora's office. Who are you?" He cringed at how rude it was to burst into someone's office without permission and then ask who they were, but it had just slipped out. But that wasn't right. He knew this was Aurora's office, and he knew everyone in the stronghold by face at least, if not by name.

She stared at him silently for a long moment before saying, "This was her office, yes, until I arrived last night. I decided to take temporary command of this outpost while we audit Aurora's performance these last few months. I'll be your commander for the foreseeable future. Who are you?"

Seth was acutely aware that she still hadn't identified herself. He wasn't sure what to do, though. There wasn't anyone else around to validate that this woman was supposed to be here. Was she an intruder? He was stuck in confused silence for a few moments before saying, very intelligently, "Who are you?"

The woman quirked a single eyebrow at Seth, and he finally saw it. She looked just like Aurora in the face. It was that skeptical eyebrow that had triggered him to connect the dots. Aurora had said her mother was on the way, and that she was some kind of high official in the guild's structure, but he'd completely forgotten after everything that had happened in the previous twenty-four hours. She stood from her chair and said, "My name is Liora, holder of the mage seat on the high council of the Adventurers' Guild, and if you earned that red cape on your back, you're now under my command. State your name and purpose immediately, or I'll smite you where you stand!" Her voice had risen slowly in volume as she'd talked, and by the end she'd been screaming, a vein pulsing on her forehead.

Seth raised his hands in a placating gesture and said, "My name is Seth. I'm a recent addition to the guild, only about two months."

Liora glared at him for a few more moments. She said, "Seth, you're the actual adventurer then." She wasn't asking, so Seth just nodded. Apparently that news had made it all the way up to the guild's top council. "I've brought along a colleague that would like to ask your wild spirit some questions. You'll escort him down into the cave first thing tomorrow morning, understand?" Seth just nodded again and started backing out the door. Liora said nothing else, so he clicked the door shut and walked down the hall. He saw the door to Aurora's bedroom and knocked there, but there was no reply. He'd learned his lesson on opening doors without permission, so headed out to the main courtyard.

Seth asked several guild mates that he saw there if they knew where Aurora was, but none of them did. He asked after Ivon too, and one of them looked uncomfortable, saying, "I think they might've put him down in one of the cells."

Seth's exclamation of surprise could've likely been heard throughout the entire mountain fortress. He immediately headed down to the little jail room under the castle.

When he got there, he was greeted with the sight of Ivon in one of the cells, sitting on the ground but not looking injured or terribly upset by his situation. Aurora and Isaac were there too, standing outside of Ivon's cell. All three looked over as he entered.

Seth said, "What's going on?"

Aurora looked up at him, surprised that someone else had entered, and said, "My mother arrived yesterday evening. Apparently she was dissatisfied with how I've been running the chapter and assumed command. It's a right granted to her by her seat on the high council."

Ivon interrupted her then, "Liora had me thrown in here for what I did with the Howlingshields. I can't blame her." He looked down at his feet, sad.

Seth looked at Aurora. "We have to do something about this." She just opened her palms to the side and shrugged. Seth's mental wheels turned, and an idea slowly formed. He said, "Well, I need Ivon's help for a mission. So he definitely can't stay here."

Ivon said, "What quest are you talking about, boy?"

Seth said, "I met Djinia earlier today, and she gave me another quest. Where's Riley? I'd like to explain it to her as well." Seth could still feel her, somewhere to the east.

Aurora answered, "Mother told Riley and Zuh that they can't stay within the walls of Slyborn since they aren't part of the guild." She sighed, exasperated.

Seth said, "Oh, great. Well then, I can share this with you all now and tell her later." He shared the shareable quest from Djinia with all three of them and saw all of their eyes bug out as they read through it.

Ivon said, "Wow, Askua is still there, on the other side of all of those monsters? Did she explain how in the world we're supposed to clear a path there? We can't even send our most elite fighters past a certain point. And what do you need me for?"

Seth elaborated, "I do have some more info, but I'll explain all of that once we get you out of there. Ivon, we need you on this mission because we know you can be trusted. Aurora, come with me. I think we need to have another talk with your mother."

Aurora only said, "Another?"

CHAPTER 10

Seth led Aurora back to her former office. She was lagging behind, as if she didn't want to go, but he kept beckoning her on. He'd never seen her so nervous. When they finally got there, Seth knocked on the door and looked at Aurora, determined.

There was a rather long pause before Seth heard a muffled "You may enter" through the door. He opened it and went in first. Liora hadn't moved positions, though the paperwork scattered across the desk seemed even more chaotic. Seth said, "We need to talk about Ivon."

Liora looked as if she didn't know who he meant for several seconds, then said, "Oh, the traitor? What about him?"

Seth said, "He may have betrayed our location to an enemy, but that was very clearly under duress, and don't forget that he was actually one of the ones who helped kill that very same enemy."

She retorted, quick as a whip, "The man knowingly worked with an enemy which quite directly resulted in one of our most promising commanders', Ramses, death. Ramses was the favorite for the next holder of the rogue seat on the council, but his light was snuffed out much too early. You want me to forget that? I will do that for nothing short of divine intervention."

Seth knew she was being superfluous, but almost laughed at her wording. He said, "I happen to have a quest from a goddess, and I need Ivon's help." Seth shared the quest with her so she could read the details for herself.

Her eyes unfocused as she read over the prompt. She said, "So you have a real quest from a goddess. It says nothing about needing Ivon's help here." She looked at Seth, challenging.

Seth got creative. "There were a few stipulations that didn't make it into the actual quest invite. We need a priest above level sixty, and Djinia told me to be sure that I brought along some people that I trusted. I trust Ivon."

Aurora said, "Mother, you should just talk to him, you'll see that he isn't a bad person like you're thinking, he only-"

Liora looked at Aurora for what seemed like the first time since they entered and cut her off,

"Aurora, the adults are talking." She looked back at Seth, "I will not let him go just because you say you need his help on some arbitrary quest."

Seth was getting angry. He said, "Then you can forget me escorting your scholar down to talk with Pahan."

Liora retorted quickly, "I'll just order you to do it."

Seth said, "I'll quit the guild. Good luck dealing with the pissed-off wild spirit under the fortress who's actually a good friend of Ivon's too." The two of them stared at each other, stubborn and silent for what felt like thirty seconds. Aurora was looking back and forth between them, eyes wide. Seth finally broke the silence, "Look, if we can complete this quest we'll be the first unit to contact another country in hundreds of years. Think of the opportunities that might open up for us."

Liora's expression subtly changed from stubbornness to thoughtfulness. She said, "There may be some lucrative opportunities for us there. I do see a few problems with your plan, however. Firstly, there are no priests over level sixty in the guild. I do know of two at that level. One is the city administrator of Agril. Even if she was inclined to go with you, she's quite ancient and probably wouldn't be up for all the travel. The other is an extremely wealthy man named Farthon in Cragos, and I doubt he'd go on such a dangerous journey for a paltry two hundred gold, and as you can imagine, two million experience is hardly anything for someone at such a high level. Your journey may be over before it ever begins."

Aurora spoke up, "I know of another priest over level sixty. I heard that Quincy finally reached sixty last summer when some blue capes came through Bosqovar."

Liora's features switched to anger, and she said, "Quincy! He's a criminal."

Seth said, "Who is Quincy?"

Aurora said, "He's one of the three people that make up the ruling body of the Transportation Guild."

Seth remembered seeing the people in blue capes several times, and how on edge Aurora had seemed around them. He said, "What is so bad about the Transportation Guild?" He remembered Reinhold saying something about them too; the man thought they may be behind the public anger towards the Adventurers' Guild in Vardon.

Liora said, "They don't openly declare it, but they stand in our way wherever they can, minor inconveniences at every turn just to make us angry. Quincy will not have his fingers in this quest."

Seth thought in silence for a moment. "And you're sure we could sway neither of the other priests to go?"

Liora said, "I severely doubt it."

Seth said, "This quest kind of seems up the Transportation Guild's alley, though, doesn't it? Busting through monster-infested wilderness to get to a destination? If the mission was under our umbrella and we could convince Quincy and some of his men to come along too, we could stipulate that we were in charge. It might be a good opportunity to mend the rift between the two guilds. There hasn't actually been any open hostility between the two of you in years, right?"

Liora said, "I think you overestimate the man if you think he'd do anything for our benefit, but I see where you're going with that logic. It would feel good to have that man following my orders..." She gazed off into the distance for a moment, then continued, "I'll have a message sent to him and inquire about this. Ivon can be returned to his probationary status and accompany you on the quest on the condition that his entire gold reward be paid to the guild as reparations. If the quest doesn't end up going forward, I'll address Ivon's situation again at that time. Now, get out of my office."

Seth said, "One more thing, Riley, the other adventurer, I'll need her too if she's willing to come. The two of us can scout the skies and handle the more dangerous jobs. I'd like for her to be allowed to stay in the fortress until then."

Liora said, "What are you going to ask me for next, my daughter's hand? Fine, but if she does anything I don't like, it's on you. Now, out!"

Seth and Aurora started briskly walking out, but Liora said, "Aurora, your father asked that I give you this." Aurora turned around and grabbed a letter out of her mother's hand, and the two of them left the office.

As they walked down the hall, Aurora said, "I've never seen anyone speak to my mother like that and survive." Seth laughed at her joke, but she wasn't smiling.

***

They went right down to the dungeon and let Ivon out of the cell. Isaac was still with his father, and they filled them in on the new developments. Seth headed out to the main courtyard and woke Verun up. The lion made another dramatic display at his displeasure about being awoken, then Seth hopped on his back and they headed toward where Seth's party sense told him Riley was.

Seth's brain refused to comprehend what he was seeing at first, as they approached Riley's position. Situated on top of a squat stone peak a few minutes' flight from Slyborn was a full-sized, two-story medieval-looking house. Zuh, Riley's giant peacock familiar, perched on top of the house's pointed roof, head tucked under one of his wings, asleep.

The house looked like it could've been ripped right out of Bosqovar, the town where Seth had first met Aurora. The bottom floor was constructed mostly of stone, with wooden beams on all four corners, but the second floor was mostly wooden with a red-tiled roof. Smoke lazily rolled out of a squat stone chimney. Seth couldn't be sure, but he was almost positive that the house hadn't been there before. He'd flown past this spot dozens of times. Could he really have missed it?

Riley must have heard Verun's landing, because the front door opened and she emerged just as Seth was dismounting. She gave him a little cheery wave as he walked up, still taking in the building. She spoke first, "How was Djinia?"

Seth said, "Hard to talk to. How'd you know that's where I was? And whose house is this?"

Riley laughed and said, "I just assumed, since the number of people who'd completed *Impress me* had increased after you vanished. It's my house! Would you like the tour?" She didn't wait for him to answer, just turned around and headed back through the door.

Seth followed and took in the first level as he said, "Yeah, but how'd it get here?" The first level had a stone floor and was almost completely wide open. Two wooden chairs sat near the fireplace where a small fire was smoldering. A wooden table and bench sat in what Seth thought must be the dining area. There was a staircase on the left side of the room heading to the second floor, and two closed doors. Riley pointed to one of the doors and said, "The kitchen area is in there. The house even came with an enchanted box that keeps food cold. Pretty funny that they have their own versions of refrigerators here, don't you think?"

She pointed to the second door. "Through there is the bathroom, one of those fancy toilets included." Seth was familiar with the magical toilets. He hadn't started seeing them until he'd become involved with the guild, as they were apparently pretty costly. Some kind of enchantment inside the toilet made everything dropped down the hole just...cease to exist. Something like that just might put all plumbers on Earth out of business if it ever found its way back there.

Seth said, "Wait, you had a magical toilet and you let me go in the woods yesterday?"

Riley ignored the question and continued. "They're nothing special, but there are three bedrooms upstairs if you want to take a look." She smiled at him, satisfied with his level of confusion. Seth could see one of Verun's massive eyes peering through the front door, his head not able to fit through the opening.

Seth looked around in confusion for a few more moments, then said, "How? Is this your boon?" She'd refused to tell him which boon she'd picked since the first time they'd met, stating that he'd just have to wait and see. He probably bugged her about it once a week or so, but she'd never cracked, and he'd never seen her do anything that a normal mage couldn't.

She grinned at him, and said, "Yeah! Pretty rad, right?"

Seth said, "So your boon is...that you can build houses really fast?"

Riley laughed and said, "Not quite. My boon is called *Void Storage*. Here, you can read about it." At that, a prompt appeared in his log.

Void Storage
You may store a rectangular box of space in the void and retrieve it at will. Any living organisms in the box will not be transported to the void. You may store up to 1 box of space at a time. Your boxes of space may not exceed 64 cubed yards.

Owned Upgrades:
-**Capacity:** Each box of space's capacity is increased to 1000 cubed yards.

Seth read the prompt, impressed at her choice. It sounded to him like she could select a three-dimensional space and then store all nonliving matter inside of it in the void. It at least explained how she'd gotten a fully formed house all the way up into the mountains.

He didn't remember seeing that option on the list, but it sounded amazing. He narrowed his eyes at her, and said, "That's great. Where'd you get the house?"

She said, "I don't like your tone. I hope you aren't insinuating that I *stole* it. It was simply an award after I completed the first quest in the area I originally entered Morgenheim."

Seth said, "Oh, wow, I'm sorry. My first quest reward was to be allowed to sleep in someone's stable for the night. What in the world did you do to deserve an entire house?"

Riley grinned and said, "I defeated fifteen giant rats that had been eating all the town's grain. This was the mayor's house."

Seth exclaimed, "The mayor gave you his own house as a reward?!"

Riley said, "Well, I didn't say it was a freely given reward...The mayor wasn't a very nice man, I found out that he'd been stealing the farmers' grain and blaming it on the wild rats. So I thought I'd teach him a little lesson on theft before I skipped town." She tossed her head back and laughed at the memory.

Seth imagined the man coming home to find that his house was simply...gone. It must've been quite a sight. He said, "Well, I came out here to tell you that you could come back to the stronghold if you wanted, but it looks like you're doing fine as it is." She nodded, and Seth continued, explaining what had happened with Djinia and the quest. He even told her about his doubts about telling the guild, and how Ivon in the dungeon had made him feel like it was the only way. She, surprisingly, didn't poke fun at him for it, just agreed that it was a good move. They talked for around half an hour before Seth left to return to the fortress, promising

Riley updates on what happened regarding the quest to Askua. He and Verun flew away, and he looked back at the little cottage on the miniature mountain peak.

CHAPTER 11

Seth was only in Slyborn for a few minutes. He fast-walked to his room and grabbed the big seed from the chest at the foot of his bed, and headed back out to the courtyard to meet Verun.

Verun took off and Seth mentally showed him the place he had in mind. Verun headed there. He landed about fifteen minutes later. Seth found himself and Verun at the very top of one of the Broken Bones. It wasn't the one that Slyborn lay on, but one of its neighbors. The mountain was massive, and the air was chilly at the top of the mountain. Seth hopped off of Verun's back and grabbed the seed, then second guessed himself. Would it be too cold for the tree at the top of the mountain? He debated with himself in silence on the top of the mountain for a minute, then decided to go ahead with his plan. He dug a hole with his hands, a feat that was undoubtedly easier because of his huge strength score. The dirt parted like butter, and before long he had a hole about three feet wide, and four feet deep.

He lowered the Mistwood Monolith seed into the hole, patted it awkwardly a few times like a pet, and then closed the dirt around it. He looked around on the ground and found some rocks, then circled where the seed was buried so he could find it again. The deed done, Seth jumped back on Verun's back and the two of them went to see Pahan.

They went into the cave entrance outside of Slyborn, Seth not seeing a reason for the two of them to split up. Even though Seth would probably see Pahan the following morning when he escorted the guild scholar down, he wanted to have a private conversation with the spirit first. Verun could sprint through the caves by memory now, getting them to Pahan in only minutes with his wings tucked back. Seth caught glimpses of lions that looked like slightly smaller versions of Verun through the darkness as he ran, but they didn't attack.

Pahan was waiting for them when they arrived in the deepest cavern of the cave, where the huge white crystal floated above the fountain. Seth hugged the big lion around his enormous neck, and Verun playfully butted his head against his father's chest. Pahan rumbled in satisfaction, then said, <I saw you plant the tree. I can feel it there, it's strange, but not so complex that I can't figure out how it was made. I'll see if I can make it grow a bit faster. Hopefully without killing it.>

Seth beamed at him and said, "I have something for you too, though I'm sure you already know that." Pahan just bobbed his massive head as Seth swapped outfits and fished the champion preservation device from his *Fortified Fanny Pack*. He set it on Pahan's fountain and watched it dissolve, then read the strange logs to Pahan that had appeared immediately after he'd inserted the Wandering Arborist's finger.

Pahan said, <Perhaps the logs were just so confused because I gave you some etherean enchanted items, so it expected you to be one of us. Our magic works differently.>

"That does sound plausible," Seth said, "but then Djinia blocked the error for some reason, and when we spoke, it seemed like she thought I'd figured some big secret out. Then she dropped it when she realized that you gave me the device. I just don't understand."

Pahan said, <You probably aren't meant to. Tell me what it was like meeting her.> Seth recounted the story of the fancy office and meeting Djinia.

Pahan didn't have any ideas as to what she might've been talking about, but he was excited to start paying attention to the tissue sample, so Seth started to leave. Then he remembered the scholar that had come with Liora, and said, "Oh, and I think I'll bring down that scholar to talk to you tomorrow. Is that alright?"

Pahan didn't sound enthused, but he said, <That will be fine, as long as he doesn't waste too much of my time.>

Seth and Verun headed back topside, Seth just in time to catch dinner.

***

Seth and Siestal, the guild scholar who'd arrived with Liora, walked down the stone path toward Pahan's main cavern. The man was probably in his seventies, with frail features and thinning white hair. He wouldn't let Seth hear the end of how he shouldn't have to walk to the bottom of some "Easium-forsaken cave" just to meet with the spirit who could manifest itself anywhere inside its domain. The man had a somewhat nasal voice, which just served to make him sound whinier.

Seth tried to keep a smile plastered on his face but it was difficult. He said, "So your specialty is the wild spirits?"

The man huffed and said, "Specialty is an understatement. I've written dozens of volumes on the subject, and read a dozen times that. I will say though, I've never actually had the chance to speak to one in the flesh. I've seen several of their crystals in person, but they always refuse to appear and speak to us." The man suddenly seemed refreshed, as if the thought of speaking with Pahan had knocked off a decade. He began walking faster.

He marveled at the glimpses of constructs as they walked. "Did you know that the spirits can both directly control the constructs they create, or give them a form of lower intelligence? It's quite fascinating."

Seth said, "Like artificial intelligence?"

The translation magic running in his head made it come out as roughly *inauthentic intelligence,* and Siestal said, "I've not heard that term, but I suppose it could work. The constructs are not really self aware like we are."

Seth remembered the kobolds he'd fought on the first day he met Aurora. It seemed like it had been years before, but he knew it was only a few months. He said, "I met a kobold chief once that was a construct, but he seemed genuinely intelligent. And what of Pahan before he supplanted the previous spirit here, he wasn't self aware?"

Siestal said, "I've only read of familiars before meeting you, and I hear there's another adventurer in Slyborn with a familiar too? I would imagine that there may be some process of giving them a self when they're captured in the summoning device, but I really can't say. As far as the kobold chief you met, I can only say that some of the constructs can be wildly convincing, but in reality, only the wild spirit is self aware. Perhaps that individual had given a huge percentage of itself to that chief, or was controlling it directly when you encountered it."

Seth mulled over what the scholar had said, but wasn't entirely convinced. Most of the monsters he'd encountered over his time in Morgenheim had seemed somewhat mindless, but not all of them.

They reached the main cavern some time later, but Pahan wasn't there. The old scholar said, "I never get tired of seeing their crystals. A thing of immense magical power and beauty." He walked over to the fountain below Pahan's crystal and sat, taking the weight off of his legs. Seth did feel somewhat bad for the man; perhaps he should have asked Verun to carry him down.

Siestal said, "His name is Pahan, you said? Hello Pahan, it's nice to make your acquaintance. May we speak?" The man was looking at the giant levitating crystal, as if attempting to make eye contact with the absent Pahan.

Wind whistled through the cavern, and Pahan formed his massive lion form behind the man. His voice said, <Hello, mortal. You may bask in my glory.>

Siestal whirled around, suddenly on his feet as if his knees hadn't been hurting him just moments before. He said, "Incredible! I have so many questions, thank you for being willing to speak with me! You are quite impressive in the flesh."

Pahan looked at Seth and said, <I think I like this pitiful human. You may leave him with me, one of my constructs will return him to the surface when we're through.>

Seth just laughed and started the hike back to Slyborn. If Siestal kept up the compliments, Pahan may never tire of the man.

CHAPTER 12

Around a week passed without much change. Liora had a messenger carry a letter to Quincy, the Transportation Guild member, giving him vague details about an expedition outside of the country but not much more, and asking if he would consider joining them for a hefty gold reward. Quincy's reply came, and he said he wanted to hear more.

Liora, like most, was frustrated with the slow rate of exchange, but didn't want to commit to travelling all the way to Cragos, where Quincy was, just to negotiate with the man. She'd found the whisper sigils framed on the wall of Aurora's office when she decided to take it over, and had the brilliant idea of having Seth and Verun fly one of them to Quincy so he and Liora could talk live. Seth felt a little irritated at being turned into a literal errand boy, but couldn't really argue the logic in the plan. He and Verun set off early in the morning, hoping to make the long flight in two days. He briefly considered inviting Riley to go, if only to have a portable house, but it turned out she'd gotten herself killed again jumping from some high place right after hitting level thirty-eight again, meaning she'd be gone for a day and a half more.

The flight to Cragos was beautiful, after crossing the Broken Bones away from Vardon they crossed over a dense forest so tightly packed with trees that it almost looked like you could walk on top of them. The occasional gaps in the canopy revealed small lakes for the most part, and Seth began to worry that they would have trouble finding a place for Verun to rest his wings. They'd decided to fly straight to the city instead of flying over the road, as it meandered around the forest.

After three hours in the air, they made it to a small lone mountain that protruded from the canopy, and rested there as the sun neared its zenith. It was only another hour of flight or so before the dense forest ended abruptly as they soared over a wide, slow-moving river. The land whooshing by below them was primarily wild plains after that, the tall grasses moving with the wind, looking like ocean currents from high in the sky.

At one point, Verun had to veer high to avoid a low-hanging storm cloud. When they'd passed over it, Seth started to spot farms below, their straight lines of crops a stark contrast to the thick, uncontrolled grasses.

The adventurer and lion spent the night in a small copse of trees they spotted, not too near to any of the farms. The trees did a good job blocking the winds that rampaged over the plains. Seth ate some of the salted meat he'd brought for the journey; it had a slightly tangy flavor, and Seth was thankful that Slyborn had a cook with a high-level cooking skill.

Verun seemed unfazed by the long day of flight, aside from his breaks every few hours. Seth, on the other hand, was exhausted. He felt like he was more tired than he should've been for just sitting on Verun's back the whole day, but wasn't able to explain it. He fell asleep almost instantly when night came.

The night was uneventful, though Seth was woken up once to the noise of something walking through the brush. Whatever it was, it decided Verun was above its pay-grade, and made a hasty retreat into the small wooded area.

The two of them took to the sky again the next morning, and began to see many more farms than the previous day, even seeing some small towns around the size of Bosqovar. It was early afternoon when Cragos came into view. The city was markedly different from Vardon, the only other big city Seth had ever been to in Morgenheim.

Where Vardon was all tall yellow stone walls, Cragos was squat and dark. The city had walls around it, too, though not as tall. They were made out of some dark-gray stone, so dark it could've been mistaken for black if the sun wasn't high in the sky. Huge pointy metal finishings attached to the outside of the wall gave it a vaguely gothic appearance in Seth's opinion.

Inside the wall he could see crowded streets that didn't look too different to the interior of Vardon, except that the structures were almost all made of dark wood. On the horizon to his right, Seth could see a dark blob that he thought may have been another of the impenetrable forests, and figured it must be where the city got all of their wood.

He'd been given instructions on how to find the Adventurers' Guild headquarters before he left, and planned on leaving Verun there while he talked with the Transportation Guild. He and Verun flew high over the city's walls and headed for the center of the city. Seth saw several guards on the wall point to him, but his red cape must have put them at ease, as none of them went running for reinforcements.

Near the center of Cragos was a huge, dark cathedral, made of the same black stone that composed the city walls. It was surrounded by a large square, as if the bustle of buildings in the rest of the city were afraid to approach.

One of the buildings on the square, or rather several right next to each other, constituted the Adventurers' Guild headquarters in the city. Aurora had hinted that this was extremely valuable property.

Verun banked his huge white-red wings and landed just in front of the group of buildings. They were easy to pick out due to the bright-red banners that hung draped from the dark stone walls. Seth hopped off of Verun's back as two guild members exited the building, looking a bit bewildered at Verun's appearance. Aside from them, there wasn't much foot traffic near the buildings. Seth waved awkwardly at the approaching members, scanning their faces and outfits to try and glean more information.

On the left was an unusually short woman with an unusually large bow slung across her back, almost dragging the ground. Seth put her somewhere in her late thirties; she had an easygoing look on her face, but he couldn't help thinking her eyes didn't miss a thing. Her cape was red on the outside like normal Adventurers' Guild member cloaks, but the inside was a mottled green and brown camo pattern. She had long, dark hair pulled into a tight braid down her back, and Seth saw a dagger handle sticking out the top of each of her leather boots.

On the right was an ancient, richly dressed man. He hardly had any hair left on his head, though a sharp goatee adorned his face. His cape was short, only falling to the middle of his back, and there was a thick gold stripe around the outside, perfectly matching the many gold rings on his fingers.

The woman spoke first, "Hello there, Seth, I presume?" Seth just nodded. Did everyone already know who he was? Why had he thought the guild would keep his existence close to the vest? She continued, "Nice to meet you. I'm Meadow, guild spymaster." She elbowed the old man, and he jerked his gaze away from Verun to address Seth.

"Hello, Seth, you can call me Alder. I'm the guild's merchant master."

Meadow spoke again, "What brings you to Cragos? Last I was updated, you were stationed out at Slyborn with the white wit- I mean, with Liora."

Seth tried not to chuckle at the way Alder's eyes bulged at the thinly veiled insult to Liora, and said, "Yeah, Liora sent me to deliver our whisper sigil to Quincy in the Transportation Guild so they can negotiate."

Meadow and Alder both looked like they'd just bitten into a sour lemon, and Alder said, "Delivering one of our most priceless artifacts into the hand of the enemy. I'll have no part in this." With that, he simply turned and walked back into the huge stone building. Just before he shut the wooden door, he called back, "I hope I'm not expected to pay ransom when those scoundrels decide they don't want to give it back!"

Meadow shrugged her shoulders at Seth. "Sorry about that. He's not a fan of the blue-cloaks. Can't say I like them much either, but orders are orders. Do you need someone to show you to their compound?"

"I do, I've never been to Cragos before. I was hoping Verun could stay here," Seth said, nodding at the big lion. "Would that be alright? He'll probably just curl up and sleep somewhere."

Meadow said, "Sure. Around back of the building there's a big mound of hay we use to-"

She hadn't finished her sentence when Verun said, <Great!> and beat his massive wings, flying straight over the building and disappearing behind it. His voice came again several moments later, projecting right into their heads, <Oh yeah, this is really comfortable. See you later, partner.> Through their bond, Seth had a vague sense of Verun standing on a massive mound of hay, turning in a circle and pawing at it.

Meadow looked up to where Verun had flown for a few silent seconds, then just chuckled and said, "I'll show you where the blue-cloaks' headquarters is, it's not far. I won't go in with you, though. They'd probably think I was mentally noting everything down to disseminate to our spies. They'd probably be right." She winked.

Without much ado, Meadow started walking away, around the perimeter of the great square the guild buildings faced. Seth hurried to catch up, then said, "Thanks for the help. Can you tell me about Cragos?"

Meadow looked at him without turning her head, giving him a side-eyed glance. She said, "I'll tell you about the city, but not for free. I deal in information, I've read all of your official reports, but I have a *lot* of questions about your...condition."

Seth had a sudden, overwhelming feeling that he was making a lopsided deal, but went ahead. "Sure, what do you want to know?"

Meadow grinned. "What's it like?" She suddenly had a childish glee about her, and her small stature didn't help the comparison. When she took in Seth's confused expression, she elaborated. "I mean dying."

"Oh, that," Seth said. "Well, it's not actually so bad. It hurts, sure, for a few seconds, then I just wake up...elsewhere. I call it the void. It's like an infinite black room. You can walk in any direction and nothing ever changes. There's not much to do, none of your belongings go with you there, so you just have to wait, for a time based on the level you were when you died, until you come back. I usually try to sleep or just pick a direction and walk."

Meadow nodded, intent on Seth's words like he was revealing some clandestine secret. Once she realized he was done talking, she said, "Very intriguing. Right, Cragos. It's one of the three major cities in Efril. It's been here for thousands of years, or at least that's what the historians say. It's commonly called the dark gem of Efril. I'm sure you noticed all the dark rock, it's called obstygian, and there's loads of it in the ground in this area. It's quite malleable in its natural form, but when subjected to high temperatures it grows quite hard, so it's great for building material as long as you have a fire mage around to cook it for you."

The two of them had been walking up the edge of the huge city square, which Seth was surprised was still almost completely empty except for a few people walking along the perimeters like he was. The huge cathedral in the center of the square had been looming off to his side in his peripheral vision, and just then the front of the massive building came into view.

Whereas the sides of the building were just huge dark arches, the front had a massive plate-glass mosaic. It was a man's face. Seth stopped walking, and glanced at Meadow. "Who's that?"

She clicked her tongue, then said, "Nope, it's my turn. Have you found any way to identify others of your kind by sight?"

Seth shook his head. "I haven't. From what I can tell, we're the same except for the whole reincarnation thing." His in-brain translation magic really struggled on the word *reincarnation*. Seth continued, "Though, I think Verun can tell by trying to scan people. He can apparently scan Riley and I, but not any other humans."

Meadow said, "That's interesting, though I'm not sure how helpful it'll be for us. I wonder what the reason for that is, though. A curious puzzle. Now, that." She motioned at the huge stained-glass face that looked like it was staring at them no matter where they went. "It's called the face of Easium, and it's quite old. It's nigh unbreakable, from what people can tell, though no one's tried *that hard* to break it, mind you. Supposedly it's the most accurate representation of the god's face, and we Cragotians have a lot of superstition around it. Have you noticed no one loiters around the cathedral? It's customary not to approach unless you intend to go in and pray, otherwise most people just skirt the edges or take the long way around."

Seth said, "Easium, the patron god of humans, right? I wonder what'd happen if I went in there."

Meadow chuckled and said, "Realistically? Probably nothing. But, you never know. He might smite you out of existence. Anyway, here we are." She motioned toward a building around a hundred paces away with blue banners adorning it.

Seth looked back over his shoulder, the Adventurers' Guild building still plainly in view. "Wait, it was right here? Couldn't you have just pointed?"

Meadow was already turning to head back. She said, "Sure, I could have, but then I couldn't have interrogated you. Supper is served at sundown, and we can find a bed for you if you need to stay the night. Nice meeting you!"

All Seth could muster as she retreated was, "Interrogated?"

A few minutes later Seth had approached the doorway to the huge building. He wasn't sure whether he should just walk in, so ended up knocking on the door instead. When no one answered, he tried the door and it opened, so he walked in.

The entryway took up two stories inside the building, with a huge staircase made out of the same obstygian stone leading up to a balcony that led deeper into the building. A mustachioed man in a blue cloak happened to be walking by on the second floor and glanced down to see Seth standing awkwardly in the entry area. Seth tried not to laugh at the man's over-the-top reaction, seemingly almost jumping out of his boots.

He yelled down at Seth as he descended the stairs, "You! What are you doing here, red-cape? Did you think you could sneak around our headquarters without us noticing?"

Seth held up his hands placatingly. "Hey dude, no, do you think I'd really wear my *bright-red* cape if I was trying to sneak into your building? I'm here to meet Quincy. I have to deliver a message from Liora the Light, his hands only."

The man's comically bushy eyebrows were still knit together, but he hadn't drawn his sword or anything. He said, "Letter for Quincy. I'll go check with him, please wait outside." He put his hands on his hips, indicating that he wasn't budging until Seth had vacated the premises.

Seth just nodded and walked back out the door, looking even more suspicious in his red cape loitering outside of the Transportation Guild headquarters.

It was only several minutes before the same man returned and beckoned Seth inside, saying, "He's busy at the moment, but said he will meet with you soon. Follow me."

The man led Seth up the grand staircase and then through several twisting hallways, until they arrived at a row of chairs outside of an office. The man indicated Seth should sit, then left without a word. He felt like a class clown waiting to talk to the principal. There was a man, presumably a knight due to his bulky iron plate armor, standing guard outside of the door, and he simply pretended Seth didn't exist. Occasionally a blue-cloak or two would walk by and spot Seth. All of them showed brief surprise at the red cape strapped to his back, then either completely ignored him as they passed, or leered at him.

After what felt like more than forty-five minutes, the door to Quincy's office opened, and a dark-haired woman walked out. She had a serious expression on her face, and didn't even spare a second glance for Seth after she apparently decided that he wasn't a threat.

The guard next to Quincy's door stuck his head into the office and said, "A red-cape is here with a message for you."

Seth heard a deep voice reply from within, "Send 'em in then." The guard just returned to his post, staring out into the hallway, saying nothing to Seth. Seth thought that must've been the only cue he was going to get, so he stood and entered the room.

Quincy was a large man, both tall and muscled, and Seth guessed he was probably in his fifties. He sat behind an even larger table and was reclined in his chair, dusty black boots propped on his desk and hands lazily behind his head. His head was shaved completely bald, and looked to have been done so recently that Seth couldn't even identify any stubble or hairline. His face was similarly hairless, except for slim dark eyebrows.

The man's teeth were what Seth noticed next. Morgenheim didn't have the level of dental hygiene that Seth had been used to on Earth. It was relatively common to see people missing a tooth or two, and the bright-white teeth of movie-stars were nearly unheard of. Quincy's smile looked like that of a wildly successful car-salesman, perfectly straight and white.

His clothing was different than Seth was used to seeing too. His shirt was made of a loose-fitting light-blue fabric, and there weren't any sleeves, showing bulky biceps. Quincy wore a pair of light-tan pants that were also quite loose-fitting and

tucked into his boots. Whereas other
Transportation Guild members Seth had seen
tended to wear large blue cloaks that draped over
their shoulders, Quincy's was more like a very
small cape that looked like it would only fall about
three-quarters of the way down his back, though it
was at that moment bunched up against his seat-
back. A blue sash the color of his cape was tied
around his waist, extra fabric hanging down his
front.

This man was supposedly one of the three
highest-level priests in the entire country of Efril?
Where were his robes? Seth couldn't even see a
staff anywhere.

He grinned at Seth as he entered, and said, "It's
been a long time since someone from your
organization has walked within a block of this
building, I'd wager, let alone entered it. These
certainly are strange times. How was your
journey?"

Seth hadn't been expecting the man to be so
cordial. He started to respond, "It was pretty
uneven-"

Quincy interrupted him, easy smile never
leaving his face, "Please, have a seat."

Seth nodded and sat down in one of the chairs
set near the front of the desk. He noticed that the
desk was quite clean; only three stacks of
parchment marred its beautiful finished wood
surface, and they were perfectly equidistant from
one another, edges aligned exactly with the edges

of the desk. He continued, "My journey was uneventful, thank you. I'm to deliver this to you and 'keep my gullet closed,'" Seth said as he fished around in his pack to produce the Whisper Sigil. Thankfully, he'd had enough foresight to transfer it from his Fortified Fanny Pack to his regular pack before entering the Transportation Guild base, dodging his normal awkward straining to remove the fanny pack in his plate armor.

Quincy leaned forward and took the small stone from Seth's hand. Until then, he'd had his hands behind his head, but as he reached for the sigil, Seth saw his hands for the first time. The man had what Seth could only describe as silvery brass knuckles on his hands. They were rough and beat up. What kind of priest was this man?

Quincy held the small runic stone in front of his mouth and put his thumb over the rune on one of the faces. It lit up with a soft purple glow, and he spoke, drawing out the words lazily. "Hello, Liora."

Seth could vividly imagine the sour look on the mage's face as her voice resonated through the stone. "Quincy."

Quincy glanced at Seth and, if anything, his grin only grew.

CHAPTER 13

Seth tried to leave after ten minutes of the negotiations. Liora and Quincy were already bitterly arguing over the details of their joint venture, focusing so much on the minutiae that Seth feared he might fall asleep. When he tried to excuse himself, however, Liora's voice snapped out of the whisper sigil, "Seth, you'll stay in the room with our priceless sigil at all times, understood?" He just sighed and sat back down in the hard wooden chair.

Liora never came right out and said that Quincy was her only option for the quest, but Seth thought the big man knew. He drove a hard bargain. Liora wanted him and at most two other Transportation Guild members to join a full raid of Adventurers'

Guild members. Parties could only support six members, but there was a way to get around that by forming raids, which lumped multiple parties in a larger group under a leading party, effectively raising the cap of how large a group of people could get and still be magically partied up to sixty, or ten groups of six.

Sub-parties functioned exactly like normal, but members of the leading party could feel the direction and distance of all members of the raid, and had access to some other leadership skills that Seth hadn't had fully explained yet.

Quincy was adamant that, if he was to go on the expedition out of the country, he wanted at least half of the raid made up of Transportation Guild members, though he advocated for even more than a perfect split, citing that his guild was more experienced when it came to fighting monsters on the road.

The two argued for hours, and when the sun began setting outside of Quincy's window, Seth hoped they'd wrap it up. Instead, Liora, via the whisper sigil, instructed Seth to take it with him, spend the night at the Cragos guild headquarters, and bring it back to Quincy the next morning.

Seth stood and exited the room, stiff joints, feeling like a zombie. Quincy cheerily waved goodbye, seemingly invigorated by the hours of debate and negotiation. "See you bright and early!"

Seth returned to the Adventurers' Guild buildings, skirting the edge of the huge square like he and Meadow had earlier in the day. He couldn't help but stare at the huge effigy of Easium's face rendered in stained glass as he walked.

The guild members were welcoming for the most part, though many of them stared when they thought he couldn't see. He got a meal in the mess hall, and went to his temporary bedroom early and slept off his weariness.

The next morning was déjà vu, Seth walked the same way to the Transportation Guild headquarters and was escorted to Quincy's office yet again. He and Liora verbally sparred until sometime around midday; Seth knew because his stomach was empty and growling. Finally, the two of them came to an agreement.

Liora had broken and given Quincy the experience and gold reward values for the quest, and had Seth share it with him so he could see the details for himself. At some point, Quincy had lost his smug attitude, and Seth could hear the irritation in Liora's voice. Neither seemed completely satisfied with the compromise, but perhaps that was a sign that it wasn't a one-sided agreement.

Quincy, accompanied by nineteen other Transportation Guild members would make up exactly one-third of the raid, less than he'd wanted, but more than Liora had wanted. Quincy had originally demanded that his party be the leading party, as he was the most experienced in moving large groups of people through monster-infested territories. Liora had vehemently disagreed, and after literal hours of debate, they'd settled on splitting the leading party between three red-capes and three blue-cloaks.

The Adventurers' Guild would be responsible for providing food for the entire expedition, and the Transportation Guild would bring their *myrt,* some kind of pack animal based on the context, and some sort of all-terrain carts for them to pull to haul food and supplies. The two forces would meet at the border town nearest to Askua inside of Efril and set off on their expedition from there in three weeks' time.

Liora signed off, and Quincy returned the whisper sigil to Seth. Seth started to rise, preparing to say his goodbyes to the man, but Quincy spoke first. "Let's you and I have a chat now that all that is behind us," he said, his pearly-white grin returning.

Seth said, "Uh, alright, what do you want to talk about?" His brain wasn't working too well after the hours and hours of arguing and haggling he'd been forced to listen to.

Quincy said, "I hope you'll keep this between us." He stopped speaking and his gaze grew stern disturbingly fast. He stared at Seth in silence, waiting.

Seth said, "Yeah, sure."

Like the stern look had never happened, Quincy's face assumed its easy, grinning expression again. He continued, "I happen to have a source who's let me know about your...unique background." He didn't elaborate, apparently unwilling to come right out and say it. Quincy continued, "I've been wondering, what would it take to get you to join up with us? We can wait until after this out-of-the-country expedition if you'd like, but someone with your...situation in the ranks could do wonders for our organization."

Seth was a little thrown off, and didn't speak immediately. Quincy must have taken his silence for the strong, bargaining flavor, as he said, "We have gold available. Positions of power. Land. Magical items. Masters in every class. What'll it take?"

Seth said, "How did you find out about that?"

Quincy smirked. "Your guild isn't the only one with spies and informants. I also happen to know that there's talk about Liora's daughter being the subject of some ridiculous prophecy, too. Now, what do you want? We could have you only work two months of the year, but pay you for the whole time. How does that sound?"

Seth cringed, unsure how to respond. On one hand, he felt a good amount of loyalty to the Adventurers' Guild. They'd taken him in when he was new and he'd made good friends. On the other hand, Liora had just come in and taken away Aurora's position, and Quincy was actually pretty likable.

The silence dragged on, until Quincy cracked. "Well, keep it in mind. We'll be seeing more of each other soon." He stood and walked around the desk, patting Seth on the back as he rose to leave. Quincy walked Seth out in awkward silence, though the muscled man just absently smiled the entire time, as if he were perfectly comfortable.

About half of the daylight was left for the day, so Seth quickly met up with Verun and they headed out of Cragos, eager to get back to Slyborn as soon as possible.

CHAPTER 14

The flight back to Slyborn was uneventful for the most part, though Seth and Verun both enjoyed the gorgeous views. The day after he made it back, he found himself standing in Aurora's commandeered office.

Liora had sent messengers to the guild's chapters in Agril and Cragos, requesting dozens of guild members by name. Seth's respect for her increased when he realized she simply remembered the names and skill sets of every member she was asking for. For all of her brashness, the woman did seem to have the best interests of the guild in mind.

Liora, Aurora, Molly, and Seth stood in Liora's office, trying to decide what their leading party would look like. Seth felt intimidated being surrounded by all of the powerful women, but tried not to let it show.

Aurora crossed her arms. "I think it's clear that Seth should be in the leading party, considering it's technically his quest, and he spoke to Djinia in person so might have additional info."

Seth said, "I really don't know if I need to be-"

Liora interrupted him, "I agree Seth should be there, and I think you should too, Aurora."

Aurora said, "Me? I want to stay here and watch the fortress. I expect you'd like that job for yourself."

Liora said, "Quincy, as much as it pains me to say it, is a very accomplished priest. He'll be bringing along two of his top lieutenants, a rogue and a scout. Seth, I assume, can do some damage. That leaves two slots open on the leading party, a knight, and another damage dealer. It'd send a strong message to have you, my daughter, on the leading team as well."

Aurora quickly retorted, "So there's a damage slot on the leading party as well. And you know what'd send an even stronger message? Your presence on the team yourself! Someone else can fill the knight role, and I can stay here and hold down *my* fort."

Liora started to respond again, even more heated, but Molly cut in, "Why don't you both go, and I'll keep an eye on the fort in the interim?"

Aurora and her mother both looked aghast for a split second before saying, in unison, "No!" Then locked eyes, aghast that they'd just agreed on something.

There was silence for a moment, then Liora spoke up, "I suppose, Molly, that isn't the worst idea in the world. You were helping to administer the fortress while Ramses was in command."

Aurora said, "She's continued to be an invaluable resource since I took over. She doesn't have any official guild officer training, but these aren't necessarily normal times. If only we had a high council member here to sign an exemption." She looked at her mother and raised her eyebrows expectantly.

Liora was silent for a long stretch before sighing and saying, "Alright, I see no issue with that. And I would like to be there to keep my eyes on that scoundrel Quincy and make sure you don't get into anything you can't handle."

Aurora looked like she was going to retort but held it in, resulting in a literal clenching of her jaw. Seth said, "Well, glad that's settled then. Molly will hold down Slyborn, and the three of us will make up our half of the leading party." They all agreed, and their impromptu meeting was adjourned.

***

Seth headed down to the crafting building again after the meeting. It'd been over a week since he'd last checked with Landers, the new smith, about his project. He had a feeling he knew what the man would say when he got there.

Landers was working on a large metal beam when Seth entered this time. It took Seth a few seconds to figure out what it was: a wagon axle. He waited respectfully for a minute and spoke up when the man stood to switch tools, "Hello Landers. I've come to check on the project. Have you made any progress?"

The man just grunted and shook his head no, not making eye contact with Seth. He started to go back to his work.

Seth had had enough. It'd been over five weeks since he'd had the request put in, and Aurora had sent multiple orders telling the man to prioritize Seth's work. He snapped, "What is your problem?!" He'd shouted it unintentionally. Landers froze.

He slowly looked up at Seth and said, quietly, "My problem is that I'd rather be smote by Easium himself than lift a finger to help your kind. You're unnatural. People who die should stay dead."

Seth was stunned. It wasn't the first time he'd faced backlash over his status as one of the race of adventurers who could come back from the dead. While he didn't flaunt it like Riley, it was well known by the entire guild that Seth had died several times and returned. It unsettled some people, and had even caused a few to harbor anger towards him. After a moment, Seth said, "You realize I didn't choose to be like this, right? And you realize we're on the same side?"

The man had turned around and Seth couldn't see his face anymore. He let silence hang thick in the room for several seconds before saying, quietly, "Every time I see your face, knowing you've died and returned, I can't help but feel that you're spitting in the face of my little Mela..." He dropped his tools to the floor and turned, tears streaming down his face. He shouldered roughly past Seth, saying, "Are you happy now?" and left.

Seth considered chasing after him, trying to explain that he didn't mean any offense by his *existence,* but it was obvious the man was going through some difficult times. He stood in silence in the empty forge basement for a time, unsure of what to do next, before heading out into the courtyard and finding Verun.

The lion was awake and ready to go when Seth arrived. They'd made a habit of flying out to the Mistwood Monolith and checking on it every day since they'd planted it. So far, there wasn't any growth, but some grass was starting to creep back over the mound of dirt. The result was the same on this day, too. Seth was a little disappointed, he'd hoped that Pahan would work his magic a little... faster. He unbuckled the little waterskin from Verun's harness and drizzled some water on the dirt mound, and the two headed out, away from Slyborn, looking for some monsters to fight.

CHAPTER 15

Adventurers' Guild members started showing up to Slyborn at a rate of several per day for the following two weeks. Liora had Seth meet every one of them that she'd requested and share the quest with them. In the evenings, Seth and Verun trained in the areas bordering the Broken Bones, and Seth finally reached level forty-nine.

Seth finally received his new plate armor from Landers, though he hadn't actually talked to the man, someone had just delivered the armor for him. Seth spent several hours with the enchanting table enchanting the armor with the *Essence-Enriched Quartzite Nuggets* he'd bought in Vardon, giving it an awesome stamina boost. When he was wearing his second outfit, his health was almost one thousand points higher, and his defense was high. He could barely move when wearing it, of course, as he wasn't a knight and didn't have the skill that granted the ability to move fluidly in plate, but it was good for absorbing impacts that he saw coming.

When the time came to finally depart Slyborn and head to the town where they'd meet up with the Transportation Guild force, forty of the spots for the shareable quest had been filled, thirty-nine Adventurers' Guild members, Seth included, and Riley filling the fortieth spot.

Seth and Verun said their goodbyes to Pahan the night before. The scholar, Siestal, would be staying at Slyborn while Seth was on the expedition. Pahan was actually happy about that, as the old man still showered him with compliments, and seemed to actually be helping him puzzle out the data he'd collected from the Wandering Arborist's finger.

The force headed off down the mountain, heading for the edge of the Broken Bones. The plan at first had been for each member to carry a large pack on their back with their food for the week, and then for a single horse-drawn carriage to pull a cart with bedrolls and tents for everyone. Instead, Riley offered to let everyone store their food and sleeping arrangements in her house.

Seth hadn't actually seen her deploy the house before, and jumped like the rest of the crowd when she held out her hand and eight bright glowing balls shot out, rapidly arranging themselves into a large rectangle. There was a flicker of deep, eternal blackness for a split-second, then the house simply...was. It dropped a few inches, creaking as it settled onto the ground in the center of Slyborn's main courtyard. The guild members spent around an hour loading big crates of food and water into the house, marveling at the inside. Some members began to store their packs in the house too, but Liora spoke up, saying each member should have their sleeping arrangements and at a minimum three days' worth of food on them at all times. She didn't have to mention that Riley was prone to dying. Some shuffling was done, and everyone evacuated the packed house.

With that, Riley raised her hand again. The eight little balls sprung out, one at a time this time, floating into position around the house until they formed a rectangle encasing it. In a flash similar to when it'd appeared, the house vanished, and Seth peeked into the void he was familiar with for just a moment. Several insects fell from where they'd clung to the house an instant before, the void refusing to take any living things. The guild members oohed and aahed, and Seth tried not to cringe as he remembered accidentally picking his boon. Things had turned out alright, and his boon wasn't as useless as it'd seemed at first, but he couldn't help but feel a twinge of jealousy at Riley's choice.

The raid party marched for most of each day, starting an hour after sunrise, breaking for lunch, and then resuming until about an hour before dark. Seth typically flew reconnaissance with Verun in the mornings, watching for approaching monsters or any other threats, practicing relaying that information back to the partial raid for when they were in really high-level territory outside of the Efril border.

Riley would take over air surveillance duties for the second half of the day, and Seth would walk with the rest of the group. Forty people wasn't a huge group, so Seth had to intentionally try and stay away from Baltern, the only other member of Seth's battle team to be invited to the raid. Isaac, Dominick, Farolt, and Tela were all deemed too low-level.

Liora was drilling the group on battle formations, a feature provided by joining a raid party. The leading party could set up three party-configurations that were saved in a menu. Any leading party member could, at will, reform the entire raid into one of those three configurations. So far, Liora, Seth, and Aurora had only come up with two configurations. The user experience on the menu for creating the formations, only accessible by those in the leading party, was atrocious, but Seth got by. One of the formations they titled the *autonomous formation,* intended to make each party independently viable with at least one knight and one priest. The second formation they had created was the *champion formation,* where teams were formed based on role, like a team of five knights and one priest who'd stand in front, and entire parties of exclusively ranged damage dealers. This was the formation they'd assume when encountering a champion, or very strong construct in the wilderness. Both formations still needed to be refined once Quincy and his people joined.

Thankfully, in both formations Seth remained in the leading party, meaning he never had to work closely with Baltern. The big knight had, so far, just ignored Seth for the most part, but Seth still felt some anger toward the man every time he saw him. That'd probably have to get fixed, but Seth was feeling stubborn.

The days went by quickly. Two nights during the one-week march ended up with their camps near small towns, and some guild members enjoyed visiting the taverns, though the threat of Liora's wrath kept them from getting too unruly.

Being in the leading party with Aurora and her mother, Seth finally got a hint of why Liora's name was so renowned when he first inspected her statistics in the party interface.

Liora (Liora the Light)
Main Class: Level 58 Mage
(5,684,356/7,387,277)
Second Class: Level 33 Knight

4,149 / 4,149 Health Points
2,988 / 2,988 Mana Points
Factions: Adventurers' Guild

The woman was a monster. She had well in excess of double the health that he had, but she wasn't even a knight primary. He wondered if she preferred using fire or wind magic; she should have access to both at her high level. He was excited to see her fight.

Seth also got a little surprise when he looked at Aurora's stat page for the first time in over a month.

Aurora
Main Class: Level 33 Knight (1,658/61,610)
Second Class: Level 18 Priest
2,412 / 2,412 Health Points
1,665 / 1,665 Mana Points
Factions: Adventurers' Guild

Seth approached her as they marched and said, "Thirty-three! How'd you get so many levels?" She'd only been level twenty-eight during the battle with the Howlingshields.

Aurora said, "Pahan was spawning monsters to fight every evening for a few hours. I was pretty annoyed when Mother took over for me, but it definitely did free me up to train more often." She smiled, obviously proud someone had noticed her accomplishment.

Seth said, "Thanks for the invite," his tone dripping with sarcasm.

Her eyes rolled behind her trademark goggles, and she said, "Oh don't act like you haven't been training in the next zone over against those elephant giants. Verun told me all about it. They're higher level than Pahan can create right now, so you're getting more from that." Seth couldn't argue with her logic.

The week felt, to Seth, like it went by in a blur. Many of the guild members were already acquainted, and their teams meshed well. Seth was worried about how the dynamic might change when Quincy's group joined the raid.

The Adventurers' Guild made it to the town they were supposed to meet Quincy's force the night before the designated meeting day and set up camp outside of the town. Unlike other towns they'd stopped at along the route, this one was small and spartan; a collection of around ten houses surrounded by a ten-foot stone wall that looked more like a small castle wall than something that should surround such a small village.

There were no taverns in this town, but one of the denizens did come out and greet the Adventurers' Guild. He was a tough-looking man in his forties with shaggy black hair reaching past his jawline and an unkempt beard. A wicked scar ran down his left cheek, a somewhat rare sight for Seth, as only naturally healed wounds created scars, and almost everyone could get healing from a priest primary or secondary. Seth heard the man and Liora talking.

He said, "To what do we owe the pleasure of such a large group appearing outside our little village?" He had an odd way of speaking; he sounded educated, but spoke in a stiff, gruff voice that counteracted the impression.

Liora answered, "We're just camping here overnight, we'll be meeting with a second force and forging beyond the edge."

The man, who'd been mostly calm and collected until that point, widened his eyes almost comically before saying, "I've lived out here for seventeen years, and things have just gotten worse. We can barely eke out an existence thanks to all of the monsters. If you plan to go even further...it's your funeral."

Liora didn't answer, just crossed her arms in front of her chest and gave the man a skeptical look. He held her gaze for a moment, then nodded, and walked back to his walled village in silence.

Ivon put his hand on Seth's shoulder, and Seth jumped a little. He hadn't heard the old scout approach. He said, "Folk out here near the edge of Efril have a rough time of it. There's hardly any competition for land or resources, so it's worth the money if they can pull it off, but the mortality rate is astronomical. The monsters out here are almost always over level forty or fifty, and it's not uncommon to see them run in packs." He looked after the retreating man, sorrow on his face.

Seth said, "Why don't they just move inward? Wouldn't that be safer?"

Ivon nodded slowly, then said, "Sure, it would be safer. Many people do just that, but then the land they leave behind becomes even more infested, shrinking our country even more. These people were probably born here, and things probably weren't so bad in their parents' or grandparents' times. They don't want to leave their home."

Seth pondered Ivon's words, even after the man had gone to set up his tent. Perhaps this was just the place to test their methods.

CHAPTER 16

Quincy and the other blue-cloaks arrived the next morning a few hours after sunrise. They'd brought around a dozen hulking animals with them, called *myrt*, which were some kind of massive impala-bison hybrid, each with four horns. One rider sat atop each, steering them, and dozens of saddle bags and packs were strapped to each big animal. Each had a cart hitched to it with high walls and tough-looking wheels, though all of the carts were empty.

Seth, Liora, and Aurora met Quincy and two others in the middle of the two groups. Quincy had the same easy smile that he'd worn the first time, and how he towered over his two companions just reinforced how tall he was. To his right was a man of more average proportions, with short-cropped hair and a goatee. A huge longbow was slung across his back, accompanied by a quiver jammed full of arrows.

To Quincy's left was the woman Seth had glimpsed angrily leaving Quincy's office when they'd spoken the first time. Her blue cloak covered most of her body and was substantially larger than most of the cloaks he had seen the Transportation Guild members sport. Her long hair was dark and loose, and she had a wide-eyed alert look to her face. Something about the way she moved bothered Seth, but it only took him a moment to figure it out. She seemed...twitchy. Instead of smoothly turning her head to look at the three approaching Adventurers' Guild members, she twitched her gaze to Seth, then with little in-between motion twitched to Liora and Aurora.

Liora and Quincy exchanged greetings, neither seeming very genuine, and then Liora said, "You can join the leading party now, please invite your own people. We'll need to work on party layouts."

Liora must have invited the three of them, because suddenly Seth could *feel* their presence. His curiosity prompted him to quickly pop open all three of their stat pages,

eager to see who he'd be fighting alongside.

Quincy
Main Class: Level 60 Priest (103,294/8,144,473)

Second Class: Level 41 Warrior
3,960 / 3,960 Health Points
6,300 / 6,300 Mana Points
Factions: Transportation Guild

Sullivan
Main Class: Level 57 Scout
(4,039,284/7,035,502)
Second Class: Level 33 Mage
2,246 / 2,246 Health Points
100/100 Concentration Points
1,899 / 1,899 Mana Points
Factions: Transportation Guild

Gianna
Main Class: Level 55 Rogue
(6,035,885/6,381,408)
Second Class: Level 39 Priest
1,856/1,856 Health Points
1,980/1,980 Mana Points
100/100 Concentration Points
Factions: Transportation Guild

Seth pulled up his own stats, just to compare. It wasn't a great comparison.

Seth

Main Class: Level 49 Warrior (21,097/1,139,069)
Second Class: None
1,764/1,764 Health Points
0/100 Fury Points
Factions: Adventurers' Guild
Stamina: 98
Dexterity: 103 (99 + 4)
Strength: 174 (147 + 27)
Intelligence: 49
Wisdom: 49

Seth was one of the weaker members of the party, and he had the lowest health. Granted, that was only because Aurora was a knight, and therefore gained health at a much higher rate per level than warriors did. Seth couldn't help but think that the Adventurers' Guild half of the leading party was quite a bit weaker than the Transportation Guild.

There was an awkward silence as everyone scanned their new party members' statistics. Seth wondered how long it'd been since members of these two guilds had been in the same party. Quincy's eyebrows climbed up his forehead, probably at Liora's health pool.

Gianna, the twitchy rogue, grinned at Seth and said, "Forty-nine huh? Condolences."

Seth said, "Sorry, what?"

She just grinned bigger and said, "The levels come a *lot* slower after fifty. You've never heard how much the experience requirement jumps?" Seth shook his head but looked back at their stats page. He hadn't even noticed how high the experience requirements were. Whereas Seth needed a little more than a million experience points to get to level fifty, Gianna needed over six million to get from fifty-five to fifty-six, though by the look of her stat sheet, she was almost there.

Seth just replied, "Oh, fantastic." She laughed a fast, lilting laugh, and Sullivan, the scout, suppressed a smile with some effort.

Quincy and Liora were sizing each other up, and after a few more seconds of silence, Liora said, "Let's get some food transferred into your carts, then we're ready to depart."

Seth broke in, "Actually, I had an idea I wanted to run by you all." Liora shot daggers from her eyes, likely furious that he hadn't talked privately with her first. He continued, "Why don't we find the dungeon for the area we're in right now and do a test run before we venture outside of the country?"

Liora's angry expression vanished, and she said, "That actually does sound like a good idea."

Quincy was nodding, too. He said, "I like that idea. I haven't tried using *Purify* on a dungeon core yet, since you told me of its effects. We barely had time to get all of our supplies together and travel out here. It'd be wise to see what we're in for before we get too far from...*civilization*." The last word dripped with sarcasm as he glanced at the small walled town in the distance.

Liora side-eyed Quincy, perhaps surprised that he'd agreed with her so readily after their marathon negotiations over the whisper-sigil. She said, "Do you know where the dungeon is for this area?"

Seth grimaced. "No, I don't, but we can try to find it."

Liora nodded. "Do that, and we'll work on loading the food into the carts." Seth had hoped to see Quincy's reaction to Riley's magical house, but nodded and mentally called out to Verun. Thankfully the lion wasn't asleep somewhere, and Seth felt him take to the air, heading his way.

Moments later Verun landed a dozen paces away, huge wings stirring up loose dirt as he killed his momentum just before touchdown. Quincy, Gianna, and Sullivan didn't shrink away or draw their weapons, just looked mildly curious. Seth assumed the same source that had let them in on his existence had also disclosed Verun's.

The two of them took off and started searching. Minutes later Seth felt seventeen other people join the raid. He groaned aloud and pinched the bridge of his nose. Verun said, <More humans in the raid?>

Seth said, "Yeah, I'll get used to it in a minute." He'd had a similar reaction when all of the Adventurers' Guild members had been added to the raid. For everyone in a regular party, they could only feel the directions of the other five, like normal, but for each member of the leading party, the positions, health, and other various metrics were available for every member of the entire raid. It was a lot of information to cram into Seth's head, but he'd learned to tune it out for the most part.

Now that the raid was actually at maximum capacity with sixty members, Seth skimmed over all of the data. It appeared that the average level of the raid was probably somewhere in the high thirties, but there were people as low as thirty-two, and people as high as level forty-eight. Liora, Quincy, Sullivan, and Gianna were the only people over level fifty in the entire raid.

With Verun's help, Seth was able to identify the entrance to the nearest dungeon within half an hour. Verun circled in the air above a musty cave opening on the side of a hill. <It is there, I can feel it,> he said.

They could only see a few dozen paces into the maw of the cavern as they flew by, after which it turned a corner, heading deeper underground. Seth and Verun headed back to the main force.

The carts were loaded up, and Seth saw Riley's house disappear as he approached on Verun's back. The raid party was divided into ten rough groups. Three were completely composed of bluecapes, though one of those was only five members. A glance at the raid menu showed that Riley was the last member of that five-person party. He thought that was odd, but it looked like the other six parties were completely made of Adventurers' Guild members, leaving the leading party as the only integrated grouping.

Seth had hoped that the quest may help heal the rift between the two organizations, but it looked like they intended to be stubborn about it. He landed near the leading party and relayed the location of the dungeon entrance.

Quincy grinned. "Great! Let's go beat a dungeon."

CHAPTER 17

A party made up of five knights and a single priest from the Transportation Guild led the way into the dark cavern. Torches were passed around, and mages lit them with their *Spark* spells.

The cavern took a steep turn to the right and started descending. The tunnels opened up and weren't cramped at all, somewhat unlike the tunnels under Slyborn. The smoky stench of the torches clogged the air in the back of the column where Seth walked with Verun and the rest of the leading party.

Liora said, "It's been years since I've fought to the center of a dungeon. I wonder how long we'll go before we have our first encounter." As if spurred by her words, there was a loud clunking up ahead. Whispers rippled through the raid as shields sprang from knights' arms and scouts drew their bowstrings back, fletching between their fingers.

Out of the curtain of darkness at the edge of the torchlight a suit of armor stumbled. Two things about the armor jumped out to Seth. Firstly, it was way too large, at least twice Seth's height, and no human he'd ever seen had biceps big enough around to warrant such huge armor. Secondly, and perhaps more importantly, in the gaps of the armor where he'd expect to see skin or cloth, there was just...nothing. He could see torchlight flickering into the holes and lighting all the way to the back of the interior of the armor. It wasn't covering the construct. It *was* the construct.

The massive suit of armor drew a sword from a hidden scabbard on its back, though the blade didn't end in a point but in a square, giving it the appearance of some kind of massive butcher knife or machete.

Seth saw Baltern shove to the front of the group to stand next to the Transportation Guild knight team. Apparently the man felt like he needed to prove something. Just moments later the huge sword raised up, scraping the cave ceiling, then descended with a *whoomph,* displacing air with frightening speed.

All of the knights raised their translucent blue shields and blocked the massive blow. Seth glanced at the combat log, his position in the leading party granting him the ability to see combat statistics for anyone in the entire raid instead of just his six-person party.

> Level 46 Nightmare Armorer hits your raid
> member Jaxon for 158 damage.

Seth saw the knight who'd been hit walk backwards into the group, his shield showing a mess of cracks, and the other knights collapsed, protecting the man. Several rogues appeared behind the colossal figure, stabbing it with their daggers, but the armor was seemingly unaffected, its health bar barely moving.

Quincy's voice rose among the din, "Mages!" There was only one blue-cloak mage in the entire sixty-person raid. He responded instantly to Quincy's verbal command, letting loose a massive ball of fire that hit the towering figure directly in the chest. The effectiveness of magic was instantly apparent to Seth, as the creature halted its swing and took a step backwards. Its health bar dropped by almost a quarter from the single attack.

There were five Adventurers' Guild mages in the raid, not counting Liora or Riley, and while they'd initially not heeded Quincy's command, they did once they saw the effect of magic on the suit of armor. There was a flurry of fireballs and weak lightning spells, then the armor stand was crumpling, losing cohesion at the joints.

Riley said from Seth's left side, "Dude, I really need to get to level forty, huh?"

Seth jumped, he hadn't realized anyone was standing so close to him. For a non-rogue, she was surprisingly sneaky. The column started moving forward again, and Seth asked, "What do you mean?"

Riley said, "My fire spells are still weak until I get the second mastery skill at forty, but you can only use *Redirect Lightning* when you have clear line-of-sight to the sky. I'm kinda nerfed down here."

Seth hadn't known that. He said, "Well, you know it might help you level if you sto-"

She cut him off, "Stop dying, right. Maybe I am too risky, but you have to take risks to get ahead, not that that's something you'd understand." She laughed and slugged him in the shoulder before sauntering off toward the group of blue-cloaks she was in a party with. They side-eyed her and subconsciously stepped away as she neared. Seth was a bit befuddled. He didn't know how to handle the woman. She always left him feeling a bit dim, and he didn't think it was just because she had a massive intelligence stat.

The raid defeated twelve more giant suits of armor before reaching a massive stone door set right into a cave wall. By then, they had it down almost to a science. The knights would attract the attention of the enemy or enemies, then the mages would blast them into oblivion in less than ten seconds.

It took Seth and four other warriors all pushing in unison to get the huge stone door open. Its grinding shook the ground, and small pebbles fell from high up in the cave ceiling. Inside was a uniform tunnel stretching straight as an arrow into the darkness. The walls were so smooth that it reminded Seth of tunnels through mountains back on Earth.

The group walked in silence for several minutes before exiting the tunnel into a massive underground cavern shaped into a perfect half-sphere. Seth had the absurd notion that he was part of a football team exiting their locker room onto the field, but there were no cheers.

Opposite the tunnel they emerged from sat a glowing red crystal embedded in the cave wall around twenty feet off of the ground. It thrummed in an angry pulse as they entered, and the dungeon's champion walked out of the darkness, each footfall rumbling the entire massive cave. Several people, including Seth, had to steady themselves against the mini-earthquakes.

The champion was almost identical to the suits of armor they'd been fighting until then, but almost twice as tall and with intricate gold and white armor instead of the simple dark iron the others had been made of. It walked to the center of the room and stopped, slamming its massive sword into the stone floor, which parted like butter for the enormous weapon, then spreading its legs apart and resting its gauntlets on the pommel, waiting.

Liora spoke, "Alright, let's have team four flank to the-"

Quincy cut her off, voice loud and commanding, "Knight party, advance!"

The group of five Transportation Guild knights and one priest advanced at his command, raising their shields to the imposing armor figure. It obliged, removing its sword tip from the cavern floor and taking a huge step forward before swinging down on the central knight. For how huge the champion was, its moves were not as ponderous as Seth had expected; it seemed that its speed had scaled up as much as its size.

The central knight caught the monumental blow on his bound shield, which promptly shattered in a spray of blue sparks. The massive sword hit him in the shoulder, severing his left arm from his body. His health bar plummeted to just above ten percent, flashing an angry red in Seth's party interface.

Several things happened at once. Quincy, realizing he'd messed up said, "Gianna!" The twitchy rogue was there one moment, then simply gone. Seth saw her appear near the downed knight and drag him backwards to a priest, who crouched and went to work with a *Restore Limb* spell. Sullivan and Quincy still stood with the leading party, not making any move to join the fight.

Liora called out, her voice clearly audible above the racket, "Mages, fan out and hit it hard!" Curiously, she also didn't make any move to join in the fight, though doubtless she could do massive damage at her high level.

Aurora must have seen the confused looks that Seth was giving the two commanders, for she leaned in and said quietly, "Our job is to lead the raid, if we get bogged down fighting, we might miss important information or decisions. Unless absolutely necessary, the leading party usually refrains from fighting."

Seth said, "All six of us?" He thought it was kind of dumb, but had already seen the value with how quickly Gianna had been able to jump in and help the injured knight.

She nodded and shrugged, as if that was just the way it was. The fight didn't last that long in the end. While the champion was level forty-three, the highest level Seth had ever seen in person, it just couldn't stand up to the onslaught from an entire raid of sixty people.

The champion dropped a gorgeous set of plate armor that looked similar to its own but on a human scale when they defeated it. Liora said the leading party would distribute all loot when they camped for the night.

The whole raid walked over to the throbbing red crystal embedded in the wall. Seth said, "How are you planning to get up there?"

Quincy grinned at him and said, "I think I will manage." He walked over and simply punched the stone wall, leaving a little fist-sized crater in the stone as if he'd punched styrofoam. He made another hole a few feet up, then fit his foot into the lower hole and raised himself up, one hand in the second hole. He punched another and kept on in that fashion for around a minute before making it up to the red crystal and standing atop it. He was certainly the strangest priest Seth had ever encountered.

Quincy breathed in a deep breath and closed his eyes, and the entire raid held their breath as golden light gathered around his hands like gloves. He froze for a moment, hands glowing brighter and brighter until they almost illuminated the cavern before abruptly laying them flat on the crystal surface. A golden shockwave ran around the crystal from where he'd touched it, colliding with itself like rippling water on the opposite side.

Quincy jumped down, landing in a classic superhero pose and turning to look at his handiwork. Seth saw in the party interface that Quncy's formidable mana pool was barely above half. Apparently the spell took an insane amount of mana to cast.

There was no reaction at first, then a collective gasp when a shining white crack appeared in the red crystal. The crack spread until it covered the whole surface like spider webs, then the red shell started flaking off and falling, turning to dust before it reached the cavern floor.

Only seconds after the first piece flaked off, the rest followed suit, leaving a crystal that looked almost identical to Pahan's glowing white one under Slyborn. A small cheer went up from the raid party, though Seth noticed the red-capes and blue-cloaks still stood apart from one another, celebrating within their own groups.

Quincy shared a prompt with the leading party as the raid headed back to the surface.

You cast *Purify* on level 159 Etherean, you've cured it of *Ectocypher*.

Seth said, "Whoa, level one-fifty-nine?"

Verun's voice broke into their minds, <Etherean levels work differently than yours do. My father is already above level seventy.> He puffed his chest out in pride for Pahan.

Seth said, "You guys never told me that!"

Verun just rumbled in his version of laughter and said, <You never asked.>

***

The raid returned to the surface and gathered their beasts of burden and supplies. They didn't encounter any more suits of armor, or any constructs at all for the rest of the time they spent in that zone. They didn't return to the small village they'd camped outside the night before, but Seth hoped that Quincy's spell might make life easier for them. They camped in that same zone that night, and set off through the wilderness the next morning, struggling through completely wild landscapes with no hint of roads or human presence. Seth hoped they'd all make it back alive, something that apparently hadn't been done in centuries.

CHAPTER 18

One week into the expedition Seth was sick of the long shelf-life foods that the *myrt* carried, tired of the beasts' awful smell, and overall just tired of living on the road surrounded by so many people.

He spent much of his days flying over the raid group and scouting for monsters, and he felt like he'd hardly had any time to talk with his friends. He'd yet to participate in a single fight with a monster, as the leading party focused on orchestrating. This also meant that he hadn't seen Liora, Quincy, Sullivan, or Gianna fight yet, which he'd kind of been looking forward to.

Seth could tell it drove Quincy crazy, standing back and watching the fight. He was sure the man would break eventually and jump into the fight.

Things were looking to get more interesting though. Using old maps, Liora predicted that they could make the trek to Askua in three weeks if they continued at the pace they'd been going.

They'd finally left the formal borders of Efril four days before, but hadn't actually seen any people for a full two days before that, as the lands around the edge of the country were just too inhospitable. It really illustrated, for Seth, what Ramses had told him months ago about the wild spirits slowly constricting the area where humans could live. If a spirit spawned monster after monster, and those monsters would try to kill all humans on sight, it would take a huge investment of time and effort to bring in high-level people to slay the monsters for weeks until the wild spirit gave up on that section of territory. Wouldn't it just be easier to move a day to the west and settle there, where the monsters were lower level and not quite as hostile? This pattern, repeated for centuries, had caused the country of Efril to be surrounded on all sides by extremely high-level, extremely hostile monsters that literally no one was willing to try and fight.

The raid had repeated their dungeon cleansing tactic perhaps a dozen times in the last week, sometimes once per day, and sometimes two. It had become somewhat routine. No champions, and especially no regular monsters could stand against a group of sixty people who were all career fighters with relatively high levels. For the most part their advancement into a new zone followed a predictable pattern. They'd start to see monsters of some type, flaming rhinos for example, as they entered a new area. The terrain would often change, and even the weather sometimes. They'd fight their way forward with relative ease, the might of the raid crushing individual monsters as Seth and Riley scoured the area looking for the entrance to the dungeon.

After it was found, usually as a cave or hole in the ground, they'd enter and descend into the earth, fighting larger and tougher versions of the monsters that inhabited the wilderness in that zone. Eventually they'd come across between one and three champions, each usually in their own room, before finally gaining access to the dungeon core. There was always the angry red light and a sharp smell of vaguely expired cinnamon before Quincy cast *Purify* and it turned white. The group would then leave the dungeon and set up camp somewhere in the zone. There were hardly any monster sightings after they'd cleared an area, and when they did see them, the monsters would usually have a yellow aura around them, and retreat at the sight of so many humans.

That wasn't to say that every dungeon had been completely without surprise, however. In the group's sixth dungeon, just when they were getting used to how seemingly every one functioned, there was a surprise.

Every dungeon was aesthetically different. Where Pahan's was mostly just a dark, unlit cave with rough walls and winding turns, they'd seen one with massive purple crystals lighting the way, and they'd cleared one infested with giant snakes where every tunnel was perfectly round and smooth, likely to enable the snakes to slither around easier.

The sixth one had been a fairly normal tunnel heading straight down for a long time, followed by a truly massive open cavern, in the center of which sat a massive stone city.

The raid hadn't encountered a single monster since they'd entered the tunnel, though they had been fighting humanoid shapes made of stone once they'd entered the spirit's territory the day before.

Down in the central cavern they found themselves face to face with a literal army of stone men, several hundred strong at least, standing in rank and file, ready to fight. Liora almost ordered a retreat, but Verun used his scan ability to get details on a few of the stone men. They were only around level twenty-five. Apparently the spirit had sacrificed quality to increase quantity, and the gambit had almost worked.

The following battle was hectic, perhaps the most hectic they'd had on the entire expedition. It started off like most others. The Transportation Guild knight party advanced on the group of monsters like they normally did, with a fan of five other parties behind them, ready to strike. All five of the knights used their *Taunt* skill in rapid succession, leading to dozens of the stone men rushing them, literally tripping over one another in their desperation to attack the knights. Their shields could easily repel the tiny stone swords from the low-level constructs, but that wasn't the issue.

Aurora, standing to Seth's left near her mother, said, "Oh no."

Seth said, "What is it?"

Liora was already nodding, seeing the same thing Aurora was. Aurora answered him, "*Taunt* only affects up to ten enemies. That means the knight group can only attract up to fifty. The rest will be free to attack whoever they see fit. This could get ugly."

She was right. Seth watched as a circle of the stone men collapsed out of rank, encircling the knight group, while other sections of the huge array of constructs broke away and went after the other parties. There were entire groups with no knights at all.

Seth said, "I'm going to help." He caught a slight smile on Quincy's face. Seth didn't wait for any arguments from Liora, jogging forward toward the battle that was rapidly devolving into absolute chaos. Verun galloped next to him, huge white paws slapping the ground.

He saw two little stone men whacking their swords against a priest in a blue cloak, the stone swords acting more like heavy clubs than any blade. Seth kicked one of the constructs in the head, instantly killing it. He picked up the other one that had been hitting the priest as she healed her leg and hurled it with all his strength. It was heavier than he expected for its size, though it was probably solid stone so perhaps that made sense. Despite the surprising density, it still went flying over a hundred yards, disappearing into the stone city centered in the cave.

A stone sword thumped Seth in the left calf, and it *hurt,* there was so much weight behind the blow. He went down on his knee from the pain, and another stone sword whacked him on the back. He grunted and planted his left hand on the ground. Then Verun was there, grabbing one of the stone men and shaking it around vigorously.

Seth regained his feet and glanced at his fury meter, seeing that it was up to fifty-five. He shouldered his way deeper into the rows and rows of stone men and activated his *Bellow* skill. All around him in a circle the little men froze as if they were made of stone. He almost laughed at the thought as it went into his head, then activated his *Cyclone Whirl* skill, blowing the rest of his fury and spinning in a circle, sword flashing.

A swath of the stone men went down from the huge damage, but others were already starting to flood into the small hole, so Seth backed up towards the raid group, not wanting to get cut off from help. At a glance, it seemed like the side of the fight he was on was doing better after he'd taken so many of the enemies out, so he hopped on Verun's back and the huge lion made a wing-assisted jump over the heads of many of the raid members, landing on the other side of the group.

Verun said, <My turn to show off.> Seth jumped off of his back and Verun waded into the sea of little stone men then roared at the sky, activating his *Flock* skill. Five copies of the red-faced lion simply appeared amid the fray and joined the real Verun in wreaking destruction on the stone army. If Seth had taken out a couple dozen with his display of power, Verun was showing him up by taking out more.

The fight was over soon after, a sea of stone body parts littering the ground as the raid collected themselves, healed the wounded, and started walking toward the city. Seth returned to the leading party, and Liora gave him a withering look.

She quietly said, "The leading party needs to be able to see what's going on to instruct the rest of the raid." Her lips were pursed in a small ring.

Seth looked between her and Quincy and said, "When we're out of here, we need to work on our party structure and formations. We weren't prepared for this." He was feeling angry at the two of them. They still mostly refused to work together and consistently tried to flex their own power, contradicting the orders of the other. Quincy just shrugged, and Liora didn't acknowledge him, but he was determined to bring it up when they made camp that night.

The group then walked through the stone city. It was like a ghost city, and *everything* was made of stone. Stone doors on the stone buildings that didn't seem to open. A little market area, where all of the tents were thin stone, and all of the wares for "sale" were actually just part of the stone counters they sat on, and couldn't be picked up. It was all very spooky, Seth thought.

A huge stone pyramid rose way above the rest of the buildings in the city, and above its peak floated the blood-red crystal. It wasn't the typical pyramid that Seth would have called to mind; it looked less like one you might see in Egypt, and more like one you might see in Central or South America, back on Earth, with huge blocky steps on all sides instead of a smooth grade.

On all four sides of the pyramid, one looking in each cardinal direction, was a stone giant. They looked like scaled-up versions of the stone men that the group had fought previously, at least fifty feet tall. They were utterly motionless, but Seth and the leading party didn't fall for that trick like they had with the first stone men. They formed up, and prepared to take on the stone giant on the side closest to them, hoping the other three wouldn't come to join the fight immediately.

The knights all formed up and drew the stone giant back toward the rest of the raid, and the damagers were able to whittle its health down while the healers kept everyone at full health. One of the knights, a woman who belonged to the Adventurers' Guild, was almost killed when the giant finally fell. It landed on her after teetering forward, and she couldn't get back in time. It ended up crushing her lower body, but five warriors lifted the stone giant's corpse off of her, and the healers cast a multitude of healing spells to get her back to full health. She was whole only moments later, but looked exhausted. Aurora mentioned to Seth that massive healing spells used the recipient's strength and energy as well as that of the priest casting it. Two of the other knights, a red cape and a blue cape, carried the woman between them, her arms slung over their shoulders.

The other three statues didn't stir as the raid climbed the huge pyramid, and Quincy repeated his *Purify* technique. Seth was standing next to him as he did it, and afterwards the man muttered, "Wow, that was the highest-level spirit yet." He shared the prompt with the leading party again.

You cast *Purify* on level 342 Etherean, you've cured it of *Ectocypher*.

When the raid was almost out of the stone city and back to the tunnel to the surface, a single stone man appeared in their path. The knights started to pull their weapons out, but it simply stood there and held its hand out. Quincy pushed through the raid, breaking rank, and approached the stone man. In its hand was a perfectly formed stone flower, which it gave to him before turning and running into the stone city, disappearing between the silent buildings, stone feet making a loud tapping as it ran. Apparently, it was happy to be cured.

***

The leading party debated for hours on the composition of the raid. Finally, it seemed like Seth was getting through to them. He gestured at the array of little red and blue scraps of cloth they'd been using to discuss party layouts. "See? A mixed-guild approach gets us the best layouts for large-scale, single-target fights, and for fighting many enemies. We need to be able to quickly pivot between facing one champion, or facing an army of small monsters."

The group had erected a large tent big enough for all of them to work inside at camp. Sullivan, who was sitting on the ground in one of the corners of the tent cleaning his massive un-strung bow said, "I don't think anyone's arguing with your point, but you're overestimating how friendly the people from the guilds will be with one another. I'm honestly surprised these two haven't started slugging it out yet." He lazily gestured to Liora and

Quincy, who stood on opposite sides of a small circular table in the center of the tent.

Liora shot Sullivan a withering glare, and Quincy just chuckled and said, "I'm not quite ready to be smote out of existence, Sully." Seth found that curious. Quincy was higher level. Did he really think Liora would beat him in a fight? Aurora spoke up, "Maybe we just give it a chance for one zone, see if everyone can keep cool and work in Seth's proposed teams."

There was a pause as everyone mulled it over, then the group agreed to implement Seth's party composition the next morning. They all exited the tent, intending to head to their own tents for dinner and sleep, when they witnessed the fight break out. Seth heard yelling to his right, turned, and saw several people brawling. He'd expected it to be a bunch of muscled dudes, but it was actually four women who'd started arguing and it had devolved into blows. Thankfully, Seth didn't see any blades or magic being brandished, so at least it didn't look lethal yet.

He'd only taken two steps toward them, intending to try and break it up, when Quincy was suddenly amongst the brawling women. He hadn't moved as fast as Gianna the rogue, impossible to see, but to Seth, he'd looked like a blur as he blew past. He went behind one of the blue-cloaked women and put his hand on her shoulder, almost calmly. Seth saw firelight glint off of his brass-knuckles, then Quincy whipped his hand backwards, and the woman went tumbling a dozen yards away, stirring up dust as she rolled over the dirt. Liora reached the fight a moment later, standing in the middle of the three remaining combatants. They all three pulled their punches immediately, not wanting to strike the imposing white-haired woman, and backed off.

Quincy was helping the woman he'd thrown to her feet, clasping her hand and summoning some whirling golden light around her as he did so. He had a quiet, tense conversation with her and the other blue-cloak woman before they simply walked away into the camp looking sullen.

Liora did similar, though not as quietly. She chewed the two red-capes out and sent them to clean up *myrt* droppings before they'd be allowed to eat. She shot a look at Seth as she departed that seemed to say "I told you so."

CHAPTER 19

The next week started rough. The raid, arranged in Seth's new layout with intermingled parties, started going against harder and harder dungeons. People were getting seriously injured, but no one had died yet, including Riley. Seth was quietly in awe of that.

The party structure they'd adopted had two forms. In what Seth called *autonomous form,* each party was self-sufficient, with at least one knight and one healer. Low-level people were paired with high-level people to create teams whose average was about the same as every other. They only adopted this form when they were against large groups of enemies, however, and that was somewhat rare after the army of stone men.

The second form, how they spent most of their time, was nicknamed *cumulative form.* In this party layout, the parties each had individual jobs. The leading party was the same in both party forms, as their job tended not to change. There were two *tank* parties, each made up of five knights and a single priest. These were the two groups responsible for getting the attention of all enemies and keeping it while the rest of the groups did their work.

There were four parties dedicated exclusively to damage, two close-ranged, made up of rogues and warriors, and two long-ranged, made up of mages and scouts. Riley and Ivon were together in one of these two groups.

Two of the remaining parties were designated the *flankers,* and depending on the situation they'd either guard the flanks of the larger group or flank behind an enemy and attack it from the rear. Both of the *flanker* groups were well rounded, with their own knights and priests as well as a complement of damage dealers. Baltern led one of these.

The final group was designated the *utility* party, and it was made up of two priests and a knight who floated where they were needed, defending injured raid members and healing them, as well as three scouts whose primary job was to help the leading party disseminate orders to the larger raid in the heat of battle.

For as much thought and energy as Seth had put into coming up with the layout, it really didn't work all that well at first. People were in parties with people from outside their own guilds and didn't know how to work together, or in some cases even actively tried to sabotage their party mates.

Seth himself saw an Adventurers' Guild priest neglect to heal a warrior in his party, and heard rumors of a Transportation Guild knight in one of the two tank parties only blocking projectiles headed for themselves and other blue-cloaks in their parties.

The pettiness actually vanished pretty quickly, though, as Seth saw members of both guilds protecting, healing, and dragging out of harm's way members of the opposite group. As the childishness calmed, the efficiency of the raid layout began to present itself. The cumulative form was a power-house against champions. Knights could take a single strike on their shield and then back off, allowing another knight to take the champion's aggression, all while the ranged damage groups peppered the monsters with spells and arrows, and the close-range damagers struck around the edges of the tank parties.

Neither Liora or Quincy admitted that the strategy was working, at least to Seth's face, but the fact that they didn't demand a change in raid layout was an affirmation enough in itself. Things seemed to be going well, even though the dungeons kept increasing in average level and difficulty. One day Seth was meeting with the leading party in their large tent just after the sun rose. A red-caped scout named Diara, a member of the utility party and an expert cartographer, entered with a message about their progress through the wilderness.

"If my calculations are right, and if the mapmakers were true with their distances on the old maps we have, the next zone we pass through should be the exact midpoint between Efril and Askua."

Sullivan spoke up, "Does that mean things will get easier? They've certainly been getting harder the longer we're out here."

Liora said, "Not necessarily, but it's possible. We can't assume that it will become any easier. Thank you, Diara, you may go."

The scout made her way out of the tent, and Quincy drawled, "We can hope it lets up, I think we all could use a break."

No one argued with that, and Seth left the tent a few minutes later, looking for Riley. He knocked on her front door, always a strange thing in the middle of the dense wilderness surrounded by tents, and heard her footsteps coming down the wooden stairs inside. A moment later she opened the door, hair frazzled. "Do we really have to go so early?"

Seth just grinned and nodded, and Riley slammed the door in his face, hollering, "Fine. I'll be out soon."

Thirty minutes later Seth, Verun, Riley, and Zuh all soared through the air, heading away from the area they'd camped the night before, heading to the next zone they needed to conquer to continue their advancement toward Askua. There was almost a solid border where the grasslands they'd been in before turned to desert; it didn't look natural at all, just suddenly rolling dunes in a line. Seth had heard that ethereans could exert their will to change the weather and landscape on their environments, but he had never seen a change so dramatic.

They flew over the dunes for another fifteen minutes or so before it was visible. It was massive, and still very far away even though it had come into view. Seth yelled over the wind to Verun, "What is that?"

<I do not know, but it doesn't look natural,> he replied. They continued on, and the shape began to resolve itself. It was a massive stone tower, jutting out of the rolling dunes. It was hard to appreciate its true size with nothing around to compare it to, but it was enormous.

The spire was made of many stacked cylindrical floors, each slightly smaller in circumference than the one it sat atop, with occasional weird protrusions and add-ons that didn't look preplanned. The entire tall structure had a distinctly cobbled-together look, like it had been added onto over a large timespan. Sand had blown up on one side of it, burying the first two floors from that side. There was a bright-red light visible from the very tip of the spire.

Seth squinted his eyes and tried to count the floors as the four of them approached in the air. He thought there were around fifty floors making up the huge structure. He planned to land next to it to help get a gauge on how tall it was, but that plan was shot down, literally.

As he and Riley approached on their mounts, the red gleam at the top of the spire suddenly brightened rapidly, then a huge beam of red light discharged in a solid column. Riley and Zuh didn't have time to get out of the way. Seth screamed as his friend was incinerated, and Verun banked rapidly, attempting to whirl around and head in the exact opposite direction. Moments later another angry red beam shot out, but Verun tucked his wings back and plummeted for a few seconds, dodging it. They kept flying, fast, but it didn't shoot again.

Seth's heart was hammering, and he glanced at his logs, trying to get more information on what in the world had just happened.

Level ??? Anti-Air Enchantment **critically** hits your raid member Riley for 1206 damage.
Your raid member Riley has died.

Seth and Verun flew back to the camp, where the five leading party members were already waiting for him, doubtless having seen the death in their logs as well.

As Seth dismounted Verun, Liora demanded, "What happened?"

He explained and shared the log with the rest of them. Aurora said, "How long until she's back?" Seth explained how it was an hour per level, so she would be back in around thirty-eight hours. Quincy said, "There must be some really great treasures in that tower." He had a glassy look in his eyes, as if imagining himself diving into a mound of gold coins.

Liora said, "We don't even know if it's safe to approach on foot, though the anti-air wording does seem to indicate it might be safe to go on the ground."

Quincy said, "I'd bet it is safe to approach on the ground. Dungeons want us to come in. They eat us. No dungeon would want to be completely impenetrable. I'm sure the anti-air enchantment is just to prevent people like Seth from flying straight to the summit."

Aurora said, "Seth, why don't you try flying most of the way there and then walking the rest of the way, to see if you can get to the entrance?"

Seth laughed, then said, "Sure, I'll just go alone and hope I don't get zapped too."

He was being sarcastic, but Aurora just nodded and said, "That will be safer than anyone else, since you won't stay zapped." She was right.

The rest of the group agreed, and Seth started preparing for another flight to the spire.

***

Forty-five minutes later, Seth and Verun were on foot, approaching the spire. The sand shifted under his feet as he walked, and it made each step take him less distance than it should. The sun beat down from above, almost as if the temperature was actually warmer in this zone. Could the wild spirits affect the weather?

He looked up, and the stone structure looked like it might've extended all the way into the sky. Seth looked at Verun. "I'm pretty sure we're already closer than Riley and Zuh got, but I guess we'd better try to find the entrance."

Verun just hummed in response, his big white paws sinking into the golden red sand with every step. He wasn't happy about having to walk such a long distance when he had perfectly good wings on his back.

Seth inspected the growing tower again. It almost looked like someone had just scaled up a tiered cake, except made from stone, and with way more tiers than any sane cake decorator on Earth would try to bake.

Seth had had ample time to count on this approach, since it had taken so long. There were exactly sixty levels to the tower; his estimate of fifty had been a little low. The bottom one was huge and round, as it had to be absolutely massive to allow fifty-nine consecutively smaller floors to rise above it.

The top level looked deceptively small from so far away, and Seth thought he might see a red glint up there. Perhaps it was whatever enchantment had shot Riley down.

The levels, however, weren't like normal floors in a building. They each had to be almost fifty feet tall, and that tall consistently from what he could see, making some of the highest floors look tall and skinny. Seth couldn't spot any windows on the lower few floors, but there did appear to be some balconies or other holes in the structure above those bottom several.

Seth drew within a hundred feet of the spire, but still couldn't spot any kind of entrance on the bottom floor. He was beginning to think he'd have to walk around the base of the entire tower, but several steps later, a rumbling started. He could feel it through the sand.

Seth said, "Uh oh, no lasers please!" No lasers came, though, instead a large square hole opened in the bottom floor of the tower. It was completely dark inside. Seth walked a little closer, but the sun beating down couldn't penetrate into the darkness. He said, "We should probably go back now, right?"

Verun said, <What are you doing?>

Seth kept walking for the door. He just needed to see what was inside the spire. Then he'd leave and report his findings to the raid. He said, "One second. I just need to..."

Verun said, <I thought you just said we should go back.>

Seth didn't answer. Moments later, Verun's teeth closed over the back of Seth's shirt. Seth tried to shrug him off, but Verun was huge and implacable as he dragged Seth backwards. It wasn't until Seth was several dozens of yards farther away that the active effect disappeared, and he had control of his own faculties again.

"What was that? It's like I was hypnotized!" Seth exclaimed.

<I think it was trying to pull you in. Thankfully I was able to save you, as usual,> Verun responded.

Seth said, "You're starting to sound like your father. Let's get out of here before I try to drag us in."

***

Seth pushed his way into the leading party's tent, and Verun stuck his head through the flaps after him, his hind quarters still outside the tarp structure.

The other five members were still there, looking at maps. Seth explained that he had been able to approach the tower on foot, but told them about feeling drawn inside. He finished off with, "Overall, I have a bad feeling about the place. I think we should consider just going around it."

He hated to say it. The spire was a mystery, and an intriguing one. They'd never encountered a dungeon that went *up* rather than down, nor one with anti-flight measures or hypnotic ability to draw people in. The truth was, though, he had a feeling it may be too dangerous for them.

Liora said, "I agree. After you left we sent a few scouts to explore zones around the left or right, and the initial reports suggest they're much more like what we've seen since leaving Efril. We'll make a determination of which one seems lower effort and go that way, skirting around the desertous area containing the spire."

She said it so matter of factly, like everyone had voted and come to that conclusion, but Seth saw Quincy's eyes narrow in anger when she proclaimed it. Apparently he wasn't pleased with the plan. Seth waited for the Transportation Guild leader to speak up, but he just smirked and rose, heading for the exit of the tent. Sullivan and Gianna rose to follow him, and Seth heard Quincy say, "Good talk."

Word got out that the raid would be going around the spire, and the speculation that things would be getting easier spread to everyone in the entire group. It was decided that a feast would be thrown to celebrate going "over the hill" in terms of the difficulty of their journey.

Scouts drifted away into the wilderness surrounding the camp in the zone they'd most recently cleared. Seth wasn't confident that they'd be able to find enough wild animals, but sure enough, three strangely muscular-looking deer were dragged into camp that evening, skinned, cleaned, and roasted on impromptu spits over big fires. Riley got an exuberant cheer when she respawned, summoned her house, and returned with a large barrel of beer, arms straining to hold it up. Seth helped her carry three more barrels out, and the feast was on.

CHAPTER 20

Seth sat around one of the many bonfires with Riley, Ivon, Aurora, and Verun. He tossed his head back and took yet another swig from his drink, then sighed happily. The taste of the beer had turned him off at first, but the alcohol in it had helped him get over that. Ivon chuckled, then said, "Feeling pretty satisfied are you, boy?"

Seth said, "Well, you heard what they were saying. It's all probably downhill from here. We're making history, reconnecting the world. What's not to feel satisfied about?"

Ivon said, "I was talking about the party layout you helped concoct." He sipped his own drink.

Seth said, "Yeah, I guess the two guilds can get along better than they thought, huh? It just took a little practice."

Twenty minutes later most of the raid had circled up while two people at a time entered the impromptu ring and sparred. The bouts were friendly, and priests, if a little inebriated, were still on hand and ready to heal any wounds. Seth had walked over and started watching as two rogues had started a bout, fists only.

They were fast, but significantly lower level than Seth, both low thirties. They moved about as quick as he could, though they were both more graceful and fluid in their movements than he was. He couldn't tell for sure, but he guessed that both of their dexterity statistics were around one hundred, given that rogues gained dexterity at a rate of three per level, and they didn't look to be wearing any insanely enchanted armor. They relied more on precision than Seth would have. A single full-strength blow from his high strength score would've done a number on either of the two rogues, but they focused on high-impact areas, striking at each other's throats and joints with lightning-fast jabs before trying to dodge the counter.

One of them finally dropped below half health around two minutes in, and they stopped fighting, clasping hands and laughing while their wounds were healed. Someone shouted, "Who's next?" as the two rogues left the center of the ring.

An excited murmur rippled around the gathered crowd, and Seth saw Baltern strut into the center of the ring. He'd levelled since their fight outside of Slyborn, if you could even call it a fight. He was still even with Seth at forty-nine, and was the highest-level knight in the entire raid. Seth felt the anger bubbling up from deep in his gut as he watched the man scan the crowd, hands on his hips, looking so smug that no one wanted to fight him. Seth popped open Baltern's stat sheet.

Baltern
Main Class: Level 49 Knight (10,323/1,139,069)
Second Class: Level 22 Rogue
3,906 / 3,906 Health Points
1,764 / 1,764 Mana Points
100 / 100 Concentration Points
Factions: Adventurers' Guild

Of course no one wanted to fight him, the man's health was insane, only beaten by Liora and Quincy. Baltern was looking at him now, smiling, and Seth realized he'd stood up without consciously meaning to. Perhaps it was the beer, perhaps it was his lust for revenge, but for whatever reason, he walked out into the center of the ring.

There was an awkward murmur, then a huge cheer as everyone realized they were about to see a high-level fight, by far the highest level of anyone who'd fought that night.

Baltern laughed and said, "Finally grew a pair, eh?" He raised his fists lazily in front of himself and stood, waiting. His odd pose stuck out to Seth; the man's feet were squared under his shoulders, and the backs of his fists were toward Seth like some early twentieth-century fisticuffs boxer. It somehow made his face look even more punchable.

Seth fought the anger bubbling in the pit of his stomach. He disliked Baltern, but they were on the same side. He needed to keep the fight friendly, though that didn't mean he couldn't rough the man up a bit.

Seth exaggerated, stretching his arms, then darted in as fast as his body would take him, trying to land a punch on Baltern's cheek. Unlike the last time Seth had punched Baltern, the knight didn't just take the blow this time, but actually managed to back out of the way, dodging the blow entirely.

Seth's alcohol-clouded mind reeled; knights weren't supposed to move that quickly. It took him a moment to understand as he backed off. Knights gained one dexterity per level, but rogues gained three. Since Baltern's secondary class was rogue, he'd instead gain two dexterity per level, the average of his primary and secondary. This calculation only applied when the average was higher than the primary class's statistic. A rogue primary knight secondary would gain three dexterity per level, not two, since the average was lower.

Just another reason Seth was disadvantaged without a secondary class. He needed to get to Askua and get whatever class Djinia had in mind for him as soon as possible. Seth darted in again, and actually skimmed Baltern's ribs with a punch. The man was about the same speed as Seth. Baltern grunted when the punch connected, though his health bar barely moved.

Seth didn't react quickly enough, and a counter punch hit Seth in his left temple, sending him stumbling backwards. Surprisingly, it didn't hurt that bad, and barely chipped his health down. Baltern had insane defenses, but his offense was lacking.

Seth feigned in with another wild right hook but halted his momentum at the last second and leaned back, correctly predicting Baltern's counter punch. Baltern's fist whooshed by Seth's face, the miss throwing the knight's balance off. He took a jerking step forward and leaned to steady himself, but Seth punished the misstep with a vicious right uppercut, hitting Baltern directly in the nose. Just like when Seth had hit him back outside of

Slyborn, the punch resulted in a loud bang like a mini-thunderclap.

He'd expected the knight's nose to crumble like paper-mache under the massive blow, but instead it felt like Seth had punched a bit of protruding steel, Baltern's inflated stamina score making his body stronger than metal.

The punch did have some effect, though, and while Baltern didn't go flying into the air, lifted by his head, like a normal man might've, he did jerk upwards and take a step backwards. Seth spared a moment to glance at his adversary's health and saw that it was around eighty percent. The blow had done some damage to the seemingly indestructible man.

Baltern threw a sloppy haymaker at Seth, determined to get him back for the big hit, but Seth rapidly switched to his secondary outfit, casting Baltern's fist to slam into a pauldron on Seth's shoulder. Was it unfair? Probably, but Seth didn't care. He wanted to hurt the overly confident jerk.

The game had changed, though, when Seth used his *Quick Change* skill. They were no longer just slugging it out. Skills were tossed in the mix. Seth's next punch should've landed squarely in Baltern's jaw, but the man's left arm came up inhumanly fast to block it, much faster than he should've been able to move with his dexterity level.

> You hit level 49 knight (Baltern) for 35 damage. The damage of this strike was reduced by 90% by level 49 knight's skill *Parry*.

Seth was still trying to skim the prompt when a powerful blow hit him in the side of the head and sent him sprawling to the ground. He groggily struggled to his feet, the punch and the alcohol mingling in his brain making it even harder to get up.

> Level 49 knight (Baltern) hits you for 206 damage with *Retaliate*.

They exchanged a few more blows, Seth's dealing more raw damage than Baltern's, though this was balanced out by Baltern's huge health pool. Seth started swapping to his plate armor just before Baltern's fists landed. Likewise, Baltern used his *Parry* ability to reduce the damage from one of Seth's punches every twenty seconds or so. Seth finally reached a full fury bar from all of the blows and activated his *Berserk* skill, sending himself into a rage and doubling his strength score, but halving his stamina. Baltern's strikes started hurting a lot more, but Seth's enormous strength score shredded through the knight's defense and even started blowing him backwards, overriding his *Immovable* skill that rendered him nearly immune from knockback.

Seth was surprised when someone started pulling him away from the fight. He was still under the hazy influence of *Berserk,* so immediately whirled and tried to swing at whoever was pulling him backwards. Quincy simply let go, ducked the blow, and then grabbed Seth again, continuing to pull him away from the fight.

He said, "Get ahold of your sanity, red-cape, or you'll regret it." Seth visibly shook as he tried to calm himself. What had happened? He'd forgotten they were even in a ring fighting; he'd just wanted to bash Baltern's stupid face in. He looked at his health bar and saw that it sat at around fifty-two percent. He quickly opened Baltern's sheet from the raid menu and saw that his was just below fifty percent. He'd won and not even realized.

Just as a healing glow enveloped Seth, emanating from Quincy's hand on his shoulder, Seth saw another priest healing Baltern. The knight threw a glance at Seth as though he were taking another measure. Was he impressed?

Quincy quietly said to Seth, "You looked almost as wild as the god of war Matrox himself fighting out there. Do you have some history with the knight?"

Seth chuckled a little, still trying to calm his raging heartbeat, and said, "Yeah, I guess you could say we don't get along."

Quincy said, "Why'd you spar with him?"

Seth thought a moment, but couldn't think of anything better than, "I guess I just wanted to?"

Quincy grinned and said, "Good man. You've gotta take what you want, that's a lesson I've learned." He had a strange look on his face as he said it, as if he were talking more to himself than to Seth. Quincy patted him once more on the shoulder, then walked into the darkness toward his tent, away from the fire where another boxing match was already starting up.

***

Seth awoke the next morning, head pounding, tongue dry and swelled like a sandpaper balloon. Something else, though, felt off, hangover aside. He'd had dozens of hangovers in his life, but none had felt so...off. An absence, like something was missing.

He checked his limbs, first, but they were all where they were supposed to be. He felt with his mind for Verun, and found the lion snoozing against the outside of his tent.

He could still feel the raid members in his party sense. Wait, no. That was it. He'd grown used to the feeling of fifty-nine other people in his party sense, but there weren't that many anymore. A huge chunk of the raid was missing.

He sat up in a panic, any self-pity for his hangover evaporating as he struggled into his pants and shimmied out of the tent. People were already about, and he stumbled toward the tent where the leading party usually met, dead-center in the camp.

He pulled up his party menu just as he entered the tent. Liora looked up as he entered and confirmed it, anger on her face as she said, "They've gone. All of the blue-cloaks are gone."

CHAPTER 21

"I need to know where they went!" Liora was screaming at one of the scouts from the utility party. Seth hadn't seen her lose her cool to this extent before.

The woman cowered back for a moment, then said, "One of the watch shifts it seems was made of entirely blue capes. We think they waited until around thirty minutes before their shift ended and then just all simply left. Diara spotted their torches in the distance when she started her shift, heading toward the spire."

Liora, Aurora, Seth, and the scout were standing in Liora's tent. Liora's hands were balled into fists. Seth could have sworn he saw a white mist begin to flicker around her hands, but in moments it was gone, and he doubted that it had actually been there. Liora said, "Search Quincy's tent."

The scout ran off. About thirty seconds later, after silently fuming and muttering to herself, Liora said, "I'll just go search it myself," and stood up and exited the tent. Seth and Aurora followed her, afraid to say much and bring her wrath down on themselves.

The scout met them before they made it to Quincy's tent, though, a scrap of paper in her hand. She looked terrified as she silently handed the note to Liora. Liora scanned it and then held perfectly still, staring straight ahead for what felt like thirty seconds. Finally, she sighed, handed the note to Aurora, and said, "What do you think we should do?"

Seth poked his head over Aurora's heavy plate shoulder armor and read the note at the same time. It read:

We've gone to try to ascend the spire. Call it a hunch, but I think there is something very special up there. We'll see you when you catch up.

-Q

Aurora said after a moment, "I don't know that we have much of a choice. We could just abandon the quest and head back for Efril, but that seems like quite the waste. Aren't we already half-way? Seth, what do you think? It is your quest after all."

The scout woman interjected, "Can we not just continue without them?"

Liora, still fuming, had to visibly restrain herself from screaming at the woman. She said, "The only way we're able to safely camp is to use zones that Quincy has already purified. If he isn't with us, I don't see us making it more than two zones away from here before we're overrun in the middle of the night." Surprisingly, Liora looked at Seth, too, awaiting his input.

Seth thought for a moment, images of the giant red laser shooting Riley out of the sky in his mind's eye, then said, "I'm open to going to the spire, but I'm not sure my opinion should be weighted that heavily, because of the whole not afraid of dying thing."

Liora said, "Well, the bright side of this is that I don't have to debate with that dolt Quincy, though I can't help feeling like he's making the decision for me with his absence. We'll go to the spire and try to salvage this mission. I have some words for that bald idiot." White light subtly glowed around her balled fists.

***

Barely an hour later, the rest of the raid, consisting of thirty-nine Adventurers' Guild members and Riley, was ready to depart. Two of them would actually be staying behind to take care of the *myrt*, so the force heading to back up the Transportation Guild members was only thirty-eight strong. They started marching.

Seth hadn't actually walked the entire way to the spire the day before, so he wasn't sure how long the march would take them, but he guessed about four to five hours at a brisk walking pace.

The half-full parties had caused a bit of a logistical nightmare too, as all the blue-cloaks had left the raid, assumedly to form their own. The two flanker parties had been made up entirely of Adventurers' Guild members, but every other party had contained either two or three Transportation Guild members. Liora quickly rearranged the group into a new party system before they departed. Riley was transferred to the leading party, since there would have been seven ranged damagers with her there. One of the utility party priests had to transfer into the now single-tank party, as both tank party healers had been blue capes. That displaced one of those knights, who in turn joined the utility party.

In the end, the group structure was the four-person leading party, two flanking parties, a single-tank party, a single close-range damage party, a single long-range damage party, and a six-person utility party, two of whom were staying back at the camp in the previously cleared zone. It wasn't ideal, but Seth was grateful that they hadn't sourced all of their healers or tanks from the blue capes, otherwise they might find it extremely difficult to fight through any dungeons.

The hike across the desert was just as brutal, but much larger than the day before. Verun had flown Seth over a good portion of it, only landing and beginning the walk when they were nearing the location Riley had been killed at. Seth felt particularly bad for the knights in their large armor; it had to be hot inside there.

Verun walked next to Seth. He could have ridden on the lion's back, but preferred to walk alongside him with the others. Riley had no such compunction, and sat atop Zuh's back as the big peacock strutted through the desert. She looked bored. Seth wished he felt bored; all he felt was fear.

Was the spire the end of the entire raid? What if everyone was killed? They didn't even know how high level the monsters were inside. What if they were all over level one hundred or something? He tried to squash the panic rising in his gut, but only had some success.

The spire loomed in the distance, growing as they approached across the desert. Seth hadn't noticed last time he'd seen it, but it almost looked like the thing was leaning to one side. He said, "Leaning spire of Pisa!" Riley laughed, but no one else did. Which made sense, since they'd never heard of the tower.

Several hours later, the smaller raid, with thirty-seven people in red capes, and Riley in her green robe, was closing in on the tower. They'd been able to see that the big dark hole was open in the bottom level of the tower. Quincy, Sullivan, Gianna, and the others were nowhere to be seen.

Seth hopped on Verun's back as they closed in, and the two of them, along with Riley and Zuh, walked out in front of the main force. Since Verun had seemed immune to the strange draw of the place, Seth thought it best for him and Zuh to lead the raid into the dungeon. Liora and Aurora agreed.

Strangely, there was no pull this time; they simply walked up to the entrance and stopped, looking at the darkness looming within. Liora stepped up next to Verun and said, "I think I can help with that." She raised her hand, palm out toward the darkness inside the tower, and a white ball of light shot out, into the darkness. Instantly, they could see inside. The white ball grew and attached itself to the ceiling of the bottom floor, fifty feet up. The floor was all sand inside, and the bottom level of the tower looked completely empty and abandoned. There was a huge stone spiral staircase at the back of the room, opposite the door, though in the scope of the room it was dwarfed. Each step was a huge slab of stone connected to a central column that extended from the ground all the way through the ceiling, into the next level. There didn't look to be much in the way of support for the steps, aside from their seemingly tenuous connection to the central column.

After a few moments of deliberation on what to do next, the raid formed up, knight party in front, and advanced into the room. It felt less like being inside a structure, and more like being inside a cavern. Nothing happened at first, but as they got around halfway through the massive empty room, Seth heard Riley exclaim, "Under the sand!"

Her finger was extended, and he looked where she was pointing. There was a slight hump in the sand moving towards them, almost like a mole under a lawn. The whole raid quickly pivoted, keeping the knights facing the moving hump, warriors and rogues behind them, and scouts, mages, utility party, and leading party in the back.

Blue shimmering shields sprang out of the knights' bracers, and they all dropped into a low stance, effectively forming a wall of shields between whatever was approaching and the rest of the party. Seth saw golden light swirling around a few of the priests' hands as they prepared to heal the damage from whatever monster was about to rip free of the sand.

An audible rumble could be heard now, and Liora's voice rose above it, "Steady. Here it comes."

The sand burst outward, and a shape emerged out of it, headed right for the wall of shields. It stopped.

No one moved. A voice said, "Hello there. Welcome to my tower." It was coming from the figure that had just emerged from the sand. He was floating several inches off of the ground, and he looked mostly like a man, but his hair was light purple, and his eyes unnaturally saturated blue-green. He was encased entirely in purple armor with navy swirls on it, and his helmet was somewhat pointed, and didn't cover his face.

He said, "Are you all with the group that came in earlier? All your capes are a different color. Rivals perhaps? On a mission to be the first to reach the summit of my tower and bask in the glory? I do admire such fierce competition."

There was an awkward silence as everyone tried to process what had just happened. Seth, embarrassingly, defaulted to his favorite phrase and spoke up first. "Who are you?"

The man didn't necessarily turn to look at Seth, it was more like he just suddenly became turned, looking right at Seth through the crowd. It was disorienting, and made him seem more like some kind of glitchy hologram than an actual person. He said, "Oh, I didn't see you two back there. How intriguing. The great three races come to ascend my tower, working together. Though one is enslaved, and another is more of an... abomination." Seth shuddered at that last word. The last time he'd heard that word, it'd been from a giant angry face that was ripping a hole in the sky. The man's unsettling gaze was still on Seth, but then it pivoted, instantly again, to Riley.

She smiled at him, walked through the crowd until she was only a couple of feet away, and extended her hand for a handshake. The man looked at her hand like it might give him some kind of infection and stepped backwards a pace, ironic since they were there to potentially cure him from the Ectocypher disease. He said, "Anyway, good luck in my tower. I hope you earn yourselves much glory before my pets kill you and feed me your essence. Good day!" There was a *thunk* as the man simply dropped back into the sand, disappearing instantly.

Riley turned to the stunned group, pouting, and said, "I don't think he liked me." She feigned wiping a tear off of her face.

A second *thunk*, much larger than the previous, sounded, and Seth whirled around to see the exit had completely closed. Liora said, "Looks like the only way out is up."

CHAPTER 22

The party passed through the rest of the first floor unharmed. It seemed larger than multiple football fields and took a noticeably long time to cross. They climbed the spiral stairs at the back of the room, knights first, and ascended to the second level. The spiral staircase seemed almost precarious, being so small compared to the absolutely massive hollow space. The staircase itself was huge, large enough for perhaps ten people to walk abreast up each step. The stairs were curiously short, though, just the right height for humans to step up. There weren't any handrails on the sides, so the group walked about three abreast and stayed very close to the center. Despite Seth's fears, none of the stone slabs snapped off as the raid party headed for the next level.

After ascending for several minutes, they reached the second level. It wasn't hollow like the first had been, or at least if it was, they couldn't see it. The stair emptied into a room barely big enough for the thirty-eight people to cram into. Seth wasn't sure they'd have been able to fit the full sixty-person raid inside. Seth hopped on Verun's back and the big lion was crammed into a corner from the pressure of bodies. When they all had entered, a bluish forcefield, similar to the one that sprang from Aurora's arm when she needed her shield, appeared, blocking their retreat down the stairs. For a brief moment people started to panic and push, no one wanting to be confined to such a claustrophobic space, but then the stone that made up the opposite wall started grinding upwards, revealing the next floor. Apparently the spirit of this dungeon didn't want them going back down.

As soon as the wall was high enough for people to duck under, they started doing so, wanting out of the confining space as soon as possible. Seth had been one of the last ones up the stairs with the rest of the leading party, so he craned his neck to try and see what was inside the second level. It turned out that he'd been wrong; it was hollow, just like the first. Liora didn't even have to send up a light orb in this room though, there were massive torches the size of men burning every dozen paces on the walls around the entire rim of the room.

This level seemed to be some kind of octagon shape, not a perfect circle like the first floor had been. In the center of the room, was what Seth could only describe as a hedge maze.

The leafy walls were perhaps twelve feet high, and Seth could plainly see the opening at the center of the wall, though his view didn't go far into the maze before another leafy green wall obstructed it. Though the room was an octagon, the maze appeared to be a perfect square as the party fanned out and started scouting around the outside. A white light could be seen extending to the ceiling, almost like a spotlight at a car dealership, from the dead center of the maze. Seth assumed that was their target.

Seth, Riley, Aurora, and her mother stepped away from the rest of the raid and started trying to form a plan. They hadn't made much progress in perhaps thirty seconds when someone yelled, "Hey, look at this!"

It was one of the scouts from the utility party, Diara, holding a scrap of blue cloth. Riley said, "Looks like Quincy beat us here."

The half-empty leading party ended up reaching a decision, and the raid moved into the maze. The area between the hedges was only wide enough for two people to walk comfortably abreast, and Seth wasn't brave enough to try flying over the top on Verun's back, vivid images of the red laser erasing Riley from existence several days before flashing through his mind. Riley wasn't so affected, because she said, "I'll try it, it'd certainly make things easier for us if we could fly over the top."

Liora said, "Absolutely not, we need you alive and fighting for us."

Aurora spoke up, "No, I agree. It seems like this dungeon is really adamant that we obey the rules it has set so far, so we probably should avoid trying to cheat any of the systems."

Everyone agreed, though it looked like Riley might ignore all of their advice and hop on Zuh's back anyway. After a moment she resisted the urge.

Three knights walked up front in a triangle pattern, one in front, two behind him, Baltern in the lead as the highest-level knight. Behind him were the next two highest-level knights from the raid, sitting at forty-seven and forty. After that came a mix of the rest of the knights, warriors, and rogues, followed by the scouts and mages, including Riley on Zuh's back. At the rear was the leading party, with Liora being actually last, after Seth riding Verun. Seth almost said something about having some knights in the rear too, in case anything attacked from behind, but then he remembered how high Liora's health was, literally the highest in the entire raid party, and realized that she may have placed herself in the rear for a reason.

The human train wound through the maze, spiky green bushes occasionally snagging Verun's wings even though he tried to keep them as close to his body as he could. He growled every time it happened, and Seth shared the sentiment. He felt blind and helpless between the walls of hedges. The smell the plants put out was overpowering; it reminded Seth of the overpowering smell of car air-fresheners shaped like pine trees right after they were opened for the first time.

They progressed through the maze. The first attack came at the front of the raid before Seth was even around a corner to see what they fought. He heard it dispatched quickly, the grunting of the knights accompanied by a shrill, inhuman squealing. He did get to see the carcass before long, when the raid moved forward again. It was chopped pretty badly by multiple sword wounds, but it looked like some kind of giant spider, so wide it probably brushed the hedges on both sides. They had to go single-file around it. It made Seth want to gag, but Verun didn't seem fazed at all as he brushed it when he squeezed by.

Liora's foresight seemed to pay off quickly after that, as two of the giant spiders attacked from the back without much warning at all. They didn't even get within striking distance of Liora though. Seth heard the commotion and turned in time to see Liora thrust both of her palms towards the rushing monsters. White light burst from her hands in a radiant wave, blowing Liora's white hair around wildly and literally incinerating the spiders in an instant. There were no corpses at all that time. Seth agreed with his previous judgement of the woman; she was a monster.

Instead of randomly looking through the maze, the group had adopted the age-old Earth logic of just following the left wall. It did cause some issues when they got to dead ends, as it was quite difficult to turn around thirty-eight people in a space only wide enough for three to pass, but the party was disciplined and organized, and reversals went relatively smoothly.

After thirty minutes they reached the center. They'd ended up having to fight dozens of the massive spiders. Only two people had gotten bitten, each of them one of the first three knights in the raid. The poison took off several hundred health per second, and lasted multiple minutes. If the raid didn't have multiple healers with them, they might have run out of mana healing the knights through it before the poison wore off. One of the priests did try to use *Cleanse* to remove the poison, but it didn't work. Seth would've wagered that Quincy's *Purify* would have done the trick, so perhaps the hedge maze had been easier for them.

They hadn't seen any evidence of the blue capes since the blue scrap of cloth at the entrance. Perhaps they'd left it intentionally.

At the center of the maze was, perhaps predictably, a giant version of the spiders they'd been fighting so far. Seth muttered, "What's with everything being giant?" and Verun huffed a laugh in response.

Verun said, <I scanned it, it's a level forty-three champion.>

The giant spider sat motionless in the center of a huge square clearing. There were several other entrances to the rest of the maze from the center courtyard, so apparently there were multiple ways to solve it.

The beam of white light ascended to the ceiling directly behind the giant spider. The raid formed up with all of the knights in front, and approached. They'd barely taken ten steps when the spider seemed to notice them for the first time and charged. It was *fast*, it almost looked like the spider had used a skill similar to Seth's *Charge*. Baltern caught the spider's dripping jaws on his shield in a masterful show of speed and reaction time, but the hit literally launched him backwards, bowling over several other warriors and rogues who were waiting behind him to strike. Apparently the *Immovable* passive skill on knights only worked to a certain level of force. One of the other knights activated their *Taunt* skill before the spider could go after Baltern again, and it turned toward that knight preternaturally fast.

The rest of the raid leapt to action. Lightning and fire lanced out of the mage group, and dozens of arrows fired at an insane pace. Verun started moving around the left to get around the bulk of the raid and into the fight, and Seth followed. He didn't think the leading party could sit back and watch anymore, especially since the raid's numbers were so diminished.

The spider had knocked four of the knights down by the time Seth got into position to activate his *Charge,* but they all looked alive, and the tank group priest was casting his group heal spell. Seth burst into action, shooting across the intervening space and sliding his sword into one of the spider's huge legs. It locked up, going completely rigid for several seconds; his stun effect had landed!

Ten huge balls of glowing white light appeared in a rough circle above the spider's head, at least the size of small cars, and everyone stepped backwards out of fear of whatever attack the spider was about to unleash. Then the balls started falling onto the spider, exploding with light and energy as they landed. The spider's legs strained, then buckled under the immense forces being dropped upon it.

The ground shook with each thundering hit, chips of rock falling from the ceiling of the stone room. Seth felt like his eardrums might burst from the resounding booms. It was dead by the time the sixth ball landed, and the other four simply ceased to exist, turning into glowing white dust and settling to the ground.

Seth pulled up his logs, unable to process what had just happened.

Your party member Liora hits level 43 Spider

Queen (Champion) with *Meteor of Light* for
32,045 damage.
Your party member Liora hits level 43 Spider
Queen (Champion) with *Meteor of Light* for
30,234 damage.
Your party member Liora **critically** hits level 43
Spider Queen (Champion) with *Meteor of Light*
for 45,834 damage.
Your party member Liora hits level 43 Spider
Queen (Champion) with *Meteor of Light* for
34,356 damage.
Your party member Liora hits level 43 Spider
Queen (Champion) with *Meteor of Light* for
33,445 damage.
Your party member Liora hits level 43 Spider
Queen (Champion) with *Meteor of Light* for
30,994 damage.
Your party member Liora has slain level 43
Spider Queen (Champion).

The whole party turned and looked backwards.
Liora still had her staff in her hand and a mean
look on her face. She looked around at the crowd
staring silently at her. "What are you all looking
at?"

Riley started laughing hysterically.

CHAPTER 23

The champion dropped a dagger with a powerful poison enchantment, dealing large damage over time to anyone it cut. The utility party let all of the rogues who said they'd use it draw straws to see who would get it, and it ended up going to a rogue named Jon, who looked delighted as he strapped it to his belt. Seth just hoped he didn't accidentally poke his leg with it. The man would need to get a sheath made for it as soon as possible.

No one was particularly keen on being the first person to step into the glowing beam of light descending from the ceiling of the room, but after about thirty seconds of debate, Riley simply shoved through the crowd and walked into the light, Zuh right behind her. There was a flash, and they were both gone.

There was a collective gasp, and everyone froze. Another flash, and Riley was back, stalking out of the beam of light, looking angrily at the faces around her, saying, "It's just a teleporter to another room, idiots!" and then vanishing again. Seth noticed that she'd said "idiots" in English, which made him chuckle.

Seth and Verun were next into the portal, followed quickly by the rest of the raid. Seth took in his view of the third floor. It was another perfectly round room, at least the interior. The floor sloped downwards, toward the center of the room, which aside from a small pedestal in the center, was completely empty. The pedestal had something shiny on it, to Seth it almost looked like a clear crystal or glass. They'd all appeared in the room very close to the edge, near the ever-curving wall. Around ten paces from the wall was a dark line drawn on the floor, going around the entire room. Seth looked up to the ceiling high above, and saw an angry red crystal the size of a basketball embedded there, glowing. Was that one of the things that had shot Riley out of the sky?

People looked to Liora. She started to consider, but Riley, apparently still sick of waiting on every decision, started walking toward the pedestal at the center of the room.

Liora yelled, "Wait!" and, surprisingly, Riley stopped and turned around, still not past the dark line. Liora said, "Knights first."

The entire raid formed up behind the knights and advanced toward the center of the room. The instant the first members crossed the black line, a loud ticking sound could be heard from somewhere under the floor. Seth could feel it in the soles of his feet. Everyone tensed when the ticking started, but nothing changed, so they kept advancing toward the pedestal.

They hadn't drawn very near to the pedestal at all when the ticking sped up, doubling in speed. That only lasted for around ten seconds, and then a huge stone shell burst from the floor and thudded into place, completely shielding the pedestal.

Everyone had frozen, and no one knew what to do. Aurora said after a time of confused silence, "I have an idea, follow me everyone." She started back toward the edge of the room.

As soon as the last person stepped over the dark line near the edge of the room, the stone shield around the center pedestal receded into the floor, exposing the glinting object again. Aurora said, "Thought so."

Ivon spoke up, "Ah, it's a speed test. Did anyone catch how many times the timer ticked?" No one had.

The group decided amongst themselves that the fastest person was probably whoever had the highest dexterity. Seth suggested that Verun could run him there very quickly, but everyone was afraid that may break whatever unwritten rules were in place, so that became their backup option if no one could make the run in time. The top contenders compared, and the winner was a woman named Velri on one of the flanking parties, a level forty-eight scout with over one hundred and eighty dexterity. She stepped up to the line, looking determined. It was less pronounced with Velri, but her mildly twitchy movements reminded Seth of Gianna, Quincy's lieutenant. If this really was a speed test, Gianna had likely breezed through it.

Liora spoke quietly to her, "Now remember, if you think it may be close, err on the side of caution, we don't want that stone barrier crushing you. Try to get in, grab the crystal, and get out. If anything unexpected happens, head for us as fast as you can and we'll support."

Everyone lined up on the black line, Velri in the center. At Liora's mark, the woman dashed toward the center of the room, moving like a blur. Her arms pumped as her boots slapped the ground, and her red cape was almost horizontal behind her sprinting form. She was moving insanely fast; she looked like some kind of superhuman to Seth's eye, and he was already substantially faster than he'd ever been on Earth.

Moments later, the rest of the raid took off after her at a run, wanting to be close in case anything went wrong. It was obvious that Verun and some of the rogues or scouts were holding back to avoid rapidly pulling ahead of the rest of the raid, but Velri had no such restriction; she was already losing them.

The ticking had started again, and though it was at the same interval as the previous time, it seemed more frantic this time. Probably because they were all sprinting across the huge stone room.

Velri had drawn close when the double time ticking started. It looked like she was going to go for it and try to make the final stretch before time ran out, but at the last second she pulled up short and backpedaled, literally skidding across the floor on her heels. It was the right decision, too, since just then the huge stone sphere burst from the floor and sealed off the center.

Velri was hunched over breathing heavily when the rest of the group made it to the center of the room. Several of her guild mates patted her on the back, and Liora said, "Good call stopping where you did. We can't afford to lose anyone."

Seth remembered, then, that he had a potion that increased running speed in his bag. He spoke to Velri, "I just remembered I have a speed potion with me. Want to try one more time?"

She looked at him silently, still breathing heavily, as if to say "Why are you just now telling me this?" She did nod though, and the whole group started back toward the line ringing the room.

Seth fished out one of the *Wind Breaker Potions* and handed it to Velri, who uncorked it, sniffed it, looked at Seth suspiciously while wrinkling her nose, then downed it without protest.

She squinted her eyes and pulled a face at the taste, then stepped up to the line, crouched and ready to take off. Her clothes rippled like wind was buffeting her from behind, but Seth felt nothing.

Riley said, "Break a leg!" and Seth saw several of the guild members look at her in horror, obviously not understanding the reference.

Before Seth could try to explain the Earth-ism, Liora barked, "Move!" and Velri took off like lightning. If Seth thought she'd moved fast before, her speed now was unbelievable, boots slapping the pavement at such a quick beat that the sounds of her steps all blended together. The whole raid took off after her, just like the previous time, but she put distance between herself and everyone else at a ludicrous rate. The ticking picked up in speed, warning that it was almost over, but only got a couple ticks in before Velri shot past the small pedestal, grabbing the small glowing object from the top as she blazed by.

Seth and the rest of the group made it to the center after a bit more running. The ticking had stopped, and the center stone column was slowly sinking into the floor. Velri handed the object to Liora, and Seth and Verun inspected it over her shoulder. Liora threw an annoyed glance at Verun, whose breath was blowing her white hair about.

The object was a small clear crystal, perhaps as large as both of Seth's fists together, and had a slight light-blue glow inside. Aside from that he couldn't see anything helpful about it. Was another teleporter going to appear?

The pedestal it had been sitting on settled into the ground, now flush, and then nothing happened.

Riley voiced all of their worries, saying, "Now what?"

Ivon cleared his throat, wrinkled his mustache, and raised an arm to point to the opposite end of the room from where they'd entered. A small indention could be seen in the wall, though Seth could barely detect it at this range. The whole raid followed Liora over there, and they found that the crystal perfectly fit into the recess. Liora pushed it in and it stayed in place, like a dull lamp on the wall. A rumbling noise issued from somewhere behind the stone wall, and a section of it simply vanished, ceasing to exist. Behind the wall was another huge spiral stair, twisting upwards into darkness. At the bottom of the stairs was a small piece of blue cloth, left intentionally in view.

Liora cast some huge balls of light up into the darkness where they stuck, and the group ascended to the fourth floor.

CHAPTER 24

At the top of the stairs spiraling from the third to the fourth level was a strange white forcefield-like wall separating the stairs from the next room. Seth poked it, figuring someone could heal him if it incinerated his finger, and it went right through. He pulled it back and it wasn't missing or anything, so he decided to walk through. He walked back and said, "Seems safe enough to me for now."

The entire raid party walked through the white forcefield. This floor was square, and Seth could see another open door, identical to the one they'd just come through, white force field and all, opposite them. The whole party formed up; Liora didn't even have to say anything.

They began to cross the wide open room, and Seth noticed a very serious look on Riley's face. It made him look twice; she hardly ever looked so serious. That made him notice everyone else's faces too, they were all mirrors of hers: determined and focused on the opposing door.

Seth started wondering, did they know something about this empty floor that he didn't? Did they feel something that he couldn't? He didn't have time to wonder too much, though, because just then, a monster dropped from the ceiling.

It stood around ten feet tall, huge, to be sure, but Seth was somewhat surprised at the thing's diminutive size after all of the freakishly huge champions he'd been facing. It had dark-brown furry skin, with the body of a man and a bovine head. Its eyes glowed red, and it wore red and gold plate armor over its chest and groin. The rest of its body was exposed, and Seth saw that the thing was heavily muscled.

It had landed next to Aurora and Ivon, and Seth had a brief thought that he was glad it'd landed next to Aurora, a knight.

The thought vanished, though, as the monster simply picked her up and ripped her in two. Ivon was shouting something, but Seth couldn't make it out. He pulled an arrow back on his bow, but the beast simply *teleported* to right in front of him. It grabbed Ivon's head in one of its massive clawed hands and squeezed. Seth looked away when he saw blood spatter.

He yelled, "Verun!" but it seemed like no sound came out. He had no voice. Verun appeared, leaping over Seth and diving for the beast's throat, fangs bared wide and menacing. The champion disappeared and reappeared behind Verun and caught him midair, stopping his lunge. It held Verun up above its head, upside down. Verun roared with his claws ineffectively shredding the empty air, but Seth couldn't hear it.

Something felt off the whole time, but it was apparent with Verun's silent roar. Either Seth had gone deaf, or something else was going on. The champion cracked Verun's back across its knee in some classic wrestling move, and threw his body onto the stone floor. Seth didn't feel the ground vibrate at all, but it definitely should have with an impact like that.

He looked at his combat log, but there was nothing there. He looked around the room. Liora was standing in the back of the crowd, glaring at the monster but doing nothing. The same glare was painted on everyone's face, but they all stood motionless while one person attacked the monster at a time. It was like poorly done fight choreography in a low-budget movie.

Seth looked at his active effects and finally spotted it. A small symbol blinked there. When he looked at it, a larger description appeared.

Active Effects

> Horrific Visions - 12 minutes remaining
> *An enemy has cast* Horrific Visions *on you,*
> *you'll see terrible things happen to others*
> *around you, though none of it is real.*
>
> Deafness - 6 minutes remaining
> *An enemy has cast* Deafness *on you, you can't*
> *hear anything for the duration of this effect.*

Seth set his eyes on the exit on the other side of the room, the one opposite the door they'd entered. He stared straight at it and started walking. His friends and fellow raid members continued to be gruesomely murdered in front of him, even though he was moving. He even saw Aurora, Riley, and Ivon killed several times each, even though it defied all logic. Throughout, he could hear nothing, not even his own breathing.

He reached the other exit and passed through; both active effects were dispelled immediately. Liora and Aurora, as well as several others, were already out of the room. Seth looked back through the curtain and frowned at what he saw.

People were running around the room in various states of panic. Baltern had his sword out and roared a wordless cry while he swung his sword through nothing. Ivon had an arrow drawn back and frantically pointed it back and forth in various directions, shouting something about how,

"The bastards won't stand still." Thankfully, it didn't look like he'd shot anyone.

Verun had made it the farthest away from the rest of the group, and was at a dead sprint, chasing something that wasn't there. Seth quickly transmitted a thought to the lion, *It isn't real, Verun. Can you sense me? Come this way.*

The lion's head whipped in his direction, and he started cautiously walking towards Seth, saying, <I can hear nothing.> Seth explained the two effects and Verun kept heading in his direction, still flinching occasionally from unseen foes.

Riley and Zuh were simply standing in the center of the room. Her arms were crossed, and she looked somewhat bored. Seth mentally spoke to Zuh next, saying what he said to Verun. Zuh replied, <We know. We are waiting for the effects to wear off.>

Seth told him to head towards the opposite door, and the two of them did. One of the people still in the grip of the spell accidentally swung their sword into one of their teammates, opening a huge gash in the man's arm. Thankfully, one of those who'd made it out by that point was a priest primary, scout secondary, and had an extreme long-range heal as one of their combo-specific abilities. She cast it at the injured man, and he was healed as he continued to run around in a panic.

Several people tried to go back into the room to help others, but the spells were immediately cast on them again, deafening them and making them see horrors. Seth realized he could help, and started trying to land his *Quick Change Position* projectile spell on anyone who wandered close enough. He was able to swap positions with four people, some of the more erratic people he spotted with weapons whirling around, and then run back out of the room himself. After five more minutes, the deafness finally wore off for everyone still in the room, and those outside were able to yell instructions to them. Everyone made their way to the exit, and then everyone was out. Several people were crying. Ivon had a tear leaking down his cheek, and he walked up to Aurora and embraced her. He said, "I don't know what my boy would've done to me if I let harm come to you, girl."

Liora heard him, and said, "What?"

Aurora quickly said, "Nothing! Should we advance to the next floor?"

Liora looked at her suspiciously for a moment, then scanned the group. She said, "Let's take a break here. One hour, rotating guard shifts, flanking team one is up first for ten minutes. Go!"

***

One hour later, the mood of the entire raid had drastically improved. Seth had sat on the ground next to Ivon and Verun for a while, catching up with the scout. He'd been doing a lot of damage for the raid group, since he was with Riley in one of the ranged damage parties, and had actually advanced to level thirty-nine. He said, "I should go on missions like this more often! Once I hit level forty, I'll be able to charge anything I want to grant up-and-comers a scout secondary! Uh... Not that I wouldn't do it for free... Of course..."

The raid formed up in ranks again, everyone having been fully healed from any incidental damage in the nightmare room. Everyone had consumed snacks and drinks during the break too. There was even a side tunnel with several holes in the floor where people could relieve themselves. It was a very strange dungeon.

They advanced toward another spiral stair at the end of the smaller chamber, knights in the lead, and started their climb to the fifth floor. They emerged to see something extraordinary.

The fifth floor was circular, and had a massive white crystal embedded in the ceiling that almost replicated sunlight. The floor was grassy with real, living grass, and there were several trees interspersed throughout the open area, all oddly leaning in toward the center light source.

The twenty blue capes were lounging near the center of the room, under one of the larger trees. Quincy waved at the group as they approached, and called out, "Thanks for joining us! We expected you at least an hour ago. What took you so long?"

Seth caught a look of fury on Liora's face, and tried to distance himself from the vengeful mage before he got hurt.

CHAPTER 25

The blue capes seemed to think that the fifth floor was some sort of rest area, or safe zone. They'd scoured the place for over an hour in teams when they'd arrived, around six hours previous, and had been able to find nothing to do anyone harm. There was a wide open stair at the other end of the room that led up to the sixth floor, but they'd decided to stop and rest, and see if the rest of the raid showed up before advancing.

The fifth floor was like a little oasis. There were several pools of crystal-clear water, and a subtle wind seemed to blow across the grass. Seth lay on his back, hands behind his head for a while, and almost couldn't tell he wasn't lying in sunlight.

Everyone was a little irritated that they'd all rested down below in the stone hallway for an hour when this place had been a staircase away, but no one had any way of knowing that, and there was no denying that the entire group needed rest after the psychological attack that was the fourth floor.

Liora and Quincy walked a distance away from the rest of the group and talked. Seth had to strain just to catch some snippets of what was being said.

"...left us out there in the desert! In what ludicrous universe is that..." Liora waved her hands around as she struggled to keep her voice down, standing up on her toes to try and get in Quincy's face.

Seth couldn't see Quincy's face from this angle, but from his body language, he would bet the man was smiling like he usually was. He shrugged his shoulders then splayed his hands out at his sides in a placating gesture. "...made it here in one...you? ...very democratic...take matters into my own hands." At that last part, Quincy had grown very still, losing some of the easy friendliness he usually put off.

Gianna, who was sitting a dozen feet away on the soft grass ground perked up, slightly turning her head toward the two leaders. Seth saw Sullivan subtly lay a hand on his bow which sat alongside him on the grass. Was there about to be a fight?

There was a tension in the air as the two powerful people stared at one another, unmoving. Finally, the tension broke, and Liora dropped her shoulders a bit, breaking eye contact with Quincy. "...could have been more willing to listen to you..." Seth heard her say. Quincy loosened up again too, and the pair continued to converse quietly.

They came back together after several minutes. Seth stood up from where he'd been sitting on the grass, next to Verun, Aurora, Ivon, Riley, and Zuh. Everyone focused on Liora and Quincy.

Liora started to open her mouth to speak, then somewhat guiltily looked at Quincy and indicated he could speak. He said, "Everyone, our two groups are going to link back up. I want to formally thank the Adventurers' Guild members for coming to-" Riley burst out in an obnoxiously loud coughing fit. Quincy tried to suppress his smile and continued, "I meant to say that I want to formally thank the Adventurers' Guild members, and Riley and Zuh, for coming to join us. I apologize for how we ran ahead without you all, but we think there may be something really special going on in this tower. It is absolutely unlike anything we've ever encountered before." He stopped talking and looked to Liora, a peace offering.

She nodded and started speaking, "We're going to reform the raid as we had it before, please organize yourselves into the parties we had at the outset. The utility party will be short, but that will have to do."

The entire raid was restored, with partial red cape and partial blue cape parties for the most part. The first flanking party was set to watch, and others were allowed to rest. The plan was to move forward in thirty minutes.

Thirty minutes later, the entire group moved toward the large doors at the other end of the fifth floor. A staircase was visible in the gloom through the doors, but when the group made their way to the base of it, they saw there was something new. A white circle was emblazoned on the floor to the right of the staircase. It glowed. Seth approached it but didn't step in. As he drew near, a pop-up appeared in his vision.

You've reached floor 5. You may exit the tower via this teleporter, or continue. Once you enter the 6th floor, this teleporter will become inactive. Would you like to exit the tower?

Yes   No

Seth relayed the information to the rest of the group, and the leading party started discussing it amongst themselves, stepping away from the group.

Liora led with, "We caught up with you, you were able to see what the spire was all about, now we should leave and continue the original plan to skirt this zone."

Quincy smiled and said, "We've proven that we can handle the spire. If it's just like the last five floors the rest of the way up, we won't have any problem. I've barely had to help fight, and that's when there were only twenty of us."

Sullivan, who usually kept mostly quiet, said, "So far, this dungeon has been vastly different than any we've seen before. Perhaps the rewards will be comparatively exotic."

Liora said, "How about we take a vote?"

Seth piped up, "I'll abstain. I don't feel right voting when I'll survive anything we face up there." He pointed arbitrarily at the stone ceiling.

Liora looked mildly annoyed. Had she expected him to vote for whatever she did? She said, "All in favor of continuing up the spire?"

Quincy, Sullivan, and Gianna immediately waved their hands, and Aurora slowly raised hers as well. Liora just sighed, then said, "Alright. I hope we don't regret this."

The whole group climbed the wide spiral stair, and approached the sixth floor. The sixth floor was laid out in the shape of a hexagon. Huge gothic stone arches met in the center of the ceiling surrounding a glowing crystal, casting harsh white light on the entire space. A smoky smell assaulted Seth's nostrils as he finally entered the room, almost last in the whole raid. It was quickly apparent where the smell originated.

In the center of the room, was a large, white dragon. It appeared to be sleeping, curled into a circle with its spiny white tail resting near its snout. It was the size of one of those double decker busses that Seth remembered seeing in every movie about London. With every deep breath the dragon let out, little twisting curls of smoke escaped from its slit nostrils.

Everyone was afraid to speak, not wanting to wake the scaled behemoth. There was some whispered planning, then the raid began to move. The knights formed up in front of the group, and they advanced into the massive chamber, toward the sleeping dragon. It cracked an eye open when they approached. Its eyes were bright, shockingly blue. It raised its head, stood on its two back feet and splayed its white wings out. The roar that issued forth from the dragon shook the very foundations of the massive spire.

The dragon started flapping its huge wings and took to the air. Seth searched the ceiling, but didn't see any angry red stones embedded there, just the single white one.

Seth nodded at Verun, who leapt into the air, beating his huge wings and propelling himself toward the dragon. He thought of his blunder with the elephant men, and of Liora chastising him for fighting the stone army, and decided to stay back and help by observing the fight.

Seth saw Riley and Zuh take to the air too, but Zuh wouldn't be able to fight. That didn't matter though, as Seth saw a ball of lightning leap from Riley's outstretched arm and slam into the airborne dragon. It left a small dark burn, but didn't seem to have done much lasting damage.

More magic, and some well-aimed arrows shot out of the two ranged damage parties toward the middle of the raid group.

The dragon was moving very quickly through the air already, flapping its huge wings and turning tight in the restricted space of the spire level. Seth thought it may just crash its huge body into the bulk of his party members, but instead it slammed onto the ground in front of the knights after one of them screamed a *Taunt* at it, throwing its weight into their shields. Two of the knights went flying, but Seth saw them surrounded by golden light as priests from the raid kept their health pools up.

Verun whooshed low past the dragon's back, raking his claws along its white scales. Huge balls of light appeared above it, then slammed down into it, cast by Liora. Seth saw Quincy at the front lines, among the knights. The man cocked back and then straight up *punched* the dragon right in the face. The force of the blow knocked the dragon back at least ten feet.

Seth felt a little silly, not participating himself while Liora and Quincy both fought, but he was determined to at least try it their way, and tried to watch for any details others might miss.

The dragon roared at the ceiling, a strange mix of deep tones and hissing sounds, then lunged forward, stretching its neck out like a snake at Quincy. It happened so fast that none of the knights had time to use another *Taunt*. The dragon's gleaming white maw closed over Quincy's left leg. Its head retracted back away as he landed another punishing punch on its snout, and Quincy was left on the ground, leg missing from just below the knee.

He cursed, then golden light bloomed around his bleeding stump. Seth saw his mana bar jump downwards with the high cost of the spell, then his leg reformed out of golden light and snapped back into existence, bootless. He stood and threw himself back into the fight, an angry grimace on his features. Seth was impressed, to say the least.

The champion's health wasn't deteriorating as fast as Seth would have expected, especially so, since the two guild leaders were participating in the fight. He picked a log at random from the sea of logs streaming past and read it.

Your raid member Velri hits Level 45 White Dragon with Blue Eyes (Champion) for 28 damage. Damage reduced by 90% due to Champion's passive ability *Hardscale.*

Maybe this was something he could help with. He looked at the dragon again, cringing at the red blood staining its wicked teeth as it snapped at the cracked blue shields of one of the knights. The blue eyes stuck out to him again, and he had an idea.

He saw Ivon, standing with a few scouts and mages that made up his ranged damage party, and yelled at him, "Ivon, go for the eyes!"

Ivon's mustache shimmied in irritation and he snapped back with, "Sure, boy, it's the easiest thing in the world!" Despite the sarcasm, Seth saw Ivon take a deep breath, focus while he drew back his bow, and fire a single shot.

Seth tracked the arrow as it streaked through the intervening space and slammed into one of the dragon's bright-blue eyes.

The effect was immediate. The dragon lurched backwards like it'd been hit by a dump truck, not a tiny arrow, and its health jumped down to just under fifty percent. The one arrow had taken out almost half of its health! Seth tried to yell, "Hit the other eye!" But his words were drowned out as the dragon flapped its wings and took off flying in huge circles around the cavernous room again.

On its second pass through, it opened its maw and a solid beam of white light, like some science fiction death laser, blasted out and slammed into the wall of the spire. It went straight through. For a brief few seconds, Seth could actually see the sky outside, but then the stone of the spire started knitting itself back together again, as if it were being rebuilt in time-lapse.

The dragon let out two more of the insanely strong attacks, the second missed again, spearing a wall, but the third did clip the shield of one of the knights. The shield shattered instantly, and one of the man's arms simply didn't exist after the attack. He flopped to the ground, unconscious but not dead, and Seth saw a priest running up to stabilize the mortally wounded man.

The dragon made one more erratic loop over the raid, then a huge whip that looked like it was made of pure light lashed out from the ground and wound itself around the beast's snout. Seth traced the whip to Liora, who was skidding across the ground on her heels as she tried to stop the dragon's momentum. She choked out, "Seth!" and he ran over, grabbing onto the energy whip and pulling with all of his strength.

The whip felt like warm, fuzzy rope, not exactly what he was expecting, but Seth's help made the difference. The dragon crashed to the ground, throwing stone chips and dust into the air, but the light-whip stayed attached, and with Seth and Liora holding onto it, they were able to hold the dragon's head still.

Its one remaining blue eye looked around the room hatefully until several arrows and spells slammed into it almost simultaneously, and the creature died.

Quincy walked over toward Seth and Liora, panting but with a smirk on his face, and said, "Sometimes you just have to get your own hands dirty, huh?" Before anyone could answer, he looked over his shoulder and yelled, "Someone cut that thing's belly open and get my boot back! I refuse to go barefoot the rest of the way up this tower."

The dragon dropped around a dozen silvery white scales that could be forged into plate armor by a skilled smith. All of the knights who were interested drew straws for the scales, and Aurora won. She shoved them into her backpack, a slight smile on her face. Baltern looked disappointed, and Seth felt a small perverse pleasure at that. The group advanced to the next floor.

As they ascended the spiraling stairwell, Seth quietly asked Quincy to explain how his class combination worked. He'd been happy to explain. Apparently, priest primary, warrior secondaries gained several combo skills that drastically changed how the priest class worked. They ended up losing all ranged skills, meaning they couldn't even heal their teammates from a distance; they had to actually lay a hand on someone to heal them. To counteract this handicap, the priest warrior gained several hand to hand attacks, drastically increased speed, and increased strength. Quincy's tactic ended up being to run around the battlefield at insane speeds, walloping enemies and tapping his party members on the shoulder or back to heal them. Seth thanked the man for the explanation, eager to see him in action even more. The ascension continued.

The seventh floor was an inferno. There didn't seem to be anything for them to fight, but no one was sure how they were supposed to make it to the other side of the huge room. Only the small exit hall from the stair was safe, but the heat generated from the huge gouts of flame inside the room were enough to make sweat spring from Seth's brow as soon as he reached the top of the stairs.

No one was sure what to make of the floor. One brave knight stuck his hand over the fire for the barest moment and had to have the burns healed away by a priest. Finally, Riley walked up and cast her level thirty-five skill, *Windstorm*, blasting furious winds at the impenetrable wall of flame. It forged a tunnel into the inferno, but Riley dropped the spell after just a few seconds. Wind continued to blow for five seconds after she let go of the spell, then the furious fire raged back in, filling the gap almost immediately.

A plan was formed. Several more types of magic were thrown into the room. Fire, lightning, and Liora's light magic didn't have any effect on the inferno, but all of the priests had access to a spell called *Riptide,* which did calm the fire for around two seconds per cast.

Aside from Riley, there were four other mages in the raid that were levelled high enough to use *Windstorm*. The tunnel the spell created through the flames was only wide enough for two people to walk abreast, and not long enough for the entire raid to fit inside. The mages were divided into two groups. The first group of three would rotate, keeping the wind tunnel open while the other two mages walked into the tunnel and extended it. All five mages had an aide with them, random lower-level members, who were responsible for literally tipping mana potions into their mouths if they went below half. The priests were interspersed throughout the formation, ready to throw down *Riptide* spells if anything went wrong with the mages to give the group a bit more time to escape the inferno. Seth wasn't very confident that a volley of the water spells would do much to save them from the insane heat, though.

There were no test runs, no dress rehearsals. The first three mages, including Riley, started their rotation, each casting their spells until they reached half mana. They'd yell, stop, and the next mage would take over before the five seconds were up and the spell wore off.

The rest of the raid, led by Liora and a level forty-seven mage from the Transportation Guild, advanced into the tunnel punched into the flame. Seth and Verun were some of the last of the group into the room, sweat dripping freely down Seth's face, tasting salty in his mouth and stinging his eyes as the powerful wind spells buffeted him from behind. He had to focus on not walking too fast and crashing into the people in front of him.

His leather boots let off little puffs of steam with each step, the floor retaining some of the heat from the hellfire surrounding them on all sides. Seth walked past Liora, who'd reached the end of Riley's group's range of effectiveness and stopped, casting their own wind tunnels. The first group started walking forward as they cast, the tunnel closing up behind them in flame as they advanced on Liora's position.

There was an awkward shuffle as the first group of mages had to pass the second one while maintaining their spell rotation, and another one when they reversed again, keeping the flames away from the rest of the group.

Finally, blessedly, the far wall of the room came into view. There was only one problem, however. The exit wasn't there.

They'd all assumed that the exit would be straight across from the entrance; that's how it'd been on every other floor they'd seen so far. The flames had blocked their view, so they hadn't been able to see, but when they crossed the room, it was just a bare stone wall, blackened by the flames.

Seth locked up, unsure what to do, but then he heard Ivon shouting over the din, "It's to the left! I glimpsed it through the flames!"

Another scout yelled, "I think I saw it too! Another door to the left."

A panicked muttering could be heard mixing with the sounds of the raging fire all around. Everyone was drenched in sweat and many had a wild look in their eye, trapped between certain death on all sides.

Seth heard Liora yell a command. "Slow pivot left in ten seconds! Ready!"

Quincy pushed through the crowd to the front of the line. Seth saw a gout of flame lick his shoulder as he drew a little too close to the edge of the wind tunnel, then his brass-knuckled hand whipped up and soothed it with a puff of golden light. He got very near the front of the group then started yelling too, "Get ready! Those farthest from the mages will have to move the quickest."

Liora counted down aloud from three, then the wind tunnel began to move, scything the flames to the left, but allowing the flames on the right to lick back in, singeing anyone who didn't move quickly enough. The tunnel through the flames now made a large L-shape, and it was getting hard to breathe, the inferno burning up all of the oxygen now that their cleared path wasn't attached to any entrance or exit.

The mages shuffled through the crowd and extended the tunnel again, searching the left wall, but still not finding it.

Finally, after one more alternation, the exit door came into view, almost identical to the entrance to the room. Everyone struggled to remain calm until they could all get out, and when the last mages walked out of the fire and dropped their wind spells, almost everyone slumped against a wall or sat down on the stone ground. They'd done it, but it had seemed a near thing.

The group took a several-hour break, lounging on the stairs leading to the eighth floor, before continuing up the spire, beat up and exhausted.

CHAPTER 26

Immediately upon passing the barrier to the eighth floor, the entrance snapped shut behind the group, rumbling the stone ground, and everyone was hit with a mute effect, suddenly unable to speak. Seth saw a log appear, but it didn't make much sense as he read over it.

> The bottom-right peg should be rotated three times to the right, but only after all other corners have been modified.

He wasn't sure what it meant until the group silently approached the exit from the room. The exit, directly across from the entrance, was a sealed stone door, a dozen feet to a side. Seth tried in vain to shove on it, but even with his huge strength score, it didn't budge.

Arrayed on the giant door was a grid pattern. There were twenty-five cells in the grid, five rows of five. Each cell contained a wooden peg, around the thickness of Seth's bicep, protruding out from the stone for around six inches. They had indecipherable runes burned into their faces, and for once Seth's magical translation ability did nothing to help.

The group eventually puzzled out, wordlessly, that the challenge of this floor was to correctly manipulate all of the various pegs in the right order to open the exit, without the use of language, all based on the vague instruction logs that only some of the members had received. Seth thought it would be easy, and sent a thought to Verun, but the big lion didn't respond. Apparently the mute debuff even extended to mental voices.

The puzzle took an extremely long time to figure out. Only twenty-five people were actually given instructions, which made Seth wonder what would have happened if there had been less than twenty-five, like if Quincy's team had made it this far alone with only twenty. After much hand waving and angry glaring, the group had been separated into two groups, one of twenty-five people who had some kind of instruction, and the other full of spectators. Liora, apparently, hadn't been given any instruction and so had taken the helm of trying to orchestrate everything. Quincy and

Sullivan were in the same group as Seth, meaning they had a log, and Gianna and Aurora were standing with the spectator group.

The first three people went, apparently having some kind of instructions that told them it was their time to go. As they turned their pegs a certain direction and a certain amount of times, the hole the wooden peg protruded from would light up blue. The fourth person went up, but did something incorrectly; their peg turned an angry red for a moment before all of the pegs quickly clacked back to their original positions and their blue lights dimmed. Liora threw an angry look at the woman who'd gone up fourth, and the whole process restarted.

It took them fifteen tries to get it right. Everyone breathed a huge sigh of relief when all of the pegs lit up blue and the huge stone wall sank into the floor. Seth heard a few people whispering and realized the mute debuff was gone. Having not spoken for so long, he too had a strange compulsion to whisper instead of talk at full volume.

The ninth floor was a three-dimensional stone maze that took them left, right, up, and down through cramped stone passageways for hours. There was some arguing over whether the huge raid should split up or continue as one group, but in the end no one wanted to be the last ones in the maze and unable to find a way out, so they all continued in one huge line. Verun struggled to fit through the passageways, and Riley had already banished Zuh for the time being. Seth asked the lion if he wanted to stay and he said something about needing to protect Seth; Seth assumed the lion was still just uncomfortable being in the void, so let him stay and shove through the stone tunnels.

By Seth's count they spent upwards of six hours on the ninth floor. There weren't any monsters to fight, but there were numerous traps like poisoned darts flying from the walls, spike pits, and huge logs or boulders suspended from the ceiling and ready to crush anyone who tripped a barely visible wire. The raid's highest-level rogues, Gianna, and Jon, the Adventurers' Guild member who'd received the poisonous spider dagger, led the group and were able to spot almost every trap before it was triggered. There were several people who ended up with poison darts in their arms, but the poison was weaker than the spider poison from the hedge maze and the priests were able to keep those people healed through the poison's duration.

Tensions had risen in the maze, but everyone was relieved when the group entered the tenth floor and saw what looked like another oasis. Where the fifth floor had been designed to look like a prairie with the occasional tree, the tenth floor simulated rolling hills covered in wildflowers. Liora didn't let anyone rest easy immediately though. The entire raid lined up in formation and they circled the rim of the room as a group, on guard. Seth thought she was paranoid, but couldn't really blame her with how strange the spire had been so far.

There were four windows looking out of the spire, almost the entire height of the floor, one in each cardinal direction from the center of the room. The windows were made of some kind of clear crystal and weren't perfectly flat, so they somewhat warped the view of the desert outside. It was clear that the sun was setting, though.

After the raid ascertained that there wasn't anything waiting to jump out and eat them, they all headed to the center of the room. Liora assigned watch shifts by party, and everyone else started taking a break. They were going to spend the night on the floor.

The leading party wouldn't take watch until sometime in the middle of the night, so Seth went and found Ivon. The old scout had found a hill to lie on facing the huge crystal window that framed the sunset. He said, "Well, boy, what do you make of all this?" He waved his hand around, indicating all around them.

Seth said, "This level, or the spire as a whole?"

Ivon's mustache shimmied a bit. "Either, both."

Seth said, "I think this must be the most industrious wild spirit in the history of Morgenheim. We thought the stone city was impressive, but this spire would absolutely dwarf it. I can't seem to figure out what the spirit's play is here. If every level tried to kill us it would almost make more sense, but some of them are just puzzles that won't necessarily hurt us unless we get stuck and starve. Then there's these oasis levels. Why provide those at all?"

Ivon hummed for a moment, thinking, and said, "Perhaps if there weren't any places to relax, no one would ever continue up the tower. They'd just focus on getting out, either via those teleporters or some more destructive means." He nodded toward where Liora, Quincy, and Gianna were in a quiet discussion. "D'you really think this tower could hold them if they were determined to get out?"

Seth said, "I guess not. I had no idea there were people so powerful out there."

"Liora's famous in the guild for how tough she is," Ivon said. "She still to this day spends a huge amount of her time levelling. Never satisfied with where they are, those kinds of people." There was a pause as the two of them watched the Adventurers' Guild and Transportation Guild leaders conferring, then Ivon spoke again, "Listen, boy." He stopped himself. "Sorry, Seth, I wanted to thank you for getting me out of that cell at Slyborn. I'm honestly not sure that I really deserve to be out and be here, but I can't say I'd pick the cell if given the choice. You didn't have to do what you did."

Seth wasn't sure what to say. After an awkward silence, he said, "Well, it is what friends do, isn't it? I just hope you've learned that if you ever find yourself being blackmailed again, you can tell me.

And it isn't just me." He nodded to where Aurora was speaking with Baltern.

Ivon scrunched his mustache up. "Yes, I do know that. Thank you, and the same goes for you. If you ever feel like you can't tell someone something, you can trust me. I won't betray you again."

Seth patted him on the shoulder and said, "I know, Ivon." The words didn't seem to make Ivon feel any better. They sat together in companionable silence for a while, both lost in their own thoughts. Seth finally stood and stretched, saying, "I'm going to see what Riley is up to." Ivon just grunted and nodded his head, eyes unfocused as he stared into the distance.

Seth saw Riley's house sitting on top of a small hillock, and tried to hold in his jealousy as he thought of his thin bedroll and the lumpy ground beneath it. He headed towards the house.

Riley, Verun, and Zuh were sitting outside of the house around a small campfire of scavenged sticks from around the oasis floor. Seth greeted them, then said to Riley, "Why'd you set up way over here so far from everyone else?"

She nudged Zuh and said, "I think we make some of the group nervous, so just trying to respect that."

Seth had certainly felt that before, but it hadn't crossed his mind in a while. He said, "I think they've gotten used to our presence by now. At least that's the impression I've gotten recently."

She said, "Oh, no, I don't mean our glorified zombie routine, I meant because Zuh and I don't fall into either one of their little cape cliques."

"Why do you think that?" Seth said, subliminally noting he'd fallen back into speaking English like she'd been doing.

Riley said, "I think they're all very comfortable in their roles. They know what to expect from members of their guild, and they know what to expect from their rivals, but I'm some kind of unknown to them. At least that's my theory."

Seth said, "Well you know the Adventurers' Guild would take you in, if you were interested, right? And I bet Quincy would too, he'd probably jump at the chance to have someone from Earth in his guild to balance my presence."

She said, "Yeah, I realize, I'm just not interested." She looked back down at her hands and kept working. Seth saw that she was weaving some of the wide-bladed grass together into a flat square. He couldn't tell what she planned to make out of it.

After some silence, Seth said, "Why aren't you interested?"

Riley looked up like she'd forgotten he was there already, and said, "Well, you've heard why the two guilds came about, right?"

Seth said, "Because people like us all disappeared?"

Riley replied, "Correct. So now that we're back, I'm not super interested in joining a group that may not be necessary for very long. If there was a group with a better mission, I might join up." She smiled at him like it was some kind of an inside joke, but he didn't get it.

After a moment Seth said, "Well, that's totally up to you, but I think there are people out there right now that I can help by being with the guild."

Riley said, "I didn't mean to criticize your decision, I'm only speaking for Zuh and I. We just haven't found the right group yet. Perhaps we never will. It all depends..." Seth wasn't sure what to say, but Riley changed the subject. "So are you romantically interested in Aurora?"

Seth felt blindsided. He was only able to reply with, "What?!" Riley didn't respond, just stared at him, her weaving paused in her lap. Seth could feel his face heating up, but he wasn't even sure why. He said, "No, I'm not interested in her...that...way...Why do you ask?"

She smiled and looked back down at her weaving, saying, "Oh, no reason. Just being nosy, I guess."

Seth was confused where she would've gotten the idea, but she didn't elaborate or bring it up again, instead changing the subject again to movies back on Earth. The two of them chatted for a while, before Seth finally went and found his campsite for the night, next to the sleeping form of Verun.

***

The group continued to ascend the spire at a healthy speed, getting at least five levels per day, but sometimes ten. A pattern had emerged with how the massive dungeon worked. Every fifth level was some kind of safe zone where the raid could camp or rest between the slog through the other levels. The other four of every five levels were a mix of champion fights, puzzles, ever more difficult to navigate mazes, and a few that broke the mold.

Being in the dungeon for so long was starting to weigh on people's emotions. Until the spire, the longest they'd ever spent in one was the better part of a day. Sleep was restless and meals were less fulfilling when they knew they were just trapped in a comically large tower.

There was another of the hallucination floors on level twenty-three. This one both projected horrifying images into everyone's minds, but also had sound. Thankfully, Quincy's *Purify* spell dispelled both the horrifying images debuff, and the horrifying sounds debuff. Unfortunately, the *Purify* spell was the highest-level spell that Quincy had, and he only had enough mana to cast it six times in quick succession before he was out of mana and had to let it recharge. He cured the entire leading party and then one of the lower-level mages from the long-range damage party who'd been slinging fireballs at the apparitions he was seeing.

Seth was able to communicate with Verun and Zuh. Verun headed toward the exit, still flinching and dodging whatever he saw. Riley and Zuh had been sitting perfectly still in the center of the room, just like the last time they'd come across this kind of hallucination.

Ivon and several others seemed to realize what was going on before they could even be *Purified,* and were heading toward the exit at varying speeds. The leading party grouped up and was trying to stop anyone from hurting each other as they lived through their nightmares, Liora and Aurora escorting the people who remained calm to the exit. Quincy was casting *Purify* every time he gained enough mana, but it was slow going.

Seth wondered if he'd been given the hallucination debuff again when the monster appeared amongst the still-hallucinating raid members, but there was nothing in his active effects screen.

It looked like some kind of super-sized werewolf, with freakishly large clawed hands. Seth started running toward the monster as it picked up one of the rogues in a fist, but Seth was thrown back when Baltern bashed his shield at some hallucination and accidentally hit him, knocking him to the ground. The rogue who'd been picked up by the monster was screaming, but so was everyone else, seeing horrors. The monster wrapped its other hand around the rogue's head and looked like it was going to try and twist his head off when Quincy appeared in front of it, having moved so fast that Seth barely saw it. He punched the monster in the thigh with a massive right hook, and the monster's thigh bone simply snapped like a twig. It roared and dropped the rogue, who stood quickly and ran the other direction, swinging his daggers at nothing.

The monster had fallen onto all fours, but it swiped a huge claw at Quincy and caught him, sending him spinning backwards. Seth could see golden light surrounding him before he even stood, so he appeared to be alright. Gianna ran at the monster and started slashing her daggers at its uninjured leg.

She was insanely fast, she looked like a blur to Seth, but the monster was fast too, and was able to rake its claws down her side, tearing open a gash through her leather armor and into her ribs. She hissed and backed off for a second before launching back in. A bright-red glow appeared around her right-hand dagger as she plunged it into the monster's shoulder, and it roared as red light started leaching out of it and into Gianna. The red light travelled up Gianna's arm and down her side, and the gash quickly knit together. Was she stealing the monster's life essence to heal herself?

The gargantuan werewolf shoved Gianna back, and the red light cut off, but it looked like the wound on her side had completely closed, leaving just a scar where it had been. Seth didn't normally see scars in Morgenheim when wounds were healed, so perhaps her power worked differently than normal priest healing.

Before the werewolf could do much damage, nine flaming arrows slammed into it, all finding a critical point in its body. One in each knee, one in each arm, one in each eye, two in the chest, and a final one in the center of its monstrous forehead. It didn't even whimper before it fell, dead. Seth traced their smoking paths back through the air and saw Sullivan, smoke rising around his bow, a focused expression on his face.

He almost yelled a congratulations to Sullivan, but then saw what the scout was doing: he was looking for more attackers. The giant werewolf had seemingly appeared from nowhere; were there more?

Seth scanned the room, too, but couldn't see anything. Had the werewolf been invisible like rogues could be? The leading party formed up and kept watch on the mayhem in the room, and Quincy *Purified* two more people before sending them toward the exit door, where others had been heading.

No more champions appeared, and Quincy focused on using his skill to *Purify* the people who were panicking the most. Many of the people eventually realized it was a much more convincing replica of the earlier floor when they were completely uninjured by all the carnage around them, and started heading for the exit. Before long, it was all over, everyone had exited the large room and was preparing to advance to the twenty-fourth.

Now that they were approaching the halfway marker up the sixty-floor tower, the rooms had gotten noticeably smaller, since each room had to be smaller than the one below it. Where the first few floors had seemed as big as football stadiums, the twenty-third floor was more like the size of a football field, though the ceilings were still around fifty feet high, or more.

Windows had become more common, and people in the raid had taken a liking to staring out of the windows over the empty desert. Skyscrapers didn't exist in Morgenheim, so people weren't used to views from so high up.

Everyone took a break and looked out of the window and mentally recuperated for almost an hour; the hallucination floors had been scarring to people, but everyone was anxious to pass the twenty-fourth floor and reach the twenty-fifth before nightfall, so they advanced.

The twenty-fourth floor was one of the stranger ones. A feline humanoid with an uncomfortably large head sat at a table in the center of the room, a game board set up in front of it. The same voice of the man in the purple-whorled armor from the first floor blasted out as if from loudspeakers when they entered the floor, saying, "One from your party must defeat my most intelligent creation at *King and Country* before you may advance to the next floor. Any player who loses immediately forfeits their life. You have as many attempts as you have lives to spend."

There was some murmuring amongst the crowd, and Seth was able to ascertain that this was a game several of the people were familiar with, and apparently quite ancient. Liora, no surprise, had a lot of experience in the game, but Seth was surprised when Ivon stepped forward too, saying, "I'm quite good at the game, not to toot my own horn." He hadn't actually said, "toot my own horn," but it was the closest thing Seth's mental translator was able to come up with.

Seth said, "Riley and I could try?"

Liora said, "Have either of you ever played?" Seth and Riley both shook their heads.

Ivon spoke up, "It takes years to get even a passable level of skill."

Liora nodded along with Ivon. "You'd just be throwing your lives away, and who knows if you'd even be able to get back into the tower once you were reborn. It needs to be one of us."

Ivon and Liora stepped away and talked quietly back and forth for several minutes, and eventually the woman nodded in defeat, and Ivon approached the table. He sat down, and the game began. The voice boomed out above once more, saying, "You may approach, but you may not interfere with the game in any way, or your player will be disqualified immediately. I do not like cheaters."

Seth and the rest of the group circled up in a half moon behind Ivon, no one wanting to stand next to the freaky-looking cat man. Ivon was allowed to go first.

The game appeared to be played on a custom-shaped map made out of small, interlocking tiles with six sides, three concave and three convex. In each tile were holes where pegs from different pieces could be inserted. The game forged ahead, with each player collecting little metal pieces representing resources like wood, metal, and food, and then spending those things to either build structures on the map, or hire military.

Seth had trouble keeping up; he'd have to ask Ivon to teach him the rules of the game at some point. The cat man grew more and more confident as they played, and Seth saw a small frown forming on Liora's face. Both Ivon and his opponent were adding height to their main kingdom piece by stacking more pieces atop it, though Ivon's wasn't growing as quickly. Finally, the game ended, though Seth wasn't sure what had signaled the end of the game as both players still had buildings protecting their kingdoms, and Ivon had even built several tiny walls around his.

The two laid out their excess resources, and each was awarded a gold coin through some kind of points system. It looked like the cat man had two more gold pieces than Ivon, but then Ivon flipped over three cards that he'd had face down, and was awarded three more gold pieces. The cat hissed at Ivon for a brief moment before simply vanishing in a puff of smoke. The huge stone slab that had been covering the exit at the other end of the room ground out of the way, shaking the floor as it went.

The whole raid surrounded Ivon, congratulating him and slapping him on the back. He tried to hide his smile under a scowl and his mustache, but Seth could still see a grin breaking through. Liora even shook Ivon's hand, and Seth hoped she'd changed her mind on the man.

The group ascended to the twenty-fifth floor. Liora insisted they walk a circuit of the entire floor before they rest, as she'd done on every other oasis level before. After that, Seth lay down on the dirt next to Verun and was asleep in moments, dreading when he would be woken up for his shift.

CHAPTER 27

Seth was woken in the middle of the night by screams. It was still very dark on the twenty-fifth floor, with hardly any light coming in through the huge crystal windows.

Seth shimmied out of his bedroll and stood as quickly as he could, still addled from sleep, and started running toward the screaming, grabbing for his sword. People were standing in a loose cluster, with one man, the source of the hysterical shouting, standing in the center, waving what looked like a piece of parchment above his head.

Seth shouldered through the crowd, surprisingly easy to do with his strength score being one of the highest in the entire raid, and caught the end of what the man was saying, "-and they're gone! Our leaders have been taken! It says it right here!"

Seth finally reached the man, and saw Aurora appear through the throng on the opposite side, Seth said, "Stop that. What is going on?!" He snatched the paper out of the man's hand.

The man, a mage named Dycer from one of the flanking teams with Baltern, looked at Seth like he'd been slapped. His affront quickly turned to anger, and he said, "You read it then!" and pushed away through the crowd. Seth looked at the paper.

It seems your raid was slightly too strong for my tower. Teams should not make it to the twenty-fifth floor without losing any members. I've taken your strongest two members and imprisoned them on floor 60.

Seth handed it to Aurora, he said out loud, "Who's missing?"

Aurora quickly scanned the note, tucked it into a pouch on her belt, and said, "I haven't seen my mother."

Gianna and Sullivan appeared next to Seth in the center of the loosening crowd, and Gianna spoke, "Quincy is missing." She looked grave.

Seth looked around at all the faces of the raid; they were begging him to say something. He said, "I..." He didn't know what to say. They had to keep going, but would it be possible without their strongest damage dealer and best healer?

Thankfully, Aurora spoke up, "Everyone stay calm. If this note is to be believed, Quincy and Mother are being held up on the sixtieth floor. We were going there anyway, so we will continue our ascension with the same speed and fervor with which we've possessed this far."

It did the trick to an extent, and everyone seemed to relax a bit now that someone had taken charge. Seth felt bad that he wasn't able to do it himself.

Aurora continued, "Now that we're all awake anyway, let's go ahead and prepare to head out in thirty. Utility team, I want you to get some torches burning so we can see what's going on, there might be some downed branches under those trees. Flanking parties one and two, you're on guard duty until we depart, starting in three minutes. Everyone else, meet here in thirty."

She started to turn and walk away, but stopped and turned when someone yelled, "What if we want to leave? There's no way we can get to the top floor without Quincy! I don't want to die just because he decided he wanted to satisfy his curiosity." Seth saw that it was one of the blue capes speaking; he didn't know the man's name by heart. Sullivan had walked behind the man and was looming behind him. He clapped his hand on one of the man's shoulders, and the man nearly jumped out of his boots.

Sullivan looked at Aurora and everyone held still, not wanting to draw the high-level scout's ire.

After a moment he said, "Any Transportation Guild members who want to leave may do so, but if I make it back to Efril alive, you'll have no place in the guild. I happen to know for a fact that Quincy would risk his life to save each and every one of his guildmates, regardless of how they got into a situation. Let that settle before you make a decision." He turned and walked away into the darkness.

Seth thought Aurora might say something similar, but she kept silent. Perhaps the spirit of rivalry between the two guilds would be enough to motivate the red capes to stick around just to prove they didn't need it said.

The raid, down to fifty-six members, moved out thirty minutes later. Seth saw quite a few people eye-balling the glowing circle that would teleport people down to the exit, but no one actually stepped inside.

Aurora, seemingly emulating her mother, ran the raid hard. They advanced all the way to the thirty-fifth floor that day, gaining ten floors. Fights were different without the massive damage output from Liora, and without Quincy's ability to remove almost every negative effect, but they got by. Seth, Gianna, and Sullivan were responsible for the lion's share of the damage output on single enemies. One of the champions they fought that day spawned hundreds of cat-sized minions when it reached fifty percent health, but they were very individually weak. Seth used his *Cyclone Whirl*, and Riley used her *Windstorm* skill to decimate dozens of them at a time.

The raid had their first death on floor thirty-four. There were no enemies there, but the floor was divided into a huge grid, and many of them had traps. Gianna led the way; being the highest-level rogue, she was the best at detecting traps. The whole group followed behind her like some giant game of *Snake*, following in her footsteps exactly. They'd made it around eighty percent across the room completely unscathed when someone towards the back of the line stumbled and stepped onto one of the trapped tiles. A pillar of fire shot straight up, strangely staying within the bounds of the square it was coming from, killing the person who'd fallen in instantly. Aurora's voice thundered over the group. "No one move! Stay calm, follow the plan!"

People made terrified noises, but no one tried to break rank or escape, and before long the last person in line, Sullivan, exited the tile maze into the safe zone at the other end of the room. Seth and Riley both resummoned their mounts, as it'd been decided they were too large to try navigating the maze themselves, and the angry red crystal on the ceiling deterred them from just flying across.

The person who'd been killed was Dycer, the mage who'd found the note from the etherean who lived in the spire. The person who'd been behind him said he'd just tripped over his own feet, and no one had been able to catch him in time.

A depressed mood settled over the raid group, and Aurora, Sullivan, and Gianna decided that the group could take a ten-hour break overnight, so everyone would get eight hours of sleep and two hours on watch. Seth barely got any sleep.

The next day, they only made it to the fortieth floor. The thirty-eighth ended up taking them almost nine hours to get through. It was a timed maze. Once anyone passed the entrance, a loud ticking began, and continued for around fifteen minutes. After the fifteen minutes, anyone still in the maze was teleported back to the beginning.

Gianna had made it through on her first attempt, but there wasn't any way for her to deactivate the timer on the other side. In the end, Gianna ended up having to teach everyone the path, running at much slower than her top speed, to get the bulk of the group across.

Even then, though, there were eight members who just couldn't make the run in the allotted time, even though they had memorized it perfectly. They were all knights, slow due to their huge armor, or magic users, not terribly high in any physical statistics that might make the run easier.

In the end, Seth and the second-highest-level warrior, a man named Mazain, had to carry the slower members on their backs, using their high strength scores to their advantage. Seth was drenched in sweat when he finished his last ferry ride. Aurora patted him awkwardly on his back as she hopped off, her heavy iron armor clanking as she stretched. She said, "Thanks for the ride," and walked off.

Seth saw Riley eyeballing him from across the room, what was that all about?

The thirty-ninth floor was a traditional champion fight, though the tentacled monstrosity seemed completely immune to any *Taunt* spells, and would just seek out whoever had done the most damage to it, ignoring all of the knights who tried to grab its attention.

Aurora yelled for all of the mages and scouts to stop damaging the champion, and the rogues, warriors, and knights finished it off at close range, the knights doing their best to intercept strikes meant for the others.

The fortieth floor had water several inches deep over the entire space, with small grassy islands jutting up all across the room. Aurora stuck to her mother's habit of forcing the whole raid to do a circuit of the entire room, made even more necessary after Liora and Quincy had been abducted from a supposedly safe floor.

No enemies were spotted, and the bulk of the raid group, now down to fifty-five members, tried to sleep while the group on shift for guard duty fought to stay awake.

CHAPTER 28

Three people left that night. They'd been sighted heading toward the stairs to the forty-first level, though everyone was confident they'd gone there to use the teleporter to the exit as opposed to going ahead alone. Surprisingly, the trio consisted of two Adventurers' Guild members and one Transportation Guild member. Apparently they weren't opposed to working together when it came to deserting. The group was two scouts and a priest from the second ranged damage party, the one that Ivon and Riley weren't part of.

Aurora didn't seem fazed at all when the guard told her, and in fact later told Seth quietly, "I'm surprised it wasn't more."

The raid, down to fifty-two people, advanced up the spire. The levels became more challenging, even forcing the group to retreat several times. The fights got harder, and the puzzles became increasingly more frustrating. The forty-sixth floor was a memory puzzle that only allowed two attempts per day. It took them six tries, their highest-level mage (aside from Liora) finally remembering the dozens of meaningless sigils in perfect order, like memorizing a shuffled deck of cards, having never seen a deck of cards before. The group was frustrated at the first failures, but Seth sensed a quiet thanks as they descended back down to the oasis on forty-five to rest until they could try again.

Seth's mind kept drifting back to Slyborn. He wondered if Pahan was alright, if Siestal, the scholar, was learning anything interesting. Had Pahan been able to create a champion yet? He thought of his new home, now far away, and tried his best to get the raid to the top of the tower.

The fifty-sixth floor held the most difficult champion they'd faced, though the difficulty was likely exacerbated by the fact that they were missing people, too.

They exited the spiral stair and grouped up just inside the room. The champion appeared to be sleeping. Seth gasped when he realized what it was, and Riley confirmed when she whispered, "It looks like the sphinx in Egypt!"

It did, though markedly smaller and in much better shape. It had a nose, for one, and the hood that surrounded its face was colored in gold and black stripes. Its eyes snapped open, then, focusing on the red and blue-caped humans standing just inside the doorway.

Almost all of the champions they'd fought had waited for the group to approach before attacking, but apparently the sphinx was different. It stood, stone limbs grinding together as it raised itself to all fours. The tower floor shook with the motion, but Seth found himself oddly unfazed by the giant monster. Had he been desensitized by the tower?

The knights formed up at the front of the raid, their blue translucent shields popping into existence attached to their forearms, forming a wall between the champion and the rest of the group.

Verun said, <A lion body but a human face. I don't like it. It's...ugly.>

Riley chuckled and said, "Aren't they supposed to ask riddles?"

The great sphinx cocked its head to one side in a surprisingly feline gesture, then its eyebrows drew down over its eyes in obvious anger. It lowered its front, hind end staying high, and pounced.

Baltern's *Taunt* skill came too late; the sphinx's head did turn towards him when he used it, but the massive creature's momentum carried it careening into the line of other knights. Their line mostly held, likely due to their *Immovable* skill, though not all of them were high enough level to have it yet. It was immediately obvious which knights were below level thirty-five, as they went catapulting back towards the rest of the raid like bowling pins struck by a particularly heavy ball.

The knights were helped to their feet, healed if they needed it, and shoved back into position surrounding Baltern, who was single-handedly holding the attention of the beast for the moment.

The fight was normal until the sphinx's health hit the seventy-five percent mark. It started levitating, rising out of reach of the melee fighters within moments. An angry purple glow emanated from its eyes, and sand started to trickle in little rivulets across the floor before flying upwards to collect around the champion. The sand seemed to be seeping through cracks in the walls; was it coming from the desert outside?

The ranged damage dealers continued throwing arrows and magic at the creature, but it shrugged off the damage, focused solely on its spell. After several more seconds of collecting sand, it roared, and the sand blasted out at hypersonic speeds in a perfect sphere centered on the champion.

It hit almost everyone. The knights were somewhat protected, as their shields covered a good portion of their bodies. Seth reflexively swapped to his plate armor, standing near the back of the raid with the rest of the leading party giving him a microsecond more to react, but it still hurt.

Little holes like pinpricks had punched straight through his solid iron armor and into his body. He choked at the sheer pain of it and fell to a knee, already feeling the blood from dozens of tiny wounds seeping down his body under his clothes.

His whole awareness had shrunk, the giant raging sphinx not even on his mind as he fought the pain. Why couldn't he move? He was dully aware of over seven hundred points of his health bar missing, bringing him down near half. Suddenly he felt a hand on his back and golden light swarmed around him, numbing the pain immediately and giving him the uncomfortable sensation of dozens of tiny holes healing all over his body.

He realized he was still in his plate armor, which was why he couldn't move very much, so subconsciously switched back to his normal armor. Gianna had healed him, and she reached out a hand to help him up. There was blood on her face, but it looked like she had healed her own wounds too.

Aurora was nearby casting a healing spell on Sullivan, who'd also fallen to the ground after the massive attack.

The knights were still engaging with the sphinx, who'd fallen back to the floor and was biting and clawing at them again. Seth's eyes flicked over the raid list. There were several people dangerously low on health, but it looked like the blast had hit everyone for exactly seven-hundred-fifty health points, and no one had less health than that in the raid. Seth was suddenly very glad Isaac hadn't come, as his health was somewhere right around that number.

The group reformed somewhat slowly, the priests doing their best to keep the knights who were engaging with the massive champion healthy at the same time as trying to bring everyone else back up to full health.

After what felt like minutes, but was probably less than fifteen seconds, everyone was back to full health and the attack resumed in earnest, ranged damagers hurling arrows and magic, rogues darting around for backstabs, their daggers somehow piercing the stone skin of the sphinx, and the warriors and knights hacking at the thing's front with their swords.

Seth found himself up in the thick of it, generating fury with the slashes of his sword, occasionally using it up to land several massive attacks in a row. He got brave when the sphinx turned somewhat away from him, looking at the knight who'd most recently taken over the beast's attention with their *Taunt* skill, giving Baltern a rest.

Seth took a few steps forward, getting very close to the front of the sphinx's chest, almost underneath it, and pressed the point of his sword against the center of it, where a strange whorling symbol looked painted onto the stone creature.

He activated his *Quick Change Pierce* skill, his longer sword and plate armor flitting into existence for barely a second before disappearing again.

The effect was instantaneous. The sphinx roared, a sound like massive boulders grinding against one another, and locked its eyes on Seth. He didn't have time to move before a stone paw larger than him swatted him away. He went tumbling, head over foot, then skidded to a halt dozens of feet away.

Level 57 Guardian Sphinx (Champion) hits you for 948 damage.

Seth crawled to his feet, wiping away blood that was bubbling out of his nose and into his mouth, tasting bitter. He wondered why he hadn't received any healing yet, but it was apparent when he finally turned and took in the fight.

His stab attack on the champion's chest had done massive damage, dropping its health down to somewhere near forty percent. It had started levitating again.

The party was scrambling, lower level people squatting behind the knights. Sand was slithering up through the air, defying gravity again, as it coalesced around the champion's bulk.

Seth's brain was a bit addled, but someone stuck out to him. A man wearing robes, holding a staff. He was standing near the back of the group, a panicked look on his face. He didn't know the man's name. He looked it up in the raid menu; it was Cynric. He was a priest primary, knight secondary, just like Seth's friend Dominick back at Slyborn.

The nagging thought finally bubbled to the top of Seth's consciousness. Dominick's use of his dome dual-class skill when he, Seth, and Aurora had fought the Wight champion under Slyborn. Had he said it made everyone inside invulnerable?

Seth tried to yell. Everyone needed to get under Cynric's dome when the sand attack went off. When he did though, a nasty wheeze just came out of his mouth, along with some spittle and blood. There was a stabbing pain in his chest, and his eyes flicked up to where active effects showed up. There was a debuff there, *Collapsed Lung*.

It would heal up, but all of the priests were too busy panicking, trying to hide from the sand attack that was coming any second. Seth was lamely limping toward the rest of the group when the attack went off.

Sand blasted out from the champion, faster than the human eye could track, punching through clothes, armor, shields, and bone. It was stronger than the first time.

Seth's brain had gone completely blank for a moment. He found himself wondering how he hadn't died. His health bar was an angry blinking red sliver. Of his nearly eighteen-hundred health, only forty-six points remained. He could hardly think, but he was able to mentally open the raid screen. Three dead. Their dull, empty health bars stood out among the huge number of people barely hanging on.

The knights, and the few who'd managed to stand right behind them, were the only people who'd endured the blast without taking crippling damage. Seth watched health bars start to rocket back up as the priests healed themselves, then others.

Seth's hands shook violently as he fished in his pocket for one of the little red vials he'd started keeping there for easy access. He was bleeding profusely from dozens of little punctures, and his forty-six health points had gone down to thirty-eight.

He felt like vomiting. The incredible pain, the avalanche of guilt at the deaths that he'd known how to prevent, he wasn't sure which was worse. If he'd stayed with Aurora, out of the fight, he'd have been able to save them. Liora had been right; the leaders needed to direct, not lead the charge.

He choked the potion down, causing his health to rocket up to over sixty percent, finally able to start walking and thinking clearly. Was Cynric still alive? A glance at the raid menu confirmed that he was. In fact, his health bar was completely full. Seth found him casting a healing spell on one of the scouts from the ranged damage party.

When Cynric finished, Seth grabbed him by the forearm and said, "Do you have the dome skill?" The man looked shocked, sweaty with panic, blood stains on his clothing. He shook his head as if shaking something loose, then said, hoarsely, "Yes. But I just used it to shield myself from that blast. I can't use it again for ten minutes."

Seth cursed and looked around, trying frantically to think of how the group could survive the next area attack. The second had been stronger than the first, so it stood to reason that the next would be even stronger. They'd already lost three people; they couldn't afford to lose any more.

The sphinx was still swiping its massive paws at the group of knights. As Seth watched, Baltern's shield shattered from one of the blows, and he staggered backwards, other knights moving into formation to keep him safe.

The champion's health was starting to move steadily down again as the priests worked to heal everyone back up to fighting condition, and the damagers started slashing and shooting. When the sphinx's health approached thirty percent, Aurora's voice carried over the cacophony of the fight, "Melee groups retreat! Knights, form a shield wall facing the champion!" She looked at Seth through the crowd, "Seth, can you teleport it to the other side of the room on my mark?"

Seth yelled in affirmation then started running past the champion. As he ran, he gestured his left hand at the sphinx and cast *Quick Change*

Position. The projectile spell collided with the monstrous form, and the timer appeared in his vision.

He was over halfway across the room when the champion's health bar hit one quarter. Their hunch had been right, and it immediately began rising into the air again, sand slithering up, weirdly organic, from the ground to coalesce around its body.

Seth reached the other side of the room and turned. There were two seconds left. He could see Aurora with her hand in the air, palm towards him, eyes locked on his. Her hand descended, like someone starting a street race, and Seth activated the skill. He was suddenly thirty feet in the air, and he started falling.

He'd only fallen for a few seconds when he collided with Verun's furry body, awkwardly draped over his back like a wet rag. Verun was rocketing toward the wall of shields that the knights had made, some high, some low, facing the champion that was now at the opposite end of the cylindrical room.

They barely made it behind the shields when a report sounded around the room like a cannon shot, followed by the sound of millions of grains of sand falling against the stone ground like rain. Seth rolled off of Verun's back and tried to regain his balance, dizzy. A quick check of the raid menu confirmed that everyone had avoided the blast, though none of the knights' shields were still intact. They'd have to regenerate for a short time before they could use them again.

The sphinx landed on the ground with a deep thud then started loping toward the raid from the far side of the room. Aurora, the only knight in the group who hadn't used her shield to block the sand spell, shoved her way to the front of the raid, summoned her translucent blue shield, and shouted, "Here!" at the monster, odd vocal distortions signaling that she'd used her *Taunt* skill to get its attention.

The monster swiped at her shield several times like an over-large cat playing with a ball of yarn. Cracks splintered through the translucent shield, but before the champion could shatter it, several other knights higher in level than Aurora finished regenerating theirs and stepped up, taking its attention. Aurora backed through the crowd, eyes alert on the battle.

When the monster hit one percent health, barely a sliver, it started to rise into the air again, but a huge flaming arrow arced away from Sullivan and exploded against the swirl pattern at the center of the creature's chest that Seth had hit earlier. It crashed to the ground in a stone heap, defeated.

No one cheered. Many of them just sat where they'd been as the fight ended. They'd won, but it didn't feel like it, and for the three bodies crumpled on the floor, it certainly wasn't a victory.

Seth ended up standing next to Aurora. He said, "I thought of Cynric's dome skill, but I was halfway across the room almost dead, so I couldn't get to him in time." He wanted reassurance, but that wasn't what she gave him.

"With my mother and Quincy missing, you're needed to help direct things. Your contributions to the fight aren't always worth the tactical advantage we have by having you direct people. Your place in the leading party, with all the extra information available, is needed." Was she blaming him?

Seth's temper spiked up. It wasn't enough that he blamed himself for the dead. Now Aurora had to blame him too. He snapped, "Yeah, that's not the first time I've heard that. Keep blaming me. You could've thought of that too. You're just like your mother."

Aurora recoiled like she'd been physically struck. He saw the brief look of absolute shock on her face before it blanked, replaced with the expressionless facade she erected so often. She looked past him, unfocused, and said, "Hm," before walking away.

Seth grimaced and went to sit by Ivon and Verun, waiting for the next level of hell.

CHAPTER 29

The fifty-seventh floor was, surprisingly, somewhat easy for the raid to pass. It was probably good, since Seth's heart wasn't in it. He'd lagged behind the group as they ascended the stairs from the previous level, the deaths weighing on his psyche. Verun had hung back and occasionally nudged him along with his snout.

They finally reached the next level. It was a puzzle, where five incredibly heavy blocks of stone were sitting on top of some glowing sigils set into the stone floor. The ceiling of the room looked like the inside of some massive clock, cogs and gears connecting in ways Seth's mind couldn't fathom.

Directly above each of the stone blocks were shining golden gears. The group formed up in case a champion appeared. Mazain, a warrior and the raid's member with the highest strength score aside from Seth or Quincy, stepped up and shoved one of the massive blocks off of the sigil, grinding over the floor as he pushed. Seth stood near the entrance, back against the wall, hardly paying attention.

The mages were right, and once Mazain had removed the stone, the gear above it started turning, driving dozens of gears and pistons in the machinery.

Mazain pushed the stone back over the sigil, and the mages all grouped up, focusing on figuring out a pattern that might work to turn the fourth huge golden gear directly above the closed exit door.

It only took them about five minutes to come up with the answer. They beckoned Seth forward, needing him to help pull off their plan. As he walked by, Riley squeezed his shoulder in a friendly gesture, her face looking somber for the first time he'd ever seen. He shrugged her off and walked over to the stone he'd been pointed to. When he was instructed to, he shoved the huge stone in the center off of its sigil. Mazain was waiting at the stone on the left, and was to push it off when a specific piston had completed fourteen cycles.

While Mazain counted the piston's revolutions, Seth walked over and got into position behind the third stone block, hands resting against its rough texture. His mind was far away, but he tried to rouse himself when he felt Mazain push the huge block, and counted to three before pushing the last one off of its space.

A nasty grinding noise emanated from the machinery, and it all halted.

One of the mages said, "Seth, you moved about nine-tenths of a second too early. Let's reset and try again."

He wasn't sure why, but the *nine-tenths* set him off. He whirled on the man, who stumbled back at the rage painted on Seth's face. He practically screamed at the man, "What's the point? Riley and I are probably the only ones who'll ever make it out of here. Our last chance to leave was probably at that last oasis floor!"

The room was eerily silent, the dozens of humans, and even Verun and Zuh holding their breath after the outburst. Riley broke the silence, disgust on her face. "Not cool, dude."

The eyes of the whole room were oppressive, and Seth felt his face heating up. He looked down at his boots and said, "Sorry, I didn't mean it. Let's just get this over with." He shoved the big stone back over its sigil, then walked toward the first one, not meeting anyone's eyes.

Less than thirty seconds later, they tried again. Seth counted to four this time, and the whole thing didn't grind to a halt. The whole group watched the gears turn and pistons punch. Other gears were raised or lowered into place at just the right moments, and after around ten seconds, the exit door started sliding open. The raid advanced, quiet and contemplative.

The fifty-eighth floor was like the inside of some massive stone engine, with huge pieces of rock rising, falling, swinging, and smashing in what seemed like a completely random order over the entire room. Gianna and Sullivan puzzled out the pattern after watching it run for almost thirty minutes. Gianna went first, and Seth held his breath as it looked like she would get crushed a dozen times over, but she casually dodged every hunk of stone as if they didn't bother her at all.

After she'd been hidden by all the machinations for around a minute and a half, everything suddenly halted, and a loud ticking started. Several of the raid members started to gingerly walk out onto the confusing floor of stone, but Aurora yelled, "Stop!" and they all halted. The group stood in silence, waiting for Gianna to return.

The ticking lasted for around thirty seconds, and then the room shook as all the stone ground into motion again, once more becoming an impenetrable wall of deadly, crushing stone. Thirty seconds later it all stopped again, and then Gianna appeared through the mess of halted rock and described what she'd found as it started back up: there was a huge lever by the exit to the next floor, but after the ticking ended and the room went into motion again, the lever raised itself and couldn't be pulled down for another thirty seconds.

Gianna and Sullivan had both spotted a relatively clear path through the mess of rock that appeared once every few minutes when all of the stone lined up perfectly, so Gianna went back through the moving maze and tried to time the lever so that the path was frozen in place. On her first attempt, she was a second too late, and the path was completely blocked by a huge piece of stone that had risen to block it right before the lever was pulled. Sullivan told everyone to hold as it all cycled again.

On Gianna's second try, she nailed it, and a perfectly straight path was visible through the shifting stones. Everyone took off in a single-file line through.

Aurora had insisted on going last, and Riley insisted on going with her. Seth, half joking, said, "Want me to carry you again?" Aurora didn't even respond, obviously still upset at what he'd said below. Zuh and Verun had both been temporarily banished to the void, as neither could fit through the slim path that led through the tons of rock.

The group sprinted through, Seth could hear the clinking of armor and swords, cursing as people squeezed through thin spaces. He was having to regulate his speed so he didn't run into the person in front of him. He was faster than most of the group.

The bulk of the group had made it across when Sullivan started shouting the count, "Five! Four! Three!" Seth crossed the threshold and spun, looking for the two women behind him. "Two!" Riley crossed the threshold.

Aurora, last in line, was more than one second from the end. She'd fallen behind, being significantly lower level than Seth, and having to lug her heavy armor. How had he not noticed? He could've easily carried her like he'd suggested at the beginning. He should have done something! Maybe he still could. He whipped his left hand out, *Quick Change Position* skill shooting out of the palm of his hand at Aurora.

At that moment, the last tick sounded, and the stone all started rumbling back into furious motion. Aurora was staring straight ahead, determined. A huge chunk of stone pushed downwards like the piston in some ludicrous engine, ready to squash Aurora like a bug.

Three things happened simultaneously. The huge piece of stone made contact with Aurora's head, pushing downward on her with incalculable force, Seth's projectile spell made contact, splashing against her left shoulder, and golden light bloomed around her as she activated her *Divine Aura* skill. Seth activated the skill to switch positions with Aurora, but nothing happened. His eyes darted to his log out of reflex.

> Your party member resists the effects of *Quick Change Position* due to their skill *Divine Aura*.

The stone kept descending. Instead of pulverizing her like it should have, it simply squashed her onto the stone floor for one second before rising again, retreating. She stood and stumbled forward, dazed but completely unhurt, and Ivon and Riley grabbed her, pulling her to the safety of the exit from the room.

She looked at them, and grinned, saying, "I'm glad that worked." The recklessness was completely out of character for her, Seth thought. The days in the dungeon were getting to everyone. Aurora didn't even acknowledge him.

The group rested for thirty minutes, then advanced to the fifty-ninth and penultimate floor of the spire. There was talk of sleeping a full eight hours in the stairwell, but it was swiftly declined by almost everyone. People wanted out of the massive dungeon in the sky, and the only way out was up.

The fifty-ninth floor was a change of pace. The dwindling raid group, battered, exhausted, and missing the outside world, entered the room to see it completely hollow and empty, except for a single human-sized figure in the center.

As the raid party approached cautiously, knights in front, Seth saw that it was the same man in purple armor that had greeted them on the first floor. He was sitting on a simple wooden stool, his legs crossed casually, smiling at them.

When they drew closer, he said, "You can put your weapons away, there will be no harm done to you on this level."

The knights looked to Aurora for confirmation. She stepped forward, past their line, and Seth, Gianna, and Sullivan followed. She said, "Where is my mother?"

The armored man looked at all four of them, seeming to ignore the question, and spoke again, "I'm quite surprised that all of you made it this far. No one's made it to the fifty-ninth floor in... hmm... over a thousand years I think. Though, in fairness, no one's entered my spire in almost as long." He frowned, looking into the distance at nothing, eyes going glassy.

After a moment, he jerked, as if surprised at the forty-seven people standing in front of him, some still with blades drawn. He said, "Oh! Where was I? Right, it's been quite some time since anyone made it this far. I'm here to offer you all a choice. The champion you'll have to fight in the final floor of my spire is *significantly* more difficult than any before it. I'm here to offer you a way out. I'll teleport any of you who wish to the exit. I'll give each of you... how much is fair... how about thirty gold to boot. The only catch is that you may *never* enter the spire again for as long as you live." He looked at Seth and Riley, then said, "And that includes *all future lives* for you two. Don't think you can circumvent my rules with a turn of phrase."

Gianna spoke up, "What about the two people you stole?"

The man's eyes focused on her in silence for a moment. He seemed like he was considering it, almost like he was surprised at the question. How could he not think that was the first thing they'd ask? His lips moved as if he was muttering, but no sound came out. He subtly nodded, then just as subtly shook his head from left to right. Finally, he said, "I'm afraid I don't know who you're talking about."

Sullivan yelled from his place near the back of the group, "What do you mean you don't know? You left us a bloody note!"

Aurora shoved her hand into her bag and produced the note, holding it out to the purple-armored man like an arrest warrant. He read it, an eerily human confusion plain on his face, then held up a palm in a clear *hold please* gesture, closing his eyes. After around two seconds he snapped them open and said, "Well, they do appear to be on the top floor, but I'm afraid I have no idea how they got there. If you'd like them back, you'll have to go get them yourselves. I'd not break my own rules, that isn't like me at all! Now, anyone who wants to take me up on my offer, you simply have to raise your hand, and it will be done. You have ten seconds to make your decision, starting... now." A loud ticking emanated from every direction at once. Seth, Aurora, Sullivan, and Gianna turned to watch the rest of the raid.

No one raised their hands. Seth was astounded. With the previous desertions, he'd expected at least a few people to take the deal, but apparently everyone who felt like sneaking away had already done it. Several people threw dirty looks Seth's way. Were they staying to spite him? As quickly as the ticking started, it stopped.

The man grimaced like he was upset that no one had taken his deal, then simply disappeared in a purple puff of dust. The wooden chair he'd sat on slowly toppled over, then melted into the floor like hot butter. The door opened on the other side of the room, showing a dim spiral stairway.

CHAPTER 30

"We need a plan," Sullivan said, absently unstringing his bow and pulling a pristine new bowstring from his pack.

Gianna quickly backed him up, "Agreed." She looked at Aurora.

Baltern spoke up, "You heard what that freak said, it's another champion fight. We've been able to defeat the champions below without too much hassle."

The sphinx flashed through Seth's mind, and he glanced at the three bodies piled by the exit of the level. They'd been carrying them up every flight of stairs.

Ivon cleared his throat, then said, "Strategically, we know more about the next level than we've ever known before. We know we'll be facing a champion. How can we use that to our advantage?"

Aurora nodded, and everyone waited for her to respond. Seth wondered when Gianna and Sullivan had decided she was the one to follow in the absence of Quincy and Liora. Finally, she said, "We should rearrange the parties. Our people can be placed more effectively. Let's build for a single-target battle, prioritize placing our strongest healers with the strongest knights in a single group that can hold the champion's attention. Ivon, can you work up a suggested party structure?" Ivon nodded solemnly.

Riley spoke up then as glowing orbs leapt out of her hand, "While he's doing that, I think we've all earned some grub before we move on." Her house appeared a few inches off of the ground, then thumped down. She disappeared inside, then returned holding several raw turkey legs. She held them in one hand and started heating them with a flame in her other. "There are more where these came from!"

A cheer rose from the whole group. Seth even struggled not to smile.

***

Seth had some people to apologize to. The cooked turkey hitting his stomach brightened his mood more than he'd have thought possible, aside from making him moderately sleepy. He found the mage he'd snapped at first, and asked if they could talk privately. The man went white, probably thinking Seth was going to berate him again, but Seth just apologized, telling him the truth, that the deaths had been his fault.

After that, he went and found Aurora. She was cleaning her sword, sitting away from everyone. Seth cleared his throat and sat next to her. "Listen, I was out of line downstairs, and I'm sorry. I do need to quit jumping into battle without thinking first, and you aren't just like your mother."

She looked at him, challenge in her eyes, then said, "Really? Please elaborate."

Seth wasn't prepared for that. He started thinking furiously. Her hair wasn't white? No, that wouldn't do. She was younger? Duh. The silence was mounting, so finally, he said, "You have a much better sense of humor."

Her face didn't change for about three seconds, then finally her mask cracked and she grinned at him and said, "Yeah, I do. Lucky answer. I know you didn't mean it. This place has been getting to all of us. Let's just focus on getting out of here alive." She raised her hand for a high-five, an Earth-ism she'd picked up from him. He obliged.

Finally, Seth found Riley. She was sitting in a rocking chair on her porch, an odd contrast to the dingy stone tower room surrounding them. Zuh and Verun were both perched on top of the house, though Verun's claws were digging into the roof just to keep him in one place. Zuh looked much more natural.

Seth did his best to apologize for shrugging her off and making the comment about her and him being the only ones to make it out alive. She acted like nothing had been wrong in the first place, but she seemed to smile more than usual, so he thought he must have done something right. They talked about nothing much for a while before several people came back for seconds, and Riley disappeared into the house.

Seth found Ivon sitting on the ground, scrawling on a piece of parchment. He said, "How's the planning going?"

Ivon looked up, mustache bristling in concentration. "Slowly, there are so many possible combinations of parties we could have just with the people we have left." Seth could see dozens of lines scrawled on the paper, and then crossed out.

A thought hit him. "How about we just work with the real thing?" With a thought, he opened the leading party menu and moved Ivon to the leading party with him. On a whim, he moved Riley there too. He grinned. "Now you can just shuffle them around in the menu."

Ivon's mustache stopped wiggling, the closest thing Seth thought he'd see to a smile, then the scout said, "Thanks, that will make things easier. Now how about you tell me how you think we should arrange everyone."

The two of them strategized and moved people around for at least half an hour, maybe more, before they finally settled on a party structure that they thought would be the best for fighting a very strong champion. The whole raid was built around a party with their three strongest knights, their two strongest priests, and Cynric, who would be in the party with the express purpose of using his dome skill if it was needed to protect their tanks.

The rest of the raid was flexible. There were groups without any healers at all, but they at least had people whose second classes were priests. The rest of the leading party signed off on their arrangement, they did some brief drilling with their new parties, distributed all of the remaining potions stored in Riley's house, then the raid ascended to the final floor of the spire. *Go time.*

CHAPTER 31

The sixtieth floor was the smallest they'd visited, which was a silly observation, Seth thought, since every floor had been continually smaller than the one it sat atop. This floor was a perfect circle, and the roof and walls were made completely out of the crystal that had formed the windows in the floors below. *Talk about a penthouse view.*

The dungeon core crystal was right in the center, as were two smaller clear crystals, in which sat the petrified versions of Quincy and Liora. Quincy appeared to be asleep, though he'd been rotated to be vertical, so apparently he had been snatched before he ever woke up. Liora had a snarl on her face, and her hands held out in front of her like she was casting a spell. Their complete lack of motion was slightly disturbing.

Seth was worried about what kind of monster would appear as the final champion, and he saw purple-red smoke pooling below the fountain that the dungeon core crystal floated above. Instead of some giant monster, though, it was simply the man from the floor below who coalesced.

The raid quickly formed into ranks as the man stalked toward them, an angry look on his smooth face. Seth couldn't tell if the subtle red glow he saw around the man's eyes was real or not.

The knights in front all brought out their bound shields, forming a wall of the translucent barriers. The armored man yelled, "You should've taken my generous offer."

As his exclamation echoed around the room, Aurora said, "Now."

The champion's eyes jerked to Aurora and stayed on her, face contorting with rage as he looked.

Five rogues who'd been invisible since halfway up the stairwell all revealed themselves at the same moment behind the champion, their five daggers plunging toward his back with surgical precision. He didn't break his death-stare at Aurora and didn't move to avoid the attack. All five daggers landed.

His health bar jumped down by almost twenty percent with the massive damage from all five sneak attacks. Seth glanced at his logs, reading the first one from the rogues, eager to know the champion's level.

> Your raid member Jon hits Level 67 Wizard of the Tower (Champion - Etherean Avatar) for 788 damage.

It was a full ten levels higher than the sphinx was. It would be difficult, but Seth felt some hope bloom in his chest. They could do this if they played it right. They just had to stick to the strategy.

A choked gasp escaped the champion's lips as he whirled, arm whipping through thin air, rogues already dancing away with their high dexterity statistics. The champion's bloody back was turned toward the bulk of the raid. Time for stage two.

Seth yelled a command, "Warriors, now!"

Four warriors activated their *Charge* skills, staggered by one second each, and leapt forward. Seth felt a pang that he wasn't one of them, but he was needed here, helping to run the show.

Mazain, the first warrior who'd charged, made contact, his sword sliding neatly into where the champion's left kidney would be if he was human. The champion's body locked up, keeping him in place for the next warrior's charge to hit home. And the next. And the next.

The champion's health was already down to seventy percent as the warriors all backpedaled.

Baltern and two other knights pushed toward the champion, a warped "Hey, ugly," *Taunt* from Baltern ensuring the champion would focus on him. Baltern closed the distance and slammed his bound shield against the champion, causing it to stumble back a few steps.

Then, something changed. The champion jumped backwards, putting a good thirty yards between himself and the knights, and said, "Enough." He didn't yell, but everyone heard it loud and clear. It was similar to how Verun's voice injected itself into all of their heads.

The champion raised his left hand, golden blood dripping from his fingers, and snapped. Just like that, his health bar was full again. He looked pristine, no evidence that there had ever been any damage. He started walking toward the knights at a brisk pace, rage gone, face calm.

Something was wrong. Everyone could feel it.

When the man was within fifteen yards, he simply swiped his hand to the side as if he were batting away a bug, and all of the knights went flying across the room, tumbling and rolling as their armor clanked on the stone floor.

Riley had reached level forty just a few floors below, and had received another beast bond token to unlock Zuh's ability to fight. She was already astride the huge bird, and Zuh leapt forward like a viper, beating his huge wings backward to propel him forward, sharp beak outstretched toward the purple armored man.

Before Zuh could make contact, though, the man backhanded him across his face, and Zuh simply vanished in a puff of blue-green mist, having taken too much damage and returned to the void. Riley landed on the ground poorly and rolled. She cried out in pain.

Mazain and his three other warriors sprinted forward toward the armored man, and two of the five rogues appeared behind the champion, popping out of invisibility for another attack. Six blades plunged toward the champion almost in sync.

The instant before all of their blades connected, the man simply vanished. Seth watched in horror as the champion appeared near the knights who were still gaining their feet, apparently still focused on Baltern due to his *Taunt*. The knight barely got his shield out in time as the champion started *punching* it, each blow sending little shockwaves through the air, sounding like fireworks.

The champion's left arm was behind his back, giving his right-handed punches a silly, casual look that belied how they shook the whole room. Ugly cracks spidered across Baltern's shield as the other two knights fell in next to him and added theirs to the wall. It was good timing, because Baltern's shattered after only a few blows.

The other knights' shields popped uncomfortably fast, too, and only Cynric appearing behind them and activating his dome saved them from being punched into a paste by the champion. Unfortunately, the spell only protected them for three seconds, and couldn't be used again for ten minutes. They didn't have ten minutes.

Scouts and mages were peppering the champion with arrows and spells, but every projectile seemed to just vanish around a foot from the man. Apparently he had some overpowered shield keeping him protected from airborne weapons.

Verun was a white blur as he flew into Seth's view and slammed into the etherean. They both went tumbling; it was the first time anyone had been able to land a hit on the man since the battle had turned. Thankfully, a two-ton lion didn't count as a projectile, even if he was airborne. In a blink, the man was standing again, as Verun struggled to get to his feet. The armored man snapped his fingers, and a hunk of crystal appeared around Verun, sealing him in place, half risen, face in a snarl.

There was golden blood running down the man's forearm, and he looked at Seth and glared, apparently blaming him for the damage dealt by Verun. A health bar appeared above his head, and there was barely a sliver missing. Had his health increased? Seth glanced at his logs to see the damage Verun had done.

Your familiar Verun hits Level 112 Enraged Wizard of the Tower (Champion - Etherean

Avatar) for 904 damage.

Level one hundred and twelve! He'd never heard of a champion increasing its own level, but apparently this one was fond of breaking rules. There was no way they could take this thing on, especially without Liora and Quincy.

His instincts screamed at him to run into the fray, to fight the champion himself, risk his own life so no more of his friends got hurt. It was an effort of will to stop himself. He'd experienced first-hand with the sphinx that running into the fight himself wasn't always the best option. Even though he didn't have a high intelligence stat, he had to *stop and think.*

He balled his fists and squeezed his eyes shut for a moment, hoping nothing skewered him, but finding no other way to tune out the battle raging close by. It was sensory overload, and the abundance of adrenaline roaring through his veins didn't help.

Seth's head whipped to look at Liora and Quincy. They were encased in some kind of clear crystal. Could he get them out? It was a vain hope, but it seemed like his only one when he saw multiple members of the raid bum rush the champion and be thrown backwards by some ghostly wind.

Seth sprinted towards the two crystals holding the guild leaders. He arrived unscathed, though the sounds of battle behind him didn't sound encouraging. He went straight to Quincy's crystal, thinking the man could help heal their allies, and slammed *Fearless* against it three times, but the metal didn't so much as chip the clear crystal. How would he break them out? If only he had something that could pierce through almost anything...

Seth resisted the urge to smack his forehead and instead pointed his sword at a chunk of crystal not occupied by any part of Quincy's body, then activated *Quick Change Pierce*. His claymore appeared for a flicker, partway through the crystal, and a loud pop echoed around the room as pieces of the crystal fell away, cracks spider-webbing through the whole like miniature lightning.

Seconds later, the whole thing crumbled to white powdery dust and Quincy fell to the ground, limp. He must have still been sleeping, or perhaps no time had passed from his perspective, because as soon as he hit, he came to, saying, "Huh-what?!" and frantically looking around. Seth almost laughed when he saw that the man had been sleeping with his brass knuckles on.

Seth said, "Tower kidnapped you, top floor, need help!" then sprinted towards Liora's prison.

Seth shattered Liora's crystal prison too, and she dropped to the ground, confusion plain on her face. He repeated his somewhat nonsensical three-second explanation to her, and then turned to see the state of the fight with the champion.

It wasn't going well. The man in the purple armor had risen up thirty feet into the air. He held a golden staff in front of himself. His eyes were closed, and what looked like sand seemed to be coalescing around him. He was going to do the same attack that the sphinx had done. Seth didn't want to think about how powerful it'd be when cast by such a high-level champion. Cynric had already used his shield.

The mages and scouts were still, vainly, trying to hit the floating man before he could release the extremely powerful spell, but none of their attacks got through, simply continuing to vanish before they reached him. Seth even saw the huge meteors of light forming above him, cast by Liora, but they also didn't penetrate, disappearing before they could strike. Zuh was out of service, and Verun was paralyzed inside a chunk of crystal. Seth couldn't get to him in time to free him and then try to stop the attack. Dozens might die from it. *Everyone* might die from it. Seth felt powerless.

Then, he saw her. Riley, flying through the air, both palms downward as wind blasted out of them, barreling right towards the man. She, incongruously, was grinning and laughing, and she zipped right through the area where the spells were vanishing, slamming into the armored etherean. He dropped his staff to the ground, and the sand that had been forming around him lost cohesion and sloughed to the floor. Riley crashed to the ground, too, but there was still a smile on her face as the man descended, glaring at her. Riley was holding both middle fingers up to the man as he arrived at her location and punched her incredibly hard, blood spattered, and it instantly shot her health to zero. Seth cringed and looked away from the gore. She was out of the fight, but she'd bought them more time.

The man waved his hands around, and at least ten more people were encased in the clear crystal, including Aurora. Liora was hurling light magic at the man, but it wasn't having any effect.

Seth had done his duty, surveying the battle from the back and getting more help in the fight, but he was out of ideas. It was time to join the fight himself. He sprinted toward the etherean, who was stooping down to pick up his fallen staff, and triggered his *Charge* skill as soon as he entered the range. He jolted forward, *Fearless* shining ahead of him, and managed to impale the etherean. Maybe it had been the fact that he was distracted retrieving his staff. Maybe it had been the speed increase *Fearless* gave his *Charge* attack. Seth's eyes flicked to his combat log.

You hit Level 112 Enraged Wizard of the Tower (Champion - Etherean Avatar) with *Charge* for 841 damage.

Level 112 Wizard of the Tower (Champion - Etherean Avatar) resists the stun effect of your

---

skill, *Charge.*

Uh oh. Seth barely had time to think it before he was flying through the air like a pinwheel. The floor greeted him soon after, forcing the air from his lungs. He squinted at the enemy.

The Wizard of the Tower made a face, clasped his palms together, then violently swiped them apart. Like a photocopy, there were suddenly two dozen of him, arrayed in a long line, standing in an identical position. The line-up only lasted an instant though, as all of them took off in different directions. The original, the only one with a staff, started levitating around ten feet off of the ground, looking downward as his clones engaged in hand-to-hand combat with the remaining raid members who weren't encased in crystal.

One of the clones jogged toward Seth, who was still trying to pull himself up off of the ground. Seth saw eight of them surrounding Liora and Quincy. The two of them stood back-to-back, Liora moving to block attacks that would've otherwise hit Quincy, Quincy occasionally tapping her on the shoulder with golden light, restoring her health back to full. Liora wrapped a whip made of solid white light around one of the clones and jerked brutally, beheading it. Quincy cocked back and punched a hole through one of their chests before yanking his hand out, covered in golden blood.

The clone heading for Seth finally reached him as he righted himself, and Seth dodged its haphazard punch and countered with a brutal slash from *Fearless*. The clones were substantially weaker than the original, as it wasn't near quick enough to dodge, and sustained a deep gash across its left shoulder.

A few more swipes dispatched the clone that was attacking him, and Seth helped a nearby priest fend off one more. He turned to see how the rest of the raid was faring. Thankfully, it looked like almost all of the clones were dealt with, but then Seth saw the original moving.

The armored champion started rising into the air again, and Seth saw sand start to coalesce around him. There was no one left who could get to him. If the blast didn't kill everyone, it would certainly take out anyone without tons of health points. Seth raised his arm and vainly tried to cast his projectile version of *Quick Change Position*, but it too disappeared in the invisible shield surrounding the armored man.

Moments before Seth thought the spell would go off, the man froze. He continued to float there for a few seconds, then the sand dispersed again harmlessly. What was he planning now? There was a subtle shift in the lighting, and Seth turned to look at the dungeon core crystal. There was a huge crack in it, and white light was shining from within.

Quincy was standing below it, panting and triumphant. Liora stood next to him, looking ready to fight off anything that came their way. Seth felt stupid that he hadn't thought of it. The man had *Purified* the crystal! But would the champion stop fighting? They'd never tried curing an etherean mid-fight. All eyes, at least those that weren't cemented in crystal, focused on the floating man. His eyes were still closed, and various expressions flashed over his face in quick succession, looking like a video of someone receiving terrible news played at three-times speed. The effect was disconcerting, human but not.

When the final piece of red crystal fell away, revealing the shining white beneath, the man opened his eyes, looking at his own dungeon core. He settled back on the ground, and Quincy backed away a few steps. The champion looked at Quincy, and said, "You cured me."

Quincy said, "I did." Then stopped. No one was sure what to say.

The man in the purple armor said, "Thank you. I knew I was infected, but it had... clouded my mind. I didn't care. I had an inkling that you might be able to cure me since you did the same to my neighbor. It was compelling me to do my best to stop you from curing me. That's why I broke the rule of the twenty-fifth floor, and took you from there. Despicable. Deplorable. Dastardly, even."

Quincy said, "So... You're going to let us go?"

The man looked around the room, taking in the dozen or so people frozen in crystal. He nodded after a moment, and waved his hand in an arc around the room. All of the crystals simply vanished, and those inside all fell to the ground in sync. The champion said, "I am. My debt to you covers that, at the very least. I should also grant you all some rewards. You didn't defeat my final floor, but you did cure me. I broke my own rules. I destroy rule-breakers. Unforgivable." He looked like he might gag. "Let me think..." He closed his eyes for a moment. Everyone was holding still, not sure yet if they were safe.

Things began to appear on the ground in front of the remaining people. In front of Quincy, first, appeared a pair of shining gold brass knuckles, the same gold as the champion's staff. In front of Liora a golden staff materialized, identical to the one that the man with purple armor held. In front of several of the warriors appeared huge golden blades or axes. Purple whorled armor appeared in front of the knights. Nothing had appeared near Seth.

The champion, or etherean, whatever he was, floated over and hovered before Seth. Seth struggled to make eye contact with the man's otherworldly gaze. He said, "Now, about you... I could just give you a weapon, like I've done for the humans here, but that seems awfully drab, given what you are, don't you agree?"

Seth, his way with words really showing up, said, "Uh...?"

The man in purple armor continued, "Let's see... I think I can make something that would help..." He held his hand out in front of him and closed his eyes, face scrunching up like he was smelling something unpleasant. A moment later, a small, intricately carved golden ball popped into existence several inches above his palm and dropped into it. The man's eyes opened and he extended his palm toward Seth.

After hesitating for a moment, Seth picked it up, and inspected it, causing a pop-up to appear in his vision.

Solidified Boon Upgrade Token

This token can be used by someone with a boon. It will grant a free boon upgrade unrelated to level.

Seth said, "Thank you. I didn't even know this was possible."

The man smiled cryptically at him, and said, "You'll be surprised with what is possible as you progress." Seth wasn't sure what it meant, but before he could decide if he wanted to inquire or not, the man had hovered over to float in front of Verun.

He looked the lion in the eyes and said, "Now, you're more difficult. You fought valiantly, and I think you deserve a reward of your own. I might be able to free you, would you like that?"

Seth felt his chest go tight. Verun deserved to be autonomous, if he wanted it, but Seth couldn't deny that it selfishly made him scared. Verun rumbled, and Seth heard his response, <I don't think I want that. I have another idea though... My father hasn't been able to create his first champion yet. Can you help?>

The man quirked a single eyebrow at Verun's use of "father" in a very human gesture, but didn't comment. He responded to the lion's question, "It will be done. Our kind is typically very secretive about our methods and sciences, but you've helped free me from hundreds of years of mind control that I didn't even realize I was under. Here, this will help immensely." At that, he extended his golden staff and touched it to the center of Verun's head for just a moment.

A new entry appeared in Seth's log.

> Your familiar Verun has been granted an etherean mental tome titled *The Thirteenth Son's Uncensored Champion Creation Guide.*

Verun shivered, like a bone-chilling cold had just settled in him, and he said, <Thank you. I will deliver this.>

The etherean was returning to float in front of Seth. Seth said, "The Thirteenth Son? Is that you?"

The man that wasn't really a man stared at him for a second without responding, then nodded, and said, "That is me. I'm one of the first ethereans. I wasn't born, but created by our father Ygzotl."

Seth shivered at the name, remembering the few moments he'd seen the god's eye staring through a hole in the clear blue sky, and the word that had shook the ground beneath him: "Abomination."

The Thirteenth Son nodded. "I see you've met. He's not fond of Djinia's children, for obvious reasons. I hadn't thought about this while I was in its snare, but I wonder if the virus can affect him, too. I'll have to try and contact my siblings, though I wonder if I'm the only one possessed of a clear mind."

Seth had so many questions for the man; why was it obvious that Ygzotl hated his kind? How old was this etherean, that he'd been created by the god himself? Before Seth could compose any more questions out of his mess of thoughts, the armored man's head whipped to look at someone behind him. Seth turned to look at what had drawn the man's attention.

Aurora stood near the back of the crowd, meeting the etherean's eyes with an easy solidity. She didn't glare, but she didn't look scared like Seth was sure he had as the ancient being had stood before him.

The etherean spoke first, his eyes glowing a deep purple all of the sudden, "My, my, how did I not notice who you were earlier? Easium's influence hangs off of you like you've just taken a swim in his fabled lake. My father would be incredibly angry if he ever found out I'd let you live. Though I wonder..." He took a step forward towards Aurora, then another. The raid members, dirty, beat up, parted away from the man in purple armor like a flock of prey, desperate to be out of the path of their predator.

He stopped walking around four feet from Aurora, and looked straight up. Seth followed his gaze, but only saw the desert sky through the crystal walls. The Thirteenth Son said, "I wondered if the big man himself might come down to protect you. I guess that would draw too much attention from my father, though. I certainly wouldn't want those two duking it out in this hemisphere... There wouldn't be much left. I do wonder, though, if I would have even been *allowed* to kill you before I was cured. Perhaps a meteor, perfectly natural, set on a very specific trajectory eons ago, might've fallen from the sky at just the right moment to end me before I finished you off." He smiled as if he'd just told the funniest joke ever formulated, his eyes bright and brows lifting high on his forehead.

As quickly as it'd come, the smile dropped away and his voice got quieter. He looked into Aurora's eyes as he spoke. "My father isn't evil. He may be misunderstood, confused, or even infected like I was. You're destined to kill him. If you can find a way to fulfill your duty without that, please try. This, I beg of you, chosen of Easium."

The silence was palpable, the emptiness after the request ringing with importance. It was as if everyone in the room was holding their breath. Seth saw Liora's face, pinched with worry and something else, wonder? So much emotion on the white-haired woman's face was out of character.

Finally, Aurora answered. "I'll do my best."

Apparently it was enough. The etherean nodded solemnly, then turned to look at Seth once more. He said, "The other one like you perished in the fight, but she'll reform an avatar. Send her to my first floor, I'll grant her and her etherean fragment rewards as well." Seth nodded in understanding.

The man looked around the room, meeting many of the eyes of the raid party, and said, "I'll be teleporting you all out, now. Be warned, I may be cured, but my tower is designed to be a challenge, if you return, I cannot guarantee your safety. Ta-ta." He snapped his fingers, and the entire group was suddenly standing at the entrance to the spire, facing away. The huge stone doorway was open behind them, but no one was keen to reenter.

The whole group started walking, vaguely shell-shocked, following the restored leading party back towards their camp in the previous zone. Seth looked at Verun, "Should we risk trying to take a flight?"

Verun looked at him, then gazed at the top of the spire, which was now shining a brilliant white instead of blood red, and said, <Let's get some distance behind us first.>

Seth opened his boon menu, keen to see what his options were with the new upgrade token.

Quick Change Artist - Upgrades available: 1

Owned Upgrades:
Position (I & II)

Available upgrades:
-Control: You gain finer control over your divine boon, and are now able to change only certain pieces of your outfit and equipment, instead of being forced to swap entire outfits at once.
-Expand: You gain access to an additional distinct outfit.
-Statistic: You gain the skill *Quick Change Statistic*. Use this skill to physically tag another living being. You and the tagged being swap values for one statistic (Stamina, Strength, Dexterity, Intelligence, Wisdom) for 30 seconds. After 30 seconds, both you and the tagged being's values return to normal.

Before Seth had seen the new *Statistic* option, he'd been sure he'd take *Control* with his next boon upgrade. Being able to only swap his sword, or the section of armor that was about to be hit sounded great, but the new option threw all his plans out the window. He imagined swapping stamina values with Baltern during their duel, or being able to run as fast as Gianna for thirty seconds. He cringed as he selected *Statistic* and gained the new skill. *Control* would have to wait. He briefly considered testing it out on someone, but thought it might serve him better if he kept it to himself for the time being.

As the group continued their trek through the desert, Seth said quietly to Quincy, "Hey, you see their level when you *Purify* them, right? What level was that one?" He remembered how impressed Quincy had been when he'd cured the one levelled somewhere in the three-hundreds.

Quincy just chuckled, shook his head, and shared the notification with Seth.

> You cast *Purify* on level 8493 Etherean (The Thirteenth Son), you've cured it of *Ectocypher*.

CHAPTER 32

Riley and Zuh returned two days later. The raid had just made it to the next zone, after resting for over twenty-four hours to recoup from the terrors of the spire. The two utility party members they'd left at the camp were still there, along with five others who'd deserted. They threw themselves at their respective leaders' feet when Quincy and Liora strode back into camp, shining golden weapons gleaming.

Surprisingly, both Liora and Quincy were more understanding than Seth had expected them to be. The five members, three Adventurers' Guild and two Transportation Guild, would receive some punishments, some garnished wages, and some kind of probationary periods, but wouldn't be completely booted from their places.

Riley headed straight for Seth when she returned. He said, "Welcome back!" as she was still around twenty feet away.

She made a strange face, and then said sarcastically, *"Why would you ever need to fly under your own power, Riley? You have Zuh! HAH!"* She kept approaching, standing right in front of him. Before he could protest, she leaned in and kissed him on the lips, before turning and walking away without even looking back. Zuh, who'd been standing behind her, let out a suspiciously human-sounding sigh and shook his feathered head back and forth before following her. Seth was still frozen in place, mouth opening and closing soundlessly like a fish. Seth wasn't sure what to say, but he couldn't say he hadn't enjoyed it.

Seth didn't see it happen, but Ivon filled him in later. Apparently Liora and Aurora had pulled Ivon aside and told him that his probation period was over, effective immediately, after his immense showing of bravery and trustworthiness during their time in the spire.

The golden weapons now seen on the hips and backs of many of the raid party had become a symbol of their survival and triumph in the spire. People with golden weapons had started calling themselves the "top floorers", and their comradery did much to assuage the rivalry that existed between the red and blue capes. They were all extremely proud of their special weapons, and with good reason; the golden weapons were *powerful.*

Seth had almost choked on his own spit when he'd first inspected Aurora's sword on the walk back to their camp after they'd been teleported out.

Etherean Gold Sword
Enchanted 1-Handed Sword
(Wielder level * 5) damage

Enchantment: If damaged, this weapon will heal itself over time.

The weapons were all scalable, meaning they grew stronger as their owners did. Even being over fifteen levels lower than him, Aurora's sword hit for more than *double* the damage that Seth's sword, *Fearless,* did. They were all like that, Seth couldn't even imagine how strong Liora would be with the golden staff in her hands. He was excited about the boon upgrade, but somewhat disappointed that he didn't have a fancy new sword.

He let those feelings slip when he told Riley about the spirit of the spire's offer to give her and Zuh rewards, later on the same day she respawned. The kiss didn't come up again, and

Seth wasn't sure how to tell her that he hadn't minded it at all.

Seth had woken the next morning to find *Fearless* missing. He was puzzled why anyone in a caravan full of swords stronger than his would care to steal his sword. He walked around the camp, looking for the shining silver pommel, but couldn't spot it. He was headed to tell Liora about the theft when he spotted Zuh on the horizon, heading to the camp from the direction of the spire.

They landed, and Riley hopped off of his back. A gold staff, a mirror of her old one aside from the shining metal, was strapped to her back, and she had a sly smile on her face as she fished something out of one of the saddlebags tied to Zuh's sides.

She pulled out Seth's sword. He said, "You're the one who stole my sword?"

She said, "I prefer the term borrowed, since I intended to give it back. Here, take a look!" She handed it to him, and he drew it from the scabbard.

While the hilt was still bright shining silver as it always had been, the blade was bright gold, matching her staff. He inspected it immediately.

Fearless (Etherean Gold Upgrade)
Enchanted 1-Handed Sword
Requirements: Warrior Only
(Wielder level * 5) damage

> Enchantment: When equipped, increase
> warrior's Charge speed by 100%. If damaged,
> this weapon will heal itself over time.

Seth was in awe. Not only had the attack gotten *much* stronger, up from a static seventy-three to a massive two hundred forty-five. He was only able to squeeze out, "H...How?"

She said, "I just took it with me when I went to get my reward, and asked if he minded upgrading ours to match the rest of the raids. Of course, I didn't bring that up until after he'd given me the boon upgrade token, and given Zuh something, too. He seemed a bit annoyed, but he did it, and you only get what you ask for, right?" She was grinning up at him.

Seth felt a lot of emotions. He didn't know if he could think of a single person in his old life who would have been so thoughtful. Riley was a great person, and sort of felt like a link to home. He needed to tell her how he felt. He said, "Riley, I..."

She interrupted him, "You want to take me out to dinner?" She grinned.

Seth laughed. "Sure, I'd be willing to bet there are some fantastic restaurants in Vardon, assuming we ever make it back to civilization."

Riley smiled. "Alright then, it's a date."

CHAPTER 33

The raid held a small funeral as soon as they left the desertous wasteland surrounding the spire. When they'd been teleported out by the etherean controlling the spire, the bodies they'd had wrapped in cloaks appeared around them too. Bodies that had been completely destroyed, like Dycer in the column of flame on the trap floor, weren't present, but they'd made a small grave for him, anyway. The service was short and somber, but it seemed that the two guilds had been united by their struggle. They rested one night, then continued on their quest for Askua.

The dungeons they faced after the spire were around the same difficulty as the ones they'd faced before encountering the spire, nowhere near as difficult as the spire itself. It seemed to have been an outlier among its neighbors. Quincy said that the spirit of the spire was the only one they'd *Purified* over level one thousand, and it had been *way* over that level.

All of the etherean gold weapons made the dungeons seem even easier, too, and the raid flew through them. Only a week after they'd left the spire, Ivon estimated that they had one, or two at maximum, zones left to clear before they made it to Askua, assuming Djinia was telling the truth and the city was still there.

Seth was starting to get nervous. How would he find his mother? Was she alright? The rest of the raid, though, was getting giddy. The massive gold and experience rewards felt like they were just around the corner. For the lower-level people in the raid, the lowest of which were in the low thirties, the two million experience reward could fetch them up to ten whole levels, which was an insane jump in power. For Seth, though, the experience would only net him one level, since the requirements got so high after level fifty.

Two hundred gold, likewise, was an extremely alluring sum of money. Seth's pay as part of the Adventurers' Guild was only twenty gold per *year,* and his was higher than average due to his high level, since the guild paid more to retain top talent. The two hundred gold would be like ten to fifteen years' salary to some of the members of the raid. Aurora had given Seth ten gold way back when she'd taken the money off of Enrique's body after he'd tried to kill her, and Seth had only managed to spend two of the gold in the months since, with the bulk of that expense going to his longsword that he kept on his second outfit. Seth wondered if Djinia had known just how high of a reward she'd set on this mission. Was she like a billionaire back on Earth, who thought that fifty dollars was a fair price for a pizza, or had she had other motives? Perhaps she wanted the two countries connected for some other reason, but tried not to let Seth in on that.

His head spun when he thought hard about it. The goddess's plans were probably so far above him that he couldn't understand them if he tried. He was likely one part of a hundred-pronged plan she'd formed. Seth still remembered what it had felt like when she'd read his mind. For the briefest instant, he'd been able to sense her's, too, and it had felt like it contained the entire universe.

That train of thought made Seth curious, and he opened his quest panel to see how many people had completed Djinia's *Impress me* quest. He was mildly surprised that it was only up to four out of one hundred claimed. Djinia had made it seem like there were quite a few adventurers in the world, but Seth had only actually met one other: Riley. Perhaps many of them just weren't doing anything...impressive? It had been tempting for Seth, just after he'd entered Morgenheim, to just stay in the Bosqovar outlying village where he'd met Thom. How many adventurers had chosen that path? How would Seth's past few months have been different if he hadn't met Aurora? Vastly, he assumed.

Seth had started noticing that people treated him and Aurora how they treated Quincy and Liora, deferring to them, looking to them for cues both in battle and out. Baltern had even clapped Seth on the shoulder after the spire, maybe slightly harder than was friendly, and said, "Getting there."

After they defeated the next dungeon, Seth and Riley, along with Verun and Zuh, went ahead to see what the next zone looked like. Riley spotted the small village first. Instead of having walls built around it, the builders had opted to instead build the little village on a raised platform with slick stone walls. Every building sat atop the dirt platform, at least fifteen feet higher than the surrounding area, and there was even a pond around the base of the raised area. Seth imagined it would be excessively difficult to gain access to the town by any means other than the single bridge to the gate. Well, at least it would be hard if he didn't have a flying familiar. All of the structures had pointed roofs that sloped in dramatic curves out to pointed edges too. It all looked vaguely Asian to Seth, and was quite a departure from the medieval aesthetic that all of the structures in Efril seemed to cling to.

Verun flew a bit closer to Zuh at Seth's request, and Seth yelled to Riley, "Do you think we should go back?"

Riley looked at him like he was crazy, and yelled back over the wind, "No way! Let's go say hi! What's the worst that could happen, they kill us?" She laughed, and Seth tried not to smile as Zuh pulled ahead and started losing altitude, heading for the town.

They ended up deciding to be at least somewhat diplomatic, and landed outside the gates. Seth could see people moving around inside the town, obviously reacting to their arrival. Riley and Seth hopped off of their familiars' backs and started walking to the thin wooden bridge. Several people started coming down the bridge from the other end, so Seth and Riley waited to meet them outside.

There were four of them, each with darkly colored skin, eyes, and hair. The first wore what Seth could only describe as samurai armor, demonic mask covering the bottom half of his face and everything. A katana hung in a slightly curved scabbard on his left hip. The second and third, a man and a woman, wore huge, bulky overlapping white robes that looked formal and starchy. Long bamboo staves poked out over their shoulders. The last man wore all black, completely covered except for a slit for his eyes. Thick, black twine was wound around his body at strategic places to hold the cloth tighter to his form, and Seth saw a myriad of small blades and pointy things strapped to his chest and stomach in easy reach. A real-life ninja.

The samurai man spoke first as he stepped off of the bridge. He kept his distance but didn't draw his sword. His eyes passed over Verun and Zuh behind the two adventurers before he started speaking. At first, Seth couldn't understand the man, it just sounded like some indecipherable foreign language, but just like the first time he'd spoken to Thom outside Bosqovar, the language started to make sense. "You come from beyond the edge, yes? I see you are both summoners." At that, he nodded to Verun and Zuh behind them.

Seth replied, "We come from Efril, we've cleared a safe path through the wilderness to reach you." As he said it, Seth heard a little ding and saw Riley jump slightly, indicating she'd heard it too. He looked at his log.

Quest complete: *Unite them*

You successfully created a safe path between Efril and Askua! 2,000,000 experience gained. You've reached level 50, 3,403,956 experience until level 51.

The man in the thick, stiff white robes spoke up, "I have read of Efril in our historical archives. We are honored to be the first to welcome you to the great country of Askua. Unfortunately, you've chosen a poor time to arrive."

CHAPTER 34

Seth walked toward the dark stone arch, stopping before he actually got within arms-reach of it. It was atop a small hill, surrounded by stone ruins that looked suspiciously like the ones he tended to respawn in when he was killed. He turned to look at the small group who'd been walking behind him. Verun walked with Aurora and Ivon. Riley, Zuh, Liora, and Quincy were there too, though Gianna and Sullivan were absent, having been left in charge back at their temporary camp.

The four they'd met in the small settlement on the border of Askua's lands were also present. Kato, the man in white robes, was a priest, and from what Seth had gathered in the last twenty-four hours, priests in Askua were identical to those in Efril, as far as skills and abilities went.

Mori, the woman in the white robes, was a summoner, one of the three classes that were exclusive to Askua and the surrounding areas. Summoners seemed to replace mages in the country, as mages simply didn't exist there. Summoners captured wild spirits, and fell into two categories. One type of summoner could use abilities related to the captured spirit, like shooting fire if they'd captured a flame spirit. The other kind could summon the spirit they'd captured to fight for them. Seth and Riley had struggled to explain to the Askuans that they weren't actually summoners, and that their familiars were unrelated to their classes.

No was the man cloaked head to toe in blank cloth. Riley had made a joke about his name when they'd first learned it, but since "No" didn't actually mean the same thing as it did in English, no one really understood it. His class was translated for Seth as ninja, he wasn't sure if that was just his in-head translator making it easy for him to understand. Ninjas seemed to replace rogues in Askua, though there were differences in the classes. They were stealthy and quick like rogues, but had more skill with mid-range projectile weapons, as opposed to the rogues of Efril who almost always preferred to be up-close and personal. He'd also seen No scale a sheer wall like it was a walk in the park.

Kodama was the last member of the group of Askuans. He was a samurai, a class that seemed to replace both warriors and knights. They were defense-oriented melee combatants, but didn't have shields. There were no knights in Askua, but Kodama had been enthralled with Aurora's armor until she'd let him try one of her greaves on. To his dismay, he'd received heavy movement penalties just like any other non-knight did when wearing plate.

The group had been very welcoming, almost suspiciously so. Eventually it had come out that their small country was on the brink of civil war, the aging king's two sons both making a bid for the throne. The settlement they'd arrived in, Hikari, was aligned with one of the sons who they called the Blade Prince. They were very eager to introduce the group from Efril to their leader, sheltering and feeding the group and more if they agreed to just meet with him.

Kodama spoke as the group stared at the stone archway. He said, "This is the gate I was telling you about. Our legends say it used to lead to your people." Riley translated the message for Liora and Quincy, who didn't speak the same language as the Askuans. She wasn't particularly fond of playing translator.

Liora cocked her head to one side. "You're right, Seth, it does look like the sculpture in the Vardon bank."

Seth took a deep breath and reached out to touch the arch. A pop-up appeared in his vision.

You feel a connection to this place.

Congratulations! You've connected with your second portal. You now have the option to teleport between connected portals. You must walk before you run. All destinations must be earned.

Previously opened portals:
Vardon, Efril

Seth mentally focused on the Vardon portal listing, and another pop up appeared.

The cost to teleport from [Hikari Outskirts, Askua] to [Vardon, Efril] is 10,000 experience. Would you like to teleport now?

Yes   No

Seth was giddy as he selected *No* and turned back to the group. He said, "I think it's going to work, it will take me to Vardon." He said it twice, first in the language of Efril, second in the language of Askua. The two groups really needed to work to learn to communicate.

The group from Efril all expressed some shock at the revelation. Had they thought he was crazy? The stone formation had come up in casual conversation as they'd discussed the fact that their two countries had been allies in the distant past, but had been cut off by ever more aggressive and powerful ethereans. Kodama was the only of the four leaders of the little village who'd even heard of Efril; apparently he was a history buff. He'd mentioned the magical gate that was rumored to lead to them, and Seth had said he needed to see it as soon as possible. It'd been a three-hour hike here this morning.

Ivon said, "Can you only go alone?"

Seth looked over the menu again and said, "I think so. It looks like you have to touch both portals to be able to use them."

Ivon nodded and looked at Aurora out of the corner of his eye. "Tell Isaac hello from all of us." Aurora stiffened but stayed silent. Did Liora still not know?

Quincy scoffed audibly, then said, "I tried to touch that sculpture in the Vardon bank once, I felt inextricably drawn to it, but that puny little bank manager yelled at me. Me! Unbelievable." He angrily worked on polishing his shining gold knuckles.

Seth chuckled and said, "You all might as well touch this one now, and maybe even have the whole raid come do it. Verun and I have some important information to get back to Pahan about

C. T. O'LEARY

creating champions, but we will come back as soon as we deliver it. We have more to do in Askua." He thought of his mother's face as he said it. Djinia had said she was here, somewhere in the small country.

Liora looked toward the Askuans and said, "We'll uphold our end of the bargain and make contact with their prince."

Seth nodded and quickly translated, then said, "I'll find you all when I get back, it shouldn't be long." They nodded at him silently. Seth struggled not to look at Riley, to search her face for approval. Instead, his eyes lingered on the sword at her hip. It had been a gift from Kodama after he'd granted his class, samurai, to her as her secondary class. She'd been adamant that she didn't want to think about it, she just knew it was the one she wanted. It had inspired Seth to action, as he felt a similar affinity to one of the Askuan classes. He looked at Mori, the summoner. He said, "I think I'm ready."

She smiled at him, eyes crinkling at the corners, "I am very humbled to be able to share our ways with you. I hope the friendship of your group and our Blade Prince will be beneficial to us all. Please kneel."

Seth did as she said, and she walked forward to lay her palm on his forehead. He had a flashback to his childhood, when his mother determined if he had a fever in the same way. A pop-up appeared and banished the thought.

> Mori, master summoner of Hikari village, would like to share her class with you. Would you like to adopt *Summoner* as your second class?
>
> Yes   No

Seth steeled himself, then selected *yes* before he could change his mind. Knowledge flooded into his brain, stinging like scalding water for a moment before rapidly dulling down to a light headache. He didn't feel much different, but he did see a new bar at the edge of his vision, only really there when he wanted to see it. Above his full health bar and his empty fury bar was a new one representing mana. He had over thirteen hundred mana points, apparently. He was excited to explore his new class and either summon more allies or use their magical skills, but that would have to wait.

Seth stood, Verun coming to stand next to him so Seth could lean against him. Mori said, "Congratulations, summoner. One tip, before you use the sight, wait until you're well rested, well fed, and far from any crowds."

Seth was about to ask what sight she meant, when he saw he had one new skill. He inspected the description.

> *Ether Sight* - Cost: 25 mana/second - Cooldown: none

Using your summoner knowledge, you peer into the ether. You're able to see the connecting magic of the ethereans.

He just nodded, and said, "I'll do that. Thank you." He looked everyone in the face one last time, even Riley, and said, "Goodbye for now. I'll see you all again soon."

They all said their goodbyes back, and Seth turned to Verun. "Ready, buddy? It will only be a few minutes, if everything goes according to plan."

The big lion bobbed his head up and down. Seth banished his familiar to the void, nodded once more at the assembled people, then touched the portal one more time. This time, when it asked if he wanted to pay the cost and teleport to Vardon, he selected yes. The world lurched around him.

***

The wind rushed through Seth's hair and the patchy beard he'd grown since leaving Slyborn; he'd been too scared to shave without a mirror. He looked down from Verun's back, watching the trees and hills roll by.

He'd been surprised, at first, when no exclamations came as he appeared in the bank building in the center of Vardon. There were several clerks talking with customers. One who wasn't working with anyone looked up from some parchment in front of himself and jumped slightly before saying, "Oh my, I didn't notice you coming in. How can I help you?"

Seth had just made an excuse and ducked out and walked through the three rings of walls surrounding the ancient building. The fact that they seemed to be backwards made more sense now, as any sane city with a portal at its center would likely want to prevent armies from appearing there.

He'd summoned Verun as soon as he was out of the bank area and taken flight, finally getting the exclamations from startled residents as a multi-ton winged lion appeared from thin air and took to the sky, wingbeats thumping the air.

They'd left the city and flown for several hours, not stopping to shop or visit the Vardon guild compound, eager to get back to Slyborn and see Pahan, Dominick, Molly, and the others. Seth was still in the raid party, and could feel the direction they were all in. They felt very far away.

He and Verun had taken one break to let the lion's muscles rest and let Seth relieve himself, and now they were on the home stretch. The mountain range was already starting to resolve itself through the atmospheric haze.

It was only a few more minutes before Seth could tell something was wrong. There was a dark shape jutting out of the top of one of the mountains in the Broken Bones range. It was hard to gauge over the huge distance, but he thought it was one of the mountains very close to the one Slyborn sat on.

It got clearer with every second as they flew closer. Verun had seen it too and had started flying faster, pushing himself. There was definitely a huge shape sticking up out of one of the mountains. It was long and roughly straight, almost reminiscent of the spire.

Seth's mind flashed back to the giant eye of Ygzotl, gazing through a hole in the sky. Had the massive god done the same here, and then stabbed a gigantic sword down into Slyborn Stronghold? Visions of the fortress in ruin flashed through his mind, Pahan's crystal all that way underground, shattered.

The shape wasn't getting any clearer as they neared; it was almost as if there was fog around the mysterious shape stretching into the sky.

Oh. Seth started laughing, almost hysterical.

Verun, the question dripping with worry through their mental link, said, <What's going on? What's funny?>

Seth wiped tears away from his eyes, cheeks hurting from his grin. He yelled over the wind as Verun kept flying, "It looks like Pahan figured out how to grow it. It's the tree. The Mistwood Monolith!"

The two of them stared in wonder at the growing shape, a tree half the height of the mountain it sprouted from, scraping the clouds, veiled in mist.

The End - To be continued in book 3!

Want a free 30 page short story set in the Quick Change universe? Sign up for my email list at authorctoleary.com and you'll get it automagically emailed to your inbox!

If you enjoyed this book, please be sure to leave a review on Amazon. I'm just an indie author, and every review helps others find out about the books. Cheers!

C. T. O'LEARY

ACKNOWLEDGMENT

I'd like to start off by thanking my beta readers, Staci, Austin, Gaius, and Sandi. Your feedback helped me make this book better than I could've on my own. Thank you.

I'd also like to thank the cover artist for this book, Jon, for his wonderful work on the art of the spire. Check his other art out at his website https://www.illustratjon.com/.

The editor for this volume, Celestian Rince, did an excellent job, including an incredible turn-around time and acknowledging one of my silly references. Thank you. Find Celestian at https://celestianrince.com/.

Finally, biggest thank you to the reader, for making it this far. The fact that anyone wants to read my ramblings continues to amaze me. I can't wait to get the next book ready!

ABOUT THE AUTHOR

C.T. O'Leary is a software engineer and fiction author from Kansas City, Missouri. He's been an avid reader of fantasy and science fiction since childhood, and has recently begun writing the Quick Change series, an ode to his love of fantasy and video games.

Learn more or sign up for updates at authorctoleary.com

LITRPG PAGES

There are several LitRPG pages or sites that I like to hang out on, or keep an eye on for new releases. Here are some links if you want to find more books in the same genre.

https://www.facebook.com/groups/LitRPGsociety/
https://www.facebook.com/groups/LitRPGAdventurers/
https://www.facebook.com/groups/LitRPG.books/
https://www.reddit.com/r/litrpg/
https://www.amazon.com/litrpg/

Made in the USA
Coppell, TX
24 October 2020

40191970R00222